THE LAST ACER

The Last Acer

ISBN: 978-1-60920-012-1
Printed in the United States of America
©2010 by McKenzie Dempsey

Cover and interior design by Isaac Publishing, Inc.

Library of Congress Cataloging-in-Publication Data

IPI
Isaac Publishing, Inc.
P.O. 342
Three Rivers, MI 49093
www.isaacpublishing.com

Please direct your inquiries to admin@isaacpublishing.com

by

McKenzie Dempsey

Isaac Publishing, Inc.

PO Box 342

Three Rivers, MI 49093

1.888.273.4JOY

www.isaacpublishing.com

ACKNOWLEDGMENTS

This book is dedicated to many people without whom this book would have never met a piece of paper.

To my teachers at St. Peter Lutheran School, especially Miss Thomas, my eighth grade teacher, for without their teaching skills and patience in class, I would have never learned how to write and enjoy it.

Thank you to all my editors, including Carol Zedaker, for correcting and reading my book, and adding extra life where it was needed.

To all my friends who read my book, and especially, my best friend, Kaylee McDonald. Without her editing help and ideas, my book would have never taken wing.

To my family, who were patient and considerate enough to listen to my explanations and plans for this book. Without their insight and enthusiasm, I would have never thought to finish this tale.

And most of all, I thank my Lord Jesus Christ for giving me my Christian education, my home, my family, my teachers, my friends, my talents, and over all for giving me his love and kindness that inspired my book.

FIRMARA

PROFUNDUM OCEAN

DERYA

•ALTASEN

MYRDDIN

CAVE OF MORALITY

OLEGRARO

UNVENTURED
LANDS

CONTENTS

PROLOGUE

A loud, thunderous roar surged through the air. The sky shattered as lightning struck. The wind howled fiercely. The clouds showed a promise of a plethora of rain. The storm was just beginning.

A lonely figure flew across the sky, its wings beating rapidly. The figure hesitated when the sky again shattered with a loud boom.

This is no weather for flying, the creature thought to itself. Even the birds know to take shelter. Of course, I wouldn't be flying in this if it were not important.

Once again, the creature took off at a ferocious speed, trying to beat the storm to its destination. Rain began to sprinkle from the sky like little bugs in a frantic dash, trying to escape the deadly fangs of a bat at night. Not far beyond the figure, a city's lights were shining brightly. Except for the storm, it was seemingly peaceful this night.

The creature took a second to look down at the object it held in its foot. The stone's red surface shimmered as another bolt of lightning flashed. The creature then clenched it in its talons, holding tight to the stone so it would not fall and be lost forever.

Then, as if the storm was not bad enough, there came an awful cry from not far behind the creature.

"Cccccrrrroooaaawwwooo!" came the cry a second time and when the creature looked back, a larger form smashed into it, causing the creature to fall a few feet. The creature regained its composure and looked to the second figure, which now hovered only a few yards from the creature's beak. There was nowhere to hide so the creature held its place. After a long silence, the stranger spoke.

"You are fassst but not evasssive Sssarora," the newcomer cackled. Then it turned its beady eyes on the leg where the creature held the object. "Give me the Crrrysssstal of Courage and maybe you'll live to sssee the founding of our sssoon-to-be-leader, Lord Trazon."

"You think I'm that stupid, Sievan?" asked the creature, named Sarora. "It would take more than any of your powers before I would consider giving it to you or your fake Lord Trazon!"

"If that isss the way it mussst be ..." Sievan smirked in evil delight, "then ssso be it!" And with that, the larger creature leapt onto Sarora and they rolled in the sky. Wings beat the air, claws scratched desperately, and talons gouged.

Finally, with all of her effort, Sarora kicked Sievan in the ribs and came down on one of his wings, ripping open the feather-covered membrane and leaving a large wound, which gushed blood over Sievan's body.

Sievan howled with frustration and agony. "You may have won thisss time but I'll be back, and the Crysssstal of Courage will be oursss!" And with a final burst of energy, Sievan sped at Sarora and raked a gash into one of her wings. He departed as quickly as he had come, speeding off until he was a speck in the horizon.

Sarora was extremely tired because of her injured wing, the fight, and the dreadful storm that now kicked up. The wind, blowing at a speed faster than a running cheetah, intensified as the rain began to turn to hail the size of a bat. Sarora headed for the air stream that she had been flying in but struggled to stay afloat. Finally, she could take it no more and Sarora plummeted to the earth. She braced herself for the impact, hit the ground, and everything went black.

A NEW DAY

Travis squinted as the bright light hit his eyes. He held his hand to his forehead to block some of the sun's intense rays. As he looked around, he found that the warm October morning seemed … well … different. But he did not know why.

After the storm the other night, everything was muddied and drenched. Several trees were completely bare because of the awful winds. The storm had been rough.

As he began to venture into the woods, Travis recalled the other night. He had been asleep for most of it but he was sure that he had heard a loud screech. At least it had sounded sort of like a screech. "Maybe I was just hallucinating," Travis mumbled to himself as he ruffled his dark brown hair. "Yeah, that was probably it. Step-dad never fed me anything that day."

Still, the noise had seemed so real. He could easily recall the sound. As he played it over in his head, Travis began to consider the different animals it could have been.

A falcon. No, that definitely wasn't it. What about a heron? That's stupid. When has a heron ever sounded like that? He knew it was most likely a bird that had made a loud screech that night, but what kind? That he wasn't sure.

Travis picked up the pace as he rounded a corner on the

trail that led through the woods. The trees were quickly turning from green to yellow, orange, and red.

He loved this time of year – mainly because he went to school five days of the week instead of staying home twenty-four seven with his step-dad. The only time Travis got to do anything during the summer was when he slipped out through his bedroom window to visit the woods.

Travis took a deep breath. The morning air was cool and refreshing. The sun had just peeked over the treetops on this beautiful Saturday. He figured he would take a walk around the woods and then visit the small pond he enjoyed so much when he needed to get away from everything in his life (his step-dad being most of the problem).

Travis spent the next hour or so looking about the woods and exploring the many trees that had fallen from the vigorous storm that had clashed the other night. It seemed that the tempest must have blown hard enough to even take down the large oak tree that had been a fixture in the forest. From a high area, the oak tree used to stand out among the pine trees and the maples, which made the best treat from their sap.

As he stopped to examine the fallen oak, he noticed a long gash in its trunk. *That's strange.* Travis thought to himself. *There is no way a buck could have rubbed that in, or any other animal could have made that. It's huge!*

Travis nervously extended his hand to feel the long mark in the oak. He found, to his surprise, that it was cut smoothly, like when you use a knife. The cut was about six inches deep and went down the trunk about a foot. There was no animal that Travis knew of that had such precision and power. The question whizzed around his head: *What made this?*

While searching for an answer, Travis looked up toward the sky. Above him, large branches had been smashed as if something big had been dropped on top of them.

"This is ridiculous," Travis mumbled to himself. "The only thing that could have possibly broken those would have fallen from the sky. That, and weigh more than any person I know, in order to break those branches," he concluded as he finished searching the ground for anything that could have caused such damage.

Travis noticed large tracks in the muddied ground, much bigger than a wolf's paws.

He bent down to study the peculiar tracks, and noticed that whatever they belonged to, they were following another pair of tracks, which seemed to resemble the tracks of a bird of some sort. The screech! Was it possible that whatever made these tracks and the creature that made the noise were one and the same? *Come on,* Travis thought to himself. *There's no possible way that they could be related. I mean, is there even such a thing known as a bird/wolf?*

Travis began to feel silly for what he was thinking. *Could something like this actually be possible?* he asked himself. At the moment, he didn't really care. He was more interested in discovering the rest of this mystery.

But still, one thing didn't fit. What was the creature that had done this damage? There only seemed to be one way to find out, and with that, Travis followed the line of tracks that led away from the oak.

The walk was long and mind-boggling, not because the tracks disappeared when the creature had walked through the leaves, but when they tended to sway from side to side like the creature had become groggy. But all this was not as agonizing as when Travis stopped for a break and more closely examined the tracks. He discovered they were covered with blood. *No wonder the creature had swaggered—it had been losing blood, and lots of it!* Travis thought to himself.

Travis picked up the pace to a brisk walk. Whatever it was, it was hurt. Not anything like a scratch but more like a large wound. A wound large enough to cause anyone to grow dizzy because of the blood lost. The thought scared him. He had once come home to find an injured cat under the front porch. After spending half an hour trying to coax it out, he struggled and finally yanked it out by its tail, which resulted in a bloody hand, a furious cat, and a ferocious old woman nagging him about hurting poor little Mr. Tinkles. After reviewing the whole experience in his head, Travis decided it best to take extreme precaution if he found this creature. Whatever he was following could be a lot worse than a ten-pound cat.

By now, the sun had passed the middle part of the sky, which told Travis it was the afternoon and that he only had around four more hours until his step-dad came home from work. Even though he still had time, he made it a habit be home exactly one hour before his step-dad would arrive, just to be safe.

Travis searched his pocket and found his lucky compass, which was cracked in the front from the time he lost it outside in the winter. The instrument was one of the last gifts his mother gave to him before she passed away. Travis held up the small, round object and turned around so it pointed north. He then searched his pocket for his jack knife, which he had inherited from his father, and made a small slit in the nearest tree heading north to mark his path back. He returned both objects to his pockets and strode off again following the tracks.

Finally, after what had seemed an eternity, the tracks lead into an underground den that had been created by the uprooting of a large tree. Travis crept quietly toward the large hole, his heart beginning to pound faster in his chest. As he inched toward the hole, he pulled out his jack knife, wanting to be prepared in case whatever it was attacked.

It was definitely a good idea, Travis found out, because not long after he reached the entrance to the cave, a deafening caterwaul blasted from it, and before Travis could move, a large figure leapt at him and pinned him to the ground. Nothing in his whole life had prepared him for what he saw standing over him.

AN ACQUAINTANCE

Travis stared at the creature in fright. It had a long, sleek, bird-like head. Its front legs had talons that clutched him firmly to the ground. Its back and rear resembled a lion. Now his question was half answered. This was the creature that had been injured.

Travis tried to roll away, but the animal was too heavy for him. The creature must have noticed his struggle because it held him down all the more firmly. Even though its golden eyes carried ferocity, they seemed equally as curious and questioning. Its beak came slowly toward him, as if to see whether or not Travis would retaliate.

Travis tried to kick the monster with his legs, but to no avail. The creature only held him tighter and tighter each time he struggled to free himself. It stared at him. Travis felt horribly frightened.

They stared at each other for what seemed like ages and then, to Travis's surprise, the creature let him up and backed away. Travis quickly scurried to stand up, only to find the creature grasp the end of his shirt and lift him into its den. Once inside, it gently let Travis down and blocked the exit to the cave. It turned again to face him, staring him down. Then, to Travis's great surprise, it spoke.

"Why did you come here?" it demanded. Its voice was

challenging but still inquiring. What did this creature want from him?

Travis nervously stared back into the creature's eyes, trying to muster up some courage. There was a long pause before he replied, "I saw the fallen tree and I decided to investigate."

"You thought wrong!" the creature boomed back. "I am Sarora and I am a gryphon."

There is the other half of my question answered. Travis couldn't help thinking. *But a gryphon?* He had never even heard of such a thing.

The creature continued, "Because you have tracked me down, prepare to take your last breath." And then, Sarora crouched down and prepared to attack.

"Wait!" Travis cried. "I didn't mean to hunt you! I was just curious." His breathing was now rapid and he could not keep the expression of fear off his face.

Sarora stood back up and looked at him. "Why should I let you live?" she asked. "Why should I give you the chance to tell everyone where I am and what I am? Why should I trust you?" Sarora emphasized the last word with a feeling a little shy of hate.

"I-I ..." Travis stammered, "I don't know. But maybe there is something that I could do for you? I saw, when I was tracking you that there were plenty enough blood stains to go around. Maybe I could help you heal? Also, I won't tell anyone where you are at. And in return, maybe you could assure me that you aren't going to kill me?" Travis added hopefully.

Sarora seemed to think about this for a moment. After

a while she said, "You solemnly swear that you won't double-cross me? Because if you do, I will shred you to pieces."

"Yes, of course." Travis said, thankful that Sarora would give him a chance. Then he raised his right hand and said, "I promise I will care for any wounds that you may have and in return you let me live. I also promise to never speak to anyone about your whereabouts or what you are." Travis finished the sentence and held out his hand to Sarora. "We got a deal?"

Looking almost regretful, Sarora reached out her front leg and shook Travis's hand, "Deal." she said firmly. "Before I do anything else with you, I must first know your name.

"I'm Travis," he replied. "I live in a small house about a quarter of a mile away from these woods."

"All right then Travis," Sarora began, "hold yourself to your promise and see what you can do with this." Then she laid down on her stomach on the ground and unfolded a wing to reveal her wound. Travis gaped in shock.

Travis stared at the large infected gash. It had puss coming from it and it reeked awfully. "That must hurt," he said.

"This one is by far the worst of all of my wounds. With it, I cannot fly," Sarora replied. Her voice had seemed to drift slower and a little dreamlike after revealing her cut.

"Well," Travis began, "I'm not a doctor, but I think the first thing I should do is get that thing cleaned up. There is a pond near here but the water isn't clean enough to help that. Give me until either late tonight or sometime early tomorrow, and I will bring something back for your wound."

"You're coming back though, right?"

"I believe so."

"How sure are you?"

"About ninety-nine percent."

"What about that other percent? Why are you not one hundred percent sure?"

"My step-dad may have other ideas."

Sarora looked away. Once again, she seemed deep in thought. Then she returned her gaze to him. "Fine," Sarora replied. "Just as long as you come back soon."

"I'll come back as soon as I can," Travis promised. "And I'll bring something to clean your wound and something to cover it up with. And after about a couple of months, you should be about good as new."

"A couple of months!" Sarora screeched. "What good will that do me? If I'm not back to where I'm supposed to be, I'll be toast!"

"Well I'm not the one who fell from the sky and has a large, gaping wound," Travis spoke back at her, working on gaining confidence. "It's this or you may never go back at all."

"Fine," Sarora finally agreed. "Just be sure to come back." Then she stood up and moved out of the way to the opening of the den. She turned to face Travis straight on. "Keep your mind focused, your reflexes sharp, and be prepared for the task ahead," she recited before him. Travis figured it was her way of saying "Stay safe, don't get in trouble, and remember your promise or else."

"No problem," Travis said, but believed the opposite. "I'll be back not any later than tomorrow afternoon."

At least I hope I will, he thought to himself. Depending

on when his step-dad left, he did not know when he would get out to the woods again.

Sarora nodded in understanding. "I'll hold you to that, Travis."

Travis then nodded to show he knew that she was serious. He walked out of the den and, without looking back, raced toward home, begging time to slow down so that he would arrive before his step-dad.

THE PAST AND THE PRESENT

Travis reached his house, out of breath, a few minutes after he had left Sarora. The sun was now sinking into the line of treetops that were beyond the silhouette of his home at the end of a large cornfield.

The house wasn't very large, and the shadows hid the home's age. Its white paint was chipping and the shingles on the roof were gray, curled and faded. The foundation was sinking into the earth and several windows were cracked and darkened from the fading light.

Travis walked around the side to his bedroom window. It was still open from when he had left. Quietly, Travis grabbed hold of the windowsill and began to pull himself into his room. As he struggled to wriggle through the small opening, a pair of headlights shone on the glass. The car quickly sped down the road toward his home, and Travis's heart skipped a beat.

Step-dad! His head screamed in fright. Travis moved faster to get himself in. Finally, he felt his body slip through the window opening and he got up off the floor and slammed his window shut. Meanwhile, the car had come even closer, but not close enough to see Travis try to get himself in. At least, he *hoped* it hadn't seen him.

The car now began to slow down and swerve into the

driveway. After it skidded to a quick stop, a large, burly man stepped out of the driver's door. He wore a black coat and a frown. Travis couldn't tell if his step-dad had seen him or not because he always wore that awful expression.

Travis's step-dad stomped toward the front door of the musty old house. This was his usual way of walking into the home, possibly because he hated the thought of having to deal with his step-son. Forcefully, Travis's step-dad flung open the door and strode inside.

Travis could hear loud footsteps coming in the house toward his small room. He quickly put the large black lock on the window, locked it, moved to his bed and worked a sad expression onto his face. Just as he found the right gloomy look, his step-dad unlocked the door and flung it open.

"I suppose it's been awful quiet around here today?" his step-father asked in his gruff voice, as he strode into the room.

"Yes sir," Travis stared at the floor and replied softly.

"What was that?" his step-father asked, cupping his hand behind his ear, "I'm afraid I didn't hear you."

"Yes sir!" he replied louder.

"That's more like it. And you haven't done anything at all today besides sit in this room?"

"Yes sir," Travis replied again.

"Good," his step-dad smiled and folded his hands before him. "Very good. Then there has been no out-of-the-ordinary occurrences for you, I presume?"

"No sir," Travis replied almost too eagerly. His step-dad must have noticed, because he leaned his head closer to

Travis's. His breath was awful—it smelled like a cross between something that had died and the cigarettes he smoked all the time.

"You haven't escaped at all, have you?"

"No sir," Travis replied slower that time and with an assuring expression.

His step-dad took a step back. "Good," he replied firmly. "That is how it should be." He turned and began to walk back toward the bedroom door. "Since you've been good, I'll be sure to give you dinner tonight." And he cackled as he walked out the bedroom and lock the door behind him.

Travis let out a sigh of relief. *That was a close one,* he said to himself. *I'll have to remember to be home earlier next time.*

As Travis began to relax, he walked around the room. The walls were painted a dull gray and the textured ceiling a plain white. His bed was small but still big enough to fit him. Next to it stood a small dresser where Travis kept his compass and pocket knife during the day when he went to school or while he was sleeping. There was no closet in the room. No matter; Travis could easily fit his possessions and clothes in a couple of plastic bags under his bed.

The only thing he really did in his room was drawing or homework. Sometimes, if he was lucky, he could sneak some sticks and rocks in and invent things or make up games to pass the time. But this only happened once in a while.

Travis went back to his bed and stared out the window. It was now very dark out—at least dark enough that Travis could only see a few feet before him.

As he stared out the window, Travis's mind went back to when he had first moved here to the old farmhouse. He remembered that it had been a beautiful day, warm and sunny. His mother's hand had been wrapped around his small, stubby fingers. He was only about seven at that time.

He remembered how nice and cozy the little house had felt when he and his mom cuddled together during story time. He had plenty of favorite stories, but the one he liked best was about a boy his mother said had been much like him.

The boy had lived in a far-off land where magical creatures came out of nowhere and people could perform many miraculous deeds with magic.

The boy trained long and hard to please his mentor, who taught him the ways of magic. The years flew by and finally, when the magical counsel deemed him old enough, he was made the ruler of all the land because of his strength and courage.

This, however, was not the only reason the boy had become the leader. The previous leader had badly mistreated the people of the land. The boy, now a young man, was expected to do great things. But sadly, just a year after he began his rule, he disappeared. Travis's mom had always said that the boy had gone back home to his family but she also told him that no one could be quite sure.

Travis also remembered how he and his mother played together on the weekends and how she enjoyed spoiling him rotten with gifts and goodies. He remembered the warm smile on her face as she told him that he might have a new father.

He also remembered his step-father's first trip to their home. He had been kind and caring back then. However,

Travis now knew that the happiness would not last forever.

He figured his mom must have known she was dying. She married his step-father, he supposed, with the hope that he would be safe when she left him forever.

The most horrible thing Travis remembered had to be the day his mother died. She had sent his step-dad to get him and bring him to her room. He remembered asking her what was going on. She had replied that he would be safe with his step-dad and that she hoped he would always love her. And just before she died, she mumbled her last breath, something that had sounded like, "I love you, Travis," and then she left him.

Alone.

Alone with a cruel step-father.

Alone without either of his true parents' comfort.

Alone without a chance to say that he loved his mother back.

Travis woke out of his thoughts and noticed he had large tears streaking down his face. He took the back of his hand and tried to wipe them away but they kept coming. Why did his mother have to leave him? Why couldn't she have lived? These questions were unanswerable to anyone Travis could have asked. Travis Wegner was all alone without any family left in the world.

Travis laid down on his bed. He heard a plate being slid under the crack of his door, but he was too upset to eat. He lay in his bed, worn and miserable, until sleep finally found him.

CARING FOR A GRYPHON

Travis woke the next morning when the sun streamed through the small window of his bedroom. As he rubbed the sleep from his eyes, he recounted yesterday's events. Travis thought as he stood up and walked over to the window.

Perfect! he thought when he saw that the driveway was empty.

He scurried out of his room after professionally picking its lock. Then, Travis ran down the hall to the bathroom and opened the door.

The bathroom was decorated in a beach theme. The wallpaper had all sorts of little seashells in the sand and the soap dispensers looked like small sand buckets.

Above the sink was a cabinet used for storing various medications. Travis reached up and opened the cabinet door and rummaged through all the contents until he found some peroxide and a few bandage rolls. He placed them on the counter and shut the cabinet door. On the front of the cabinet was a mirror. Travis looked into his own eyes and smiled. His brown hair was ruffled, not even coming close to a "neat" status. His brown eyes were bright as he gave himself a wink and continued on his way. Stretching his lean body, Travis picked up the peroxide and rolls and walked out of the bathroom.

After grabbing a snack bar from the kitchen, Travis left his home through his bedroom window once again and headed for Sarora. Today the sky was clear but the air was chilly. *Note to self: Find some gloves,* Travis told himself as he stuffed his items under his arms, rubbed his hands together, and then shoved them into his jean pockets.

When he arrived at the den, Travis saw Sarora waiting for him by its entrance. She had obviously been waiting for him for a while.

"What?" he asked her, puzzled. "Did you think I wasn't coming?"

Sarora just stared at him and motioned for him to go into the den. Travis followed her as she led him in.

The den was the same as yesterday only now it seemed less foreboding. Now that he looked around, Travis felt almost warm and at peace in the small, cozy place.

Travis watched as Sarora laid down on the dirt-covered floor and silently gazed at him.

"Well," Travis began, "I don't know if silence means more or less hostility coming from you."

"Fine." Sarora finally spoke after several seconds of silence. "I admit it. I was almost completely sure you wouldn't come back."

"And are you disappointed that I came back or disappointed that you were wrong?" Sarora stared at him in silence once more.

"Fine, fine," Travis finally said. "Don't answer that."

Sarora spoke again after Travis gave up on the question. "Well, you came for a reason so let's get to it." And with that she stretched out her wing to him. Once again, Travis was shocked by the wound. It smelled terrible and the blood that surrounded it was dried and crusty.

Travis continued to stare at the awful wound until Sarora spoke again, "You know, I really feel like having turkey tonight and isn't it convenient that one is standing right in front of me?"

Travis's eyes widened in horror at the thought and he quickly began to unscrew the cap on the peroxide. "I'm on it, I'm on it."

He took some peroxide and poured it on the injury, at which Sarora retorted by saying, "Ouch! Geez, why don't you just saw the wing right off, it would be equally as painful!"

After the peroxide had stopped bubbling, Travis took some bandage rolls and began to tightly wrap them around Sarora's large wing. It took all three rolls of bandage and plenty of patience from Sarora to get them on.

"Finally!" Sarora and Travis exclaimed together when they had finished, both tired of the whole thing.

"Try to avoid some of the trees next time you are flying, okay?" Travis jokingly suggested.

"I'm not a bad flyer!" Sarora hissed at him, examining her newly bandaged wing. "I've been living like this for a while!"

"I never said you were a bad flyer," Travis tried to cover up his joke.

"It sure sounded like you did," Sarora shot an evil glare at him.

"Well, why did you hit a tree then?" Travis asked. "Just felt like falling from the sky, did you?" His jokes now sounded more like an accusation than a jest.

Sarora stood up and stared into Travis's eyes. "Now let's see you try and fly in a storm with a dargryph on your tail!" Sarora's eyes widened with regret.

"What in the world is a dargryph?" Travis asked.

"Nothing. I've told you too much as it is." Sarora looked away from him.

"Why don't you tell me?"

"Because you don't need to know," Sarora stated loudly, and before Travis could reply, Sarora cut in. "End of discussion."

Travis finally gave up the question. "Well, I should head back for the day. Step-dad has half a day at work. I'll come and see you tomorrow."

Sarora nodded. "Come back as soon as possible."

"I will," Travis replied and with that, he headed home for the afternoon.

HOME ALONE

When Travis arrived home, his step-dad had still not returned. *I'll just grab something to entertain myself and then I'll head inside*, he told himself.

As he neared his window, Travis noticed a small tree branch, about four feet tall and about as round as his thumb.

This'll keep me busy long enough, Travis thought as he picked up the tree limb. *I'll make use of this.*

Travis gingerly ran his free hand over the top of the branch. The thin bark was still attached to the wood, but it could be easily removed while the branch was still wet.

Travis pulled his jack knife out of his pocket and began to strip off the bark of the branch. It took a little while longer than he had expected, but it was worth it when he held the bare branch in his hands.

After he had stripped the branch, Travis began to wipe the blade of the pocketknife gently and steadily down the branch. He repeated the motion over and over until all the under-bark had been removed. Next, Travis found a soft, dry place in the sunlight and left the branch out to dry.

After checking to make sure the branch would be okay on a stump near the field, Travis re-opened his bedroom window and quietly slid through it. Using his sore hands, Travis shut the window behind him and made sure that it was shut tight and locked. After that, he removed his dirty shoes and hid them under his small bed. Travis then walked to his bedroom door and picked its lock and strolled out of the room into the hallway for the second time that day.

Travis took his time walking around the house and exploring its various rooms. He noticed the way the furniture was all covered in filth—from the cigarette-singed couch to the smoke-filled curtains. The air was musty and reeked of cigarette smoke.

At the moment, Travis found himself glad that he was locked in his room. *At least I don't smell the smoke twenty-four-seven,* and since he wasn't often exposed to his smoking step-dad, Travis's lungs were as healthy as any other thirteen-year-old kid.

Travis walked out of the living room, up the stairs, and into his mom's old room. The walls were a light, rosy pink. Rose wallpaper rimmed the top of the walls by the ceiling. A beautiful flower-like light hung from the middle of the ceiling.

Slowly, Travis moved over to his mom's bed and swept his hand across the thick sheets. The large blanket was also decorated in roses, red and pink. The large green and red pillows were still propped up where he had last left them.

Travis quietly slid himself onto the bed, laid down on his back, and stared absentmindedly at the ceiling. The odorless room brought a kind of comfort to Travis as he lost himself in his memories.

Oh Mom, Travis began to speak to her through his thoughts. *I wish you were here. I needed to talk to you about my new friend.* And so, Travis began to tell his mom about

21

Sarora. He told her what she looked like and of her peculiar attitude.

Travis also let her know what he was learning in school, how his grades were doing, and, grudgingly, how his step-dad was doing.

After he was finished recounting his tale to his mom, Travis said good-bye to her, got up off the bed, re-fluffed the pillows, and walked downstairs to his bedroom.

As he shut his bedroom door and locked it, Travis reminded himself how lucky he was compared to some other kids. At least he had a home and food to eat. But his thankfulness quickly disappeared as his step-dad drove into the driveway, strode out of his dark car, and came to interrogate him once again. *If it weren't for step-dad,* he thought to himself, *I could feel a whole lot luckier.*

A PHENOMENON

The month of October flew by with many visits to Sarora's den. He now knew what she ate—things like rabbits and other small mammals—as well as the things that tick her off—like stupid questions and Travis's complaints about cleaning her wound.

Every visit went something like this: Arrive. Greet an irritable Sarora. Check the bandage rolls. Apply more disinfectant and replace bandage rolls if needed. And if he had time, sit and chat with Sarora for a while until he had to head for home.

Travis and Sarora talked about many things while in Sarora's den. He once asked her about being a gryphon.

"So," Travis had begun, "you're a cross between an eagle and a lion?" He had looked up information on gryphons while at school a couple days before.

"Not an eagle and a lion, empty head," Sarora had replied. She called him an empty head because of his many varied questions and, to her, his lack in knowledge. "I'm a hawk and a lioness. See?" She had pointed to her wings with her beak. "My feathers are a golden-brown, unlike an eagle's and," she then had pointed to her beak with her talons, "the very end of the tip of my beak is black."

"I see," Travis had replied, "and you're part lioness because you're a girl, right?"

"You actually do have something inside your thick skull, empty head!" Sarora had replied, faking a surprised expression on her face with a hint of shock in her voice. "I thought it was hollow!" And together they had laughed for a long while.

Travis woke up with a jolt as he heard a crack of thunder outside. It was very early in the morning and he had been asleep for only part of the night because his stomach's constant rumbling had kept him up.

Travis got out of bed and stretched as he walked over to the window. The dark clouds covered the sky and rain was just beginning to sprinkle the earth.

Darn it, Travis thought. *Does it have to storm on such a cold day?* He was half tempted to get back in bed and sleep the day away and not visit Sarora, but he knew better. And so, Travis got up, put on his rugged fall coat, opened his bedroom window, and headed for Sarora's den.

The icy cold rain droplets pelted his face as he sprinted across the cornfield to the woods. When he reached the woods, the trees began to provide some shelter from the rain but the wind continued to howl.

Before Travis reached the den, he spotted Sarora waiting for him under the shelter of a tree. "Quick!" she called to him. "Go to the den and I'll be with you in a minute!" Travis obeyed her orders and ran the rest of the way to the den.

The den was as warm and cozy as ever. Travis quietly sat down and began to wait for Sarora. Outside, the thunder struck and Travis felt the whole ground rumble. As he waited, he looked around the small room. Randomly, he looked to where Sarora usually laid and saw that there was a lump in the soil.

Travis moved over to the spot. As he stood over the lump, he gently uncovered a small sack from under the dirt. *Why does Sarora need this?* he asked himself. After a quick glance around the room, Travis stuck his hand in the bundle and pulled out a round, red crystal.

At first the crystal did nothing. However, as Travis held the object it began to glow and vibrate. As he looked closer, Travis saw a small flame begin to flicker inside the crystal. The crystal then let out a burst of light that engulfed the den in its wonders. Travis heard the storm outside subside.

Travis squinted his eyes until they were almost completely shut. At this moment, he had two feelings going through him—fright from the sight of the glowing crystal and a strange courage. Travis had no idea how he could feel both at once and yet, he felt it.

"What are you doing!" came a yell from the entrance of the den. Travis quickly recognized the voice—it was Sarora.

He immediately dropped the crystal. Thankfully, the object landed on top of the soft sack, which cushioned its fall. "I … I was just looking! I didn't mean to make it do that!" Travis stammered nervously, fearing Sarora's wrath.

Sarora quickly came in and put the crystal back into the bundle. "Come quickly," she said in a rushed tone and she headed out the den with the red crystal clutched in her beak.

Travis scrambled out the entrance and followed Sarora as they ran. "What's the matter?" he asked as they headed toward the cornfield.

"Listen carefully to what I say," Sarora began. "I'll stop

and wait for you by the edge of the woods while you go and grab anything in your home that is valuable to you. Then, when you are all set, come back to me and we will leave immediately. If you are not back to me in five minutes, I'm coming in for you whether I have to tear your house apart or not."

"We're leaving!?!" Travis exclaimed. "Just because I touched a stupid crystal you are kidnapping me?"

"Not kidnapping," Sarora replied. "I'm saving your behind, so get moving!" She finished off and stopped running as they reached the edge of the cornfield.

Travis debated asking her more but decided otherwise. He was completely out of breath when he reached his house.

Nimbly, he unlocked the window, scurried through it, and dug through his dresser drawer for his compass and jackknife.

After a minute's search, Travis had his jackknife, compass, a map of the northern U.S. (for no apparent reason), and a first aid kit, stuffed into his backpack. *We might need something to eat,* he thought to himself as he unlocked his bedroom and rushed into his kitchen.

He returned to his room a couple minutes later with a box of granola bars and some hamburger meat (for Sarora).

After stuffing his backpack full, Travis slid out of his bedroom window. *I ought to bring my branch,* he thought to himself, remembering the piece of wood that he had been working on the past month. Quickly, he darted to the stump where his somewhat damp branch lay, picked it up, stuffed it in the handle of the top of his backpack, and darted back to his bedroom window. As he looked out to the cornfield, he noticed Sarora running straight for him, but that's not the only thing he saw.

Behind Sarora, flying in the sky, was a large black gryphon. And just by looking at it, Travis could tell that it was not a friend of his or Sarora's. Sarora obviously had not yet seen the creature.

"Sarora!" Travis yelled. "Look behind you!"

TAKE OFF

Sarora turned to look back. At the sight of the creature, she stopped and turned around to face it.

"What are you doing?" Travis yelled out again. "Run! Get away!" But Sarora remained rooted to her spot.

Within seconds, the creature landed a few yards from the spot where Sarora was standing firm, her head down low. Now that it was closer, Travis could just make out what it appeared to be.

The giant creature was a little bigger than Sarora. Its head, like Sarora's, resembled a bird. But this bird seemed to be more like a crow and it had several sharp teeth sticking out of its beak at various areas.

It also had the wings of a crow that were a pure black, as well as a little talon at the bend on each wing. But the weirdest thing about one of its wings was that it had a large, healing wound like Sarora's.

Its legs and body looked like a big, black cat's, however, it had the tail of a snake. This creature was just crazy looking.

A low growl began in Sarora's throat. The creature stared harshly at her with its evil red eyes. It spoke in a voice that sent a shiver through Travis's body.

"Ssssooo Sssarrrorrra, we meet again," it said. "I assume you know why I am back."

"I'm gonna take a wild guess and say it is for revenge," Sarora retorted, unblinking.

The creature cackled at Sarora's retort. "We both know that you arrren't that ssstupid, Sssarrrorrra." Its expression became more serious. "I believe the rrreassson we crossed paths last time was because of the Crrryssstal of Courrrage, aren't I rrright? And the rrreassson I'm back isss because the crrryssstal has found itsss partner."

"I have no clue what you are talking about," Sarora retorted again. "After I fell, the crystal smashed and it is now in a bundle of pieces inside my den where I have been staying."

"You insssolent child!" hissed the creature, its red eyes flaring with anger. "Give me the crrryssstal orrr elssse!"

"I choose or else," Sarora replied jokingly. "It sounds more promising."

"Then face the wrrrath of I, Sssievan! Lord Trrrazon's mossst powerrrful creaturrre!" And with that, Sievan began speeding toward Sarora, fury filling his eyes.

Sarora snapped her head around to speak to Travis.

"Travis! Cover your ears!" she shouted and then turned her head back to face Sievan once again.

Travis didn't waste a second covering his ears with his hands. He already knew better than to argue with Sarora.

Travis also knew that Sarora could surprise you from every point of view but still he had no idea of what she was about to do.

Sievan was now only a few feet from Sarora, his eyes now hungering for battle. In a second, he would be upon Sarora.

Immediately, Sarora snapped open her beak and out of it came a screech that paralyzed Travis with fear.

Sievan instantly collapsed on the ground, a dazed and frightened look in his eyes. His legs were sticking out away from his body as if he was standing. It looked like he was a petrified statue.

Sarora quickly spun around and galloped toward Travis. As she passed him, she lifted him onto her back with her beak as she continued to run.

Travis had kept quiet until now but he wanted answers. "What in the world are you doing?" he asked her as she ran onto the road, faced one way, and stopped in her tracks.

"I already told you," she replied. "I'm saving your butt. Now hold this carefully," she instructed him as she passed the bundle holding the crystal to him. Travis noticed that she must have hid it under her wings when Sievan came.

"Why are we on the road then?" Travis dared to ask as he grabbed the bundle carefully and stuffed it in his backpack. "Why don't we run to the woods and run through there?" But Sarora did not reply. She only stood there, standing in silence and staring at the long unwinding road.

"Oh, I get it," Travis answered himself thoughtfully. "We can't go through the woods because there are too many trees and branches in the way."

"Thank you, Sir Obvious," Sarora replied as she began to paw the ground like an impatient horse.

"For real though," Travis began again. "What are you doing?"

"Calculating," Sarora stated shortly.

"Calculating what?"

"My takeoff distance."

His heart plummeted, "What ... what do you mean by that?" Travis asked nervously, afraid of the answer. Once again, Sarora did not reply. This made Travis even more nervous.

Silence enveloped the whole area. Only a couple of birds quietly chirped in the air. Sarora, almost silently, continued to paw the ground.

Then suddenly, Sarora took off running. Travis struggled to hold onto her feathers and keep a hold of his staff (which was still resting in the loop at the top of his backpack), as the wind whipped his face.

Then, to Travis's displeasure, Sarora began to unfold her wings. "What do you think you are doing? You can't fly!" he yelled loudly enough so she could hear him.

"We'll just see about that!" Sarora shouted back as she finished unfolding her wings. Then she began to beat them, slowly at first, but she continued to pick up her pace. Gradually, Travis and Sarora were lifted off the ground.

"I'm not so sure about this," Travis stated nervously as they continued to ascend into the sky. It felt as if he were riding a Ferris wheel, as the air seemed to suck him up higher into the sky.

"Don't start saying that," Sarora began, "because I want to fly for as long as possible."

"Great," Travis replied trying to let out a joke to calm his fears. "Why don't we just fly to a 'magical land' while we are up here? Maybe the 'magical' people can save us." He smiled.

"That's practically what we will be doing. Now hold on,"

THE LAST ACER: TAKE OFF

Sarora said. "I have to find an air current." And with that, Sarora dove.

The air whipped at Travis's face even harder. "Ah!" Travis yelled loudly at the top of his lungs. He struggled to keep a firm grip on Sarora, but this was no easy task as her feathers would loosen from the force of his pulling.

"Sorry," Sarora apologized after she had found her current. "I forgot that I have a passenger."

"You forgot?" Travis replied, flabbergasted. "I could have fallen off to my doom and you say that you forgot I was on you?"

"I said I was sorry," Sarora stated with a smirk.

"Look," Travis began, "let's get everything straight. And don't go making up excuses not to tell me. I believe that I am entitled to know." He paused for a second before continuing. "The glowing crystal says so."

"All right," Sarora replied. "Open your ears so that I don't have to repeat this again. It is a long story."

THE ACERS

"I'll bring you up to speed with the story from the beginning," Sarora said.

"Long ago, before the separate societies, there was a peace-loving land called Firmara. It was a very docile and pleasant land at the time.

"The people of Firmara needed firm and strong leaders to keep them at peace, so they turned to the magic wielders. Magic wielders were people unlike others because they could use magic to do their work for them.

"To be a magic wielder, though, you needed to first visit the cave of Morality and take a crystal from the walls.

"The journey to get to the cave, however, was filled with danger, so most mortals decided they liked themselves in one piece and figured that they could get along without magic.

"Life was wonderful for mortals and magic wielders until one of the magic wielder's apprentices sent everyone and everything into chaos.

"Against his teacher's words, the young apprentice fought the mortals, demanding that the magic wielders should become the true rulers of Firmara rather than its knights.

"And so, the magic wielders banished him from the land for taking so many innocent lives, and outside of the land he stayed for twenty years." Sarora sighed deeply before continuing.

"Everyone had thought they had seen the last of him but still he returned, as hate-filled and as greedy as ever. Over the years, he had gathered some willing followers and together they attacked the capital of Firmara. Ever since then, the mortals have not trusted magic wielders—good or bad."

"But there is more, isn't there?" Travis asked. "That can't be the end of it."

"You are correct," Sarora replied. "There is more to the story.

"Though the magic wielders were no longer trusted, they still wanted to protect the mortals, no matter the cost. And so, the strongest, who had already completed their training, came together and became what they are known today as the Acers, the legends of old.

"Every one of them had fought hard to protect Firmara from the evil hand of Lord Trazon. However, against their effort, there had only remained one faithful, and living, Acer and his apprentice—until today." Sarora turned her head sideways to look at Travis.

Travis pondered the statement for a second before questioning Sarora. "What are you saying?" he asked her. "Are you actually trying to tell me that because I touched that stone that I am some hero in training?"

"Well ..." Sarora began, "yeah. If that is the way you want to put it."

"But I can't use magic."

"Believe it or not you can," Sarora replied.

"Prove it," Travis said, not wanting to believe any more of what Sarora said.

"All right," Sarora said. "Focus on that cloud over there and hold your hand out toward it." She pointed to a large fluffy cloud to their right. "Now, whatever I say, pretend it is the cloud saying it."

"But that sounds ridiculous," Travis objected.

"I'm trying to prove something."

"Sorry. Geez."

"Okay, let's try it." And Sarora began talking in the most insulting way that anyone could have ever thought possible.

"You are a sight for the eyes. Your enemies will not cower in fear, but rather in laughter. How can you expect to become an Acer when no one cares about you?"

This made Travis's blood boil. In fact, he began to feel quite warm even though the cold winds were still blowing. Yet nothing happened to the cloud. Travis could tell that Sarora was becoming impatient. She became so irritated, in fact, that she nearly went too far with the words that came out of her mouth next.

"Your mother must have been just outrageous. If I had a choice, I would have left you alone. A dull blade must have been sharper than her knowledge or else she would have known to put you up for adoption. Why she would keep a child like you, I don't know."

"DO NOT SPEAK OF MY MOTHER THAT WAY!" Travis yelled in fury. And that is when it happened. From his hand shot a quick stream of fire that split the cloud in two.

Travis gave a yelp of surprise and looked at his hand. It

was unscathed; it wasn't even scorched from the flames.

How could this happen? Travis thought to himself.

"Puzzled aren't you?" Sarora smirked. "There is your proof. Do you need me to show you more?"

Travis shook his head. "I … I'm good," he stated, reminding himself not to doubt Sarora ever again.

"Are you positive?" Sarora asked. "I could always show you how the flames could shoot out from every point of your body. It could even come out from—"

"I'm good!" Travis yelped before Sarora could continue and she laughed.

"What's so funny?" Travis asked.

"You!" Sarora laughed again. "The look on your face was just priceless!"

They flew quietly for a couple of minutes. Travis watched his surroundings for any sign of Sievan, in case he came. "What was that creature?" Travis asked Sarora.

"He is a dargryph." Sarora replied. "A dark creature made of evil animal spirits. He was created only to serve Trazon, the dark knight as some call him now."

Is he even still alive? he thought to himself. "Is Sievan dead?" Travis asked quietly.

"What was that?" Sarora asked. "I can't hear you when you mumble, especially when the wind is so loud up here."

"Is Sievan dead?" Travis shouted so that Sarora could hear him this time.

"I'm afraid not," Sarora replied. "The screech only paralyzes the victim and puts him in a trance-like sleep. It doesn't kill them." Then Travis thought he heard her mumble something that sounded like "unfortunately."

Another question struck him. "Why were you able to screech like that this time but you hadn't before when you faced Sievan?"

"That is the downfall with that technique," Sarora replied. "I can only do it from the ground and I can only use it around once every month."

"Had you used it before he had attacked you the first time?" Travis asked.

"Yes," Sarora replied hesitantly.

"On who?"

"A person."

"What person?"

"A person I know."

"You are not being very helpful."

"It's my own business."

"Fine. Keep it all to yourself then," Travis said.

After a few moments of silence Sarora said, "You go ahead and get some sleep. It'll do you better than just sitting there."

"But what if Sievan comes?" Travis asked.

"Then I'll wake you," Sarora replied.

"Are you sure that your wing will be okay?" Travis asked.

"Stop treating me like that, I'll be fine! Now like I said, get some rest. Today's events must have tired you."

Travis nodded, finally giving in. He stretched his arms around Sarora's neck and laid his head on it. And soon, lulled by the gentle winds, Travis fell into a peaceful sleep.

A REST STOP

Travis ran through the dark woods as fast as he could. Ahead of him ran a shadowy figure, darker than the night itself. Travis continued to keep up with the form until it turned on him. In a split second, everything went pitch black.

Travis woke with a start and remembered that everything was safe and that he was with Sarora, still flying in the sky. The only thing he had to worry about was where Sarora was headed. *I hope that Sarora knows where she is going,* he thought to himself as he looked at her injury. Before the flight, the wound had finally begun to scab over, but now it began to bleed slightly. *Depending on how long we have been flying, she should rest sometime soon.*

"Sarora?" Travis began.

"Yes?" came the exhausted reply.

"I think you should take a rest soon."

"If I keep going we can make it to our destination in another couple days or so."

"Have it your way then," Travis replied. Suddenly remembering what had occurred yesterday, Travis decided that he had more questions that needed to be answered.

"So," he began, "are there other things that an Acer can do besides wield magic?"

"Well, yeah, sort of," Sarora replied. "Acers have the

power to call upon their spirit animal. But you can only call upon it at will when you have fully become an Acer."

There was a pause and then Travis spoke. "Who are you, Sarora?" he asked from out of the blue.

"Who do you think I am?" Sarora countered his question with another question.

"I'm not sure," Travis replied and then his eyes widened when a thought came to mind. "Are you my spirit animal?"

Sarora was quiet for a moment and then replied, "You could say that."

"So you will do as I say then?"

"I never said ..." she began to object, but Travis cut her off.

"But you did in the fine lines of saying *'Acers have the power to call upon* their *spirit animal.'* "

"But ... but ..." Sarora sputtered.

"Don't blame me," Travis replied. "You said it yourself. Now land somewhere safe so you can take a rest."

"But—"

"Sarora?" Travis interrupted her.

"Fine, I'll land." Sarora gave up the fight and began to circle down toward the ground. The ground below consisted of many oak trees like that of the woods at Travis's home.

Sarora circled the treetops until she found a clearing in the woods. She slowly descended and landed on the ground, though she stumbled a little during the landing.

"See," Travis began, "that's not so bad."

Sarora sat down so that Travis slid down her back down to the ground.

"Ow!" Travis said as his rear end slammed the cold earth

and his staff whacked the back of his head.

"Yeah," Sarora replied, smirking to herself. "Now it isn't so bad." Travis couldn't help smiling as well. It was impossible to stay mad at Sarora.

Sarora stood and began to walk ahead. "Come on," she said to Travis. "We should find a place to camp."

Travis quietly followed Sarora through the woods. The trees of this wood consisted of small pines and medium-sized oaks. The oaks were bare of leaves because it was November. *It won't be long until the snow comes,* Travis thought to himself.

As they continued to walk, Travis kept a sharp eye out for anything that both he and Sarora could rest in. He spotted a log over a hole and pointed it out to Sarora, who disagreed because of the fungi growing on and around it.

They kept walking until they came to a badger-sized hole in a large rock. The rock was around five feet tall and a couple of arms-length wide. It was a darker shade of gray and sparkled a little wherever rays of sunlight hit it.

Travis was curious why Sarora had stopped them there. *It is nearly impossible that both of us could fit in there, let alone get in there,* Travis thought. However, Sarora would quickly erase that thought from his mind.

"Stand back," Sarora told Travis and he hurriedly obeyed. Sarora then mumbled something under her breath that Travis could not hear. Then, without waiting another second, she quickly obliterated the front of the rock with a couple swipes of her talons.

Unbelievable! Travis shouted in his mind. Not only was it unbelievable but something was strange about the way Sarora dismantled the front of the hollow rock. It wasn't just the fact that her bird-like talons could tear through the dense object. No, it was the way the wind had whipped up, only for the time Sarora had spent opening the rock. Travis began to wonder if it was because she had mumbled something under her breath.

"How did you do that?" Travis asked Sarora, astonished.

"It was just luck ..." Sarora replied in a quiet and worn-out voice.

"Just luck?" Travis asked. "Come on. We both know that what you just did wasn't 'just luck.'" When Sarora didn't reply, Travis spoke her name, "Sarora?"

When she still did not reply, Travis walked up to Sarora's side and stroked her shoulder. He noticed how she had her head hanging low, and how her breathing was quick and shallow.

"Here," Travis began, "let me help you in."

Sarora just shook her head, "I'm just ... winded," she told him in the same quiet voice and began walking slowly into the large, hollow rock. Once again, Travis followed close behind her. Exhausted, they both settled down in the cold, hard rock.

After sitting for a long while, Travis became bored. He had tried to entertain himself but nothing seemed to work. He decided to go for a walk.

"Just don't go too far," Sarora told him as he walked away.

The woods were darkened by the night. Nocturnal animals were already out and about, trying to find food.

Even though most of the day had become clear after the crystal lit up, dark clouds had gradually covered the night sky. It was dark enough that even the brightest of stars did not show. *Winter is coming quickly,* Travis thought. *We need to get to the place that we headed towards very soon. And we also need to get there before the snow comes.*

He continued to think.

But there are several problems that will slow us down. Sarora is once again worn out and if we tried to fly in this cold weather, she could hurt herself. I don't see us taking off in a hurry anytime soon because of that.

We could try to walk there, but unless we would like to spend the rest of our lives as circus freaks, it would be better to fly. There would be no possible way for us to walk in— scratch that—there would be no possible way for us to walk around even the smallest town without remaining undetected.

While Travis racked his brain for an idea, he continued walking through the woods, remembering to use his knife to cut small notches in the trees to mark his path. Once or twice, he saw a rabbit dart across his path.

After a few minutes, Travis began the walk back to the hollow rock with a few medium-sized sticks to make a fire.

When he arrived, he found Sarora sleeping in the rock and thought it best not to disturb her, so he began to build a little fire.

Travis took the sticks, laid the smaller ones on the ground, and built a tepee around them using the larger sticks. When he had finished building the fire area inside the rock, he concentrated on the sticks, held his hand out toward it, and thought of what Sarora had said earlier.

Within a couple of seconds, a small flame shot from his hand and onto the wood tepee. Soon, the fire was glowing steadily and it began to warm the hollow rock.

Travis rubbed his hands together and held them out toward the fire. *Today has been a long day,* he thought.

As the fire continued to glow, Travis heard his stomach growl. He took his backpack off and pulled out the box of granola bars. Though they were small, they could hold off some of Travis's hunger, for as long as they lasted at least.

After devouring one of the small bars, Travis zipped up his backpack, doused the fire with a pile of dirt, and laid down for some much-deserved rest.

TO BE A HUNTER

Travis woke the next morning to find Sarora rummaging through his backpack.

"If you don't mind me asking," Travis began, "what are you doing with my backpack?"

Sarora pulled her head out of the pack and Travis watched as a granola bar wrapper fell from her mouth. Travis quickly got up, rushed to the backpack, and looked inside of it.

"You ate all of the bars!" Travis exclaimed in horror. "Now what am I supposed to eat?"

"How about that slab of raw burger you put in there?" Sarora asked, still chewing on some of the bars.

"That was for you!"

"Travis," Sarora began, "I'm a gryphon, not a monster."

Travis just rolled his eyes. "Sorry for not taking an hour to cook it, but I was in a hurry. If you wanted it cooked, you should have told me before you ate all of the granola bars. Besides, couldn't you just cook it yourself?"

"Seeing that there were no matches in the pack, that I don't have opposable thumbs, and that you're the one with the fire power, I think it would be pretty difficult for me took cook something," Sarora retorted after swallowing the rest of the bars.

"Be that as it may," Travis began, "we still have one other problem."

"And what would that be?"

"The fact that winter is nearly here and all we have left for food is a pound of hamburger meat."

"So," Sarora retorted, "go and get something to eat."

"You think that I can hunt?" Travis asked, genuinely surprised.

"No, I think that you were gifted with the ability to call all the animals of the world and ask them to jump on a stick and roast over a fire."

"You're jesting, right?"

"Duh."

"But I've never hunted before," Travis complained. "How am I going to hunt anyway? I don't have a gun or a bow and some arrows."

Sarora heaved a loud sigh and rolled her eyes. "Follow me if you are that incompetent." And she walked out of the hollow rock. Travis grumpily followed at her side.

After they had journeyed a little ways, Sarora motioned for Travis to be silent.

He craned his neck and stood on his tiptoes to try and see over Sarora. About nine yards in front of them stood a badger. The big creature was shuffling around the leaves, probably looking for bugs. Its long front claws raked the cold, hard earth as it waddled about from place to place. Thanks to the way the wind was blowing in their faces, the badger could not smell them.

Sarora crouched down low to the ground, her eyes focused on the large animal, which seemed like an ant compared to Sarora. After a long while, Sarora leapt up and landed next to the badger. Before the badger could make a run for it, Sarora grabbed it by the neck and shook it, snapping its spine.

After killing it, Sarora dropped the dead badger on the ground and looked up at Travis. "Don't give me that look," she chided Travis, who had been grimacing at the entire scene. "It was its destiny to die and become the ground, as is the destiny of everyone else."

Travis slowly walked out of the bushes and up to the badger carcass. Its eyes stared blankly at him, although they were still in a surprised shape. Its neck was crooked where Sarora had broken it.

Travis felt remorse for the poor animal. Death had come so quickly and silently for the great animal. *It isn't fair,* Travis thought. *It isn't fair that this animal was just minding its own business and now it's dead, only to hope not to be wasted away.*

Travis felt Sarora's tail run down his back. He looked away from the corpse and behind him to see Sarora standing next to him. "It's okay," Sarora said. "We do not kill for joy or for sport, we kill to live."

"It's just …" Travis began as he looked away from her, "the badger never expected his death to come. Was it fair to not warn him?"

"Travis, no one knows when their death will arrive. We do not know if it will be today, tomorrow, or a hundred years from now."

"But then what should we do about death?"

"Enjoy our life now, give thanks and pray that we live long lives, and accept it when it comes," Sarora told Travis.

"We can't dwell on the things that will happen but rather think on the things that are here in your life now."

"You speak as though you've already experienced it."

"In some ways, I already feel that I have."

Travis slowly nodded his head in understanding. It had felt like death to him when his mother had died.

"Come," Sarora told him. "Pick it up and let's be on our way back to the den."

"Why do I have to carry it?" Travis asked. "It looks like it weighs a ton!"

"Don't make me do all the work Mr. Melodramatic. It is your only source of food now."

"I feel so special ..." Travis muttered sarcastically as he hunched over and pulled hard to throw the heavy creature over his shoulder.

"And don't get the slightest idea that I'm always going to get food for you," Sarora said to him. "You'll have to find your own way of feeding yourself."

But what could I possibly use? Travis asked himself. Then the idea struck him. It may take awhile, but he knew that it was worth a shot.

When Travis and Sarora returned to the stone, Sarora showed Travis how to gut the badger. While Travis gutted the creature (a sickening task), Sarora dug a hole near the edge of the hollow rock. She dug deep down into the earth so that the meat would stay cool and fresh.

After the gruesome task was finished and the meat stored, Travis went into the rock and came back out with his staff. He then found a dry, comfortable seat near a large tree and leaned his back against it.

"What are you doing?" Sarora asked from where she was lying in the sun.

"You'll see." Travis replied as he pulled his jackknife out of his pocket and began to shave the tip of the branch down.

A WEAPON

Travis finished his work by sundown. The modified staff lay in his lap, and his tired hands lay at his side. His eyes ran over the branch again and again, studying its every feature. *This is exactly what I need.*

The staff, which had already been smoothed out and cleaned, had a newly pointed end. The tip came out at a point from the staff, giving it a pencil-like look. It may have looked ridiculous, but Travis didn't care; this was his new hunting weapon, and he was proud of it.

"What do we have here?" Sarora asked as she stood up and walked over to inspect Travis's staff.

"This," Travis began, holding up the staff, "is my way of hunting."

"It looks like a giant pencil," Sarora critiqued.

Travis shot her a nasty look. "You said I should find a way to hunt for myself and so I did. This is how I will hunt."

"Oh yeah," Sarora started, "I can picture it now. Travis, the mighty hunter, runs hard and fast, chasing the animals through the forest as they all scream together, 'Look! It's Travis and his killing pencil! Run for your lives!' "

"Oh just shut up!" Travis snapped at Sarora, for the first time. Even Sarora seemed surprised at Travis lashing back. "You'll see. It may not be pretty, and to some creature like you it may not be life-threatening, but to me, it'll be the difference between starvation and contentment."

"Contentment should be the last thing on your mind," Sarora replied. "Let's just focus on staying alive and then we'll see to your contentment."

Travis merely ignored Sarora, stood up and turned to leave. "I'll see you soon."

"Travis!" Sarora called after him. "We have enough food! You don't need to hunt!"

Travis's only response was his hand waving to her over his shoulder.

"He's a boy all right," Sarora mumbled to herself, "block-headed and eager to make a point with no purpose."

Travis took a deep breath as he steadied himself. He was kneeling, hiding in a bush and less than ten feet in front of him stood a lonely deer. Her tail swished to and fro while her all-hearing ears swiveled on top of her head.

Travis tightly gripped his staff, which was lying at his side. His palms began to sweat and his heart beat as fast as ever, pounding in his chest. *I'll show Sarora,* he thought with determination, *I'll show her I can hunt.*

The deer remained stationary in the little clearing, her head down low and her mouth focused on the grass. *It's now or never. I'll never get a shot like this again.* But something held Travis back. Something in his mind called out, reminding him of the badger that Sarora had killed.

He shook his head. *This is it. I can't back out now. I can do it, I can do it.* Travis took another deep breath and lunged.

The deer immediately threw its head and tail up and jumped sideways, away from Travis.

He landed a foot away from the deer but before he could take a second jab at it, it ran. The last thing Travis saw of the deer was its rear-end high tailing it out of the area.

Travis yelled a curse at the sky. "Darn it! I was so close!" he yelled as he pouted and jabbed his staff into the ground.

Irritated, Travis sulked back to the rock amid a darkening sky.

When he returned, Travis was hungry, tired, and defeated. To his surprise, Sarora said nothing to him at all—she didn't even ridicule him. She was just lying on the floor, staring off into space.

Travis went to the other side of the rock and sat on the floor. Quietly, he removed some of the badger meat from his backpack, lit a fire using his hands, and proceeded to drop the burger on a rock near the flames.

Sarora quietly shifted her gaze to the crackling fire. Still, she didn't utter a word. What was even weirder was that Travis noticed how her injured wing was pressed against the wall.

That's not a good sign, Travis thought. He knew she was too stubborn to tell him if she was hurting or upset. He was going to have to drill her in order to get her to tell him. *However,* Travis thought again, *she is my spirit animal, she has to listen to any order I give her.*

"So," Travis began, "would you like to tell me why you are acting so quiet and innocent all of a sudden?" Sarora just kept her gaze fixed on the flames.

This time, Travis cleared his throat, hoping to grab her full attention. "Let me *put* this more clearly," he began again. "Tell me what's going on!"

Finally, Sarora turned her gaze toward him. A hazy look covered her eyes. "Winter's coming …" she muttered quietly.

Travis rolled his eyes, "No duh. What's *really* bothering you?"

Sarora just quietly blinked at him and said nothing.

"Okay! I've had it!" Travis shouted at her. "Stand up, turn around, and let me see your wing!"

"Now?" Sarora asked tiredly.

"Yes," Travis replied impatiently, "now."

With a reluctant sigh, Sarora forced herself up and turned the other way so that Travis could look at her wing.

"Why didn't you tell me about this?" he asked cuttingly.

"Didn't want you to worry …"

"Didn't want me to worry!" A quick look revealed that Sarora's injury, which had nearly finished healing, was now once again leaking puss and scabs were crusting all over it.

"I didn't mean to upset you," Sarora replied, this time regaining her full voice. Yes, winter is coming. No, it is very unlikely that I will fly again for a great while. Yes, we must find a solution before the snow comes, if possible."

"Okay, okay, I get the picture," Travis retorted and turned to grab the first aid kit from his backpack. Travis quickly rummaged through it and tossed aside anything unneeded—scissors, a small signal flare, and a children's band-aid designed with little kittens that were carrying hospital gear.

Eventually he found a bandage roll and an alcohol wipe. Sarora grudgingly held out her wing and he wiped the scarred tissue up and down until the wipe was brownish-yellow from the puss. He proceeded to wrap as much of the bandage roll around her wing as he dared and stuck it to itself so that it would hold.

Travis let his arms hang limply at his sides. They were aching in every place possible from gutting the badger to sharpening his staff and, on top of that, cleaning up the gouge in Sarora's wing.

He looked at the fire. His meat on the rock needed to be flipped. Tired and delusional, Travis shoved his hand under the burger to flip it.

"Ah!" he screamed in pain as his hand jerked back from the burning rock. He quickly shoved his hand in his mouth in an attempt to cool it.

"Look, Empty Head is back," Sarora commented from where she lay by the fire.

"Oh, we quwaiet," Travis tried to talk through his hand-filled mouth. He looked around the room for a spatula but found only his staff, so he took his burnt hand out of his mouth and picked it up and used it to carefully flip over his dinner. *At least it is good for one thing,* he thought to himself.

Ten minutes later Travis was filling himself with the little slab of badger meat. He had offered some to Sarora but she declined, saying that she was too tired to eat.

After the small dinner, Travis grabbed his backpack and set it against the wall of the large rock to use as a pillow (and to save it from Sarora). Leaving the fire lit to put itself out, he laid back and rested his head onto the sack and steadily began to watch the flames.

"Good night," Travis whispered to Sarora.

"Good night, Empty Head," the reply came from Sarora and soon the pair were fast asleep.

THE STARRY-EYED DEER

The next few days were spent resting and strategizing. Winter was coming fast and they needed to find a way to stay warm or get to their destination without being seen or killed.

Most plans ended up being rejected because of some complication. They considered continuing on through the woods, staying on the outskirts of any towns along the way. But Sarora pointed out that their destination was still several hundred miles away and that it would be nearly impossible to walk through the woods the entire way, especially since a large city and a vast lake lay between their current location and their destination.

They considered waiting it out until Sarora had completely healed, but that thought was quickly dashed when a snow shower covered the ground with a thin blanket of powder, creating a sense of urgency for reaching the end of their journey.

One thing was certain: They must take action soon or live in the cold rock for the winter, becoming a human Popsicle or Gryphon-sicle.

Once, Travis pulled out the map he had brought with them and tried to get Sarora to point out where they were.

He laid the map across the ground outside of the hollow

rock and pointed to where his house was. "We were right there when we took off," he began, placing his finger on the top of the state of Ohio. "Would you mind showing me where we are now?"

Sarora walked over to where Travis knelt and sat beside him. "Let's see …" she started. "Well, to put it simply, if we started there, we are probably somewhere around here," she said, circling the whole top right corner of the map and some of the ground. "Does that help any?"

"You mean to tell me that you have no idea where we are?"

"Well, you asked and I showed you where I guessed where we are approximately," Sarora replied.

"But you circled the country of Canada ranging all the way off the map to where Europe should be."

"Precisely."

"Well, I guess the sooner we are off, the sooner we will find out our location," Travis sighed.

Travis also still had not given up the hope of killing his first animal with his staff. His last attempt on an animal, a rabbit, had left him with a bruised elbow.

The rabbit had been sitting in front of him, staring at him, and had been completely still. Once he had been a couple feet away, Travis had lunged and then jabbed his staff at it, aiming it at its chest. However, the rabbit was extremely fast and ran away before the blow came within an inch of its face.

But Travis figured the past was the past and that eventually he would become a hunter. He believed that it was only a matter of time before he would get his first kill.

The days had rolled into the end of November. The clouds that rolled through promised snow, and plenty of it. Any oak trees in the woods were now completely bare. The leaves that scattered the ground were coated in snow and frost. Yes, winter was upon them.

Travis woke with a start the next morning. The cold wind was blowing through the open hole in the rock along with the bright sun, shining at its best through the trees.

Travis rubbed his eyes with his numb hands. He sat up and braced himself for the cold as he pulled the badger hide off him. It was extremely cold without his makeshift badger hide blanket covering the lower half of his body.

He began to warm as he stood up and did a little jog in place to keep his flesh from numbing from head to toe. The weather wasn't always like this now. It was cold one day, snowing the next, then it would warm up and melt the snow, making the ground wet and muddy. It would get cold and start the cycle all over. The weather cycle got old quick.

Sarora began to stir on her side of the hollow rock. First one eye opened and then closed shut, and then both eyes opened and she lifted her head to look at her surroundings. She stretched her legs like a cat, starting with the front and ending in the back. She stood, walked to the center of the opening in the rock, and breathed in the morning air. This was her morning ritual. Everything in Travis's world was very repetitive right now.

"Good morning," Sarora spoke sleepily to Travis, who just nodded a good morning in reply.

"Will you get breakfast ready again? I'll go see if I can find more to replenish our food stock."

Here we go again, Travis thought, *the same thing every morning.* "Why don't *I* go and find some food today while you cook breakfast. Just to change things up."

"You are the cook here, Mr. Opposable Thumbs. Don't forget you are the one who has the ability to start the fire."

"How about this then," Travis began. "I'll cook breakfast and you sit here and watch. Then later, I'll go hunting for us and you can take the day off."

Sarora rolled her eyes. "You be the hunter if that is what you have to do, but I would prefer to eat a full meal tonight. You know, the one that fills my stomach, not that low-in-calorie, no-substance, imaginary food. Because that is what you will come home with when you finally give up on the whole idea."

Travis shot a dirty look at Sarora. Sometimes she just overdid it with her explanations and teasing. "You'll see when I come home with the largest deer you've ever seen." And then he walked outside to get some of the badger meat from the makeshift freezer.

After breakfast, Travis grabbed his staff, his compass, and his pocketknife, and said goodbye to Sarora. He planned on spending the whole afternoon or longer to get something edible to eat.

He began his walk through the woods, keeping an eye out for any sign of prey. Within the hour, Travis had spotted and scared off a few rabbits. Every time he would get close, the rabbits would just turn tail and run.

He began to grow bored and tired by the time the sun had passed the center of the sky. Deciding it best to take a break, Travis settled himself under a large tree and sat there quietly, enjoying the day.

He sat there for what he figured was around two hours. The weather had begun to grow colder and clouds began to roll in, but Travis wasn't concerned; today was all about proving himself.

Just as Travis began to stand up, he heard a couple of steps. Then another couple and he began to hear the bushes near him rustle. Travis slowly crouched down and turned his gaze to where the noise was coming from.

Again, he heard two steps together, a moment of silence, and then the other two steps and the bushes rustled. Travis held his breath. Even before he could see the animal, he knew what it was.

The deer slowly stepped into the clearing about twenty feet from Travis. Its head was held high, its ears swiveled from side to side. It took in a great whiff of the air and turned its head from side to side, but it did not seem to detect Travis.

Travis was so shocked that it took him a second to realize that he wasn't breathing. He took in quiet, deep breaths to try and settle his heart rate. Slowly, he reached his hand to his side and grabbed his staff.

His hand brushed a small leaf pile that had been on the ground. The deer stopped, and stared directly into Travis's eyes. Now that he could see the deer better in the lighter clearing, Travis knew it was a buck. But not just any little buck with four to six points on his antlers—no, this was the largest deer Travis could have ever seen. This deer had a wide rack that must have held over twelve points. That was very rare indeed.

The deer held its gaze. It knew that Travis was there but it remained. Its ears turned toward Travis. The buck held its head high and let out a snort.

Travis quickly looked to his staff, and then looked back at the deer. 'Err' snorted the deer and he bobbed his head once.

Again, Travis looked to the staff and this time quietly set it down. Travis may have wanted to prove himself, but being seriously injured by a buck was not on his agenda.

Travis returned his gaze to the buck. To his surprise, the buck took one step toward him, and then another. *What does he think he's doing?* Travis thought.

The deer held steady again and after a brief pause took two more steps toward him. They were now fifteen feet apart.

Travis was beginning to panic. He had no idea what this animal intended to do and he did not feel like sticking around to find out. However, Travis held his place.

The buck continued to move slowly toward him. Step, step, pause. Step, step, pause. Step, step, pause. Now only eight feet separated them.

While the deer came closer, Travis continued to make nervous glances around to find an escape route. Now only five feet separated them. Travis was able to see every little detail on the buck—his black, velvety snout; his white chest, underbelly and underside of his tail. These characteristics told him that the deer was a whitetail.

The buck took two more steps toward Travis and the pair stood a foot apart. The deer lowered its head so that it was face-to-face with him. Travis just quietly stared back in awe. The deer's eyes were not normal. Instead of just being a black hole, they were a darker color, flecked with gold sparkles. The sparkles danced like stars on a wavy water surface.

The buck held its position and blew its warm air in Travis's face. Immediately, Travis's eyes closed shut and a familiar dream flooded into his head …

Travis ran through the dark woods as fast as he could. Ahead of him ran a shadowy figure, now clearer than the time before. It had a long, flowing tail and mane and its hooves beat the ground. Its coat was darker than the night itself.

Travis continued to keep up with the form until it turned on him. In a split second it reared and everything went pitch black.

Travis's eyes snapped open in a flash, the memory of the dream still swarming in his head. The buck was nowhere to be seen.

A thick blanket of snow had covered the ground and Travis began to realize that he was freezing. His hands and feet were numb as could be.

Travis looked to the sky, which had grown cloud-covered and black in what had felt like a short period of time. Snow was falling heavily and steadily.

Travis tried to stand and move around but the air, compared to the blanket of snow, was so freezing that he quickly sat back down. He sat there shivering for a minute until he convinced himself to try to move again. This time, he was able to stand and began to stagger toward what he thought was the direction of the hollow rock.

Twice he tripped and fell but was able to get back up and continue walking. The wind kept increasing in speed and the snow blew into his face and blinded him. His hands and feet were so numb that he could not feel them.

Travis fell a third time and could not get back up. His limbs were too cold and his muscles hurt from shivering. He knew he could not last much longer. If someone did not find him soon, he would be a goner.

The snow quickly piled on top of Travis until he was almost completely covered. From somewhere in the distance, Travis though he heard someone call his name but he did not respond.

A minute passed and Travis heard the voice again. "Travis! Where are you?" He wanted so badly to respond but his face was numb and frozen close to the ground.

When the call came again, Travis tried to shout back. "I'm over here ..." his muffled voice said.

Whoever called must have heard him because soon he heard snow crunching beneath feet. Travis soon heard a voice next to him. "Oh, Empty Head ..." Before he could hear more, Travis blacked out.

NEW PLACE, NEW FRIEND

Travis heard dishes clang together and could smell the fresh aroma of someone frying bacon and eggs. His hands rubbed against the blanket covering him … wait a minute … blanket! Bacon! Dishes!

Travis's eyes snapped open and he looked around. He was lying on a couch in a living room. The walls were painted a yellow color that brought a cheery atmosphere to the room. Across the room was an old television set on a small table. A doorway led to the kitchen.

Travis quietly began to sit up. He had absolutely no idea where he was. This was definitely not his house or any other house he had ever been in before.

"Hello?" Travis called. "Anyone there?" Of course, he knew someone was there, he just didn't know who it was.

Travis heard the shuffling of feet and glanced toward the kitchen. There, in the open doorway, stood a man. He had silver-white hair and blue eyes. He wore an old, grease-covered apron over his blue plaid T-shirt. His blue jeans were also quite dirty and smudged with paint stains. In his one hand he held a cleaning rag and in the other a spatula.

"Well, you decided to get up now, huh?" The old man

smiled as he shifted his rag from one hand to the other. "I was just making us some breakfast. You feel well enough to get up and come to the table?" The man seemed sincere enough to trust. Besides, Travis was hungry.

"Sure," Travis began, "but where am I?"

"I'll tell you everything after a good breakfast," the man said, walking over to Travis and holding out his hand. "An old man's promise."

Travis nodded and took the man's hand. The man pulled Travis up to his feet and together they walked into the kitchen.

The kitchen was fitting of an old country home. The walls were painted a plain white while the wallpaper was a patterned blue and white. A china blue and white chicken sat on the windowsill.

A small wooden table sat in the middle of the room. On it rested a pitcher and plates with the same blue and white pattern as the chicken and the wallpaper. Two chairs sat next to the round table. The man led Travis to one of the seats and they sat down together and filled themselves with delicious bacon and eggs. Travis figured it had been the best meal he had had since nacho day at school, which had been several months ago (it was not his fault that the cooks hated cleaning the cheese off everything).

When they had finished, the old man leaned back against his chair and looked at Travis with thoughtful eyes. "All right. I promised, so I'm gonna start with the simplest part of the tale," the man said as he cleared his throat and began. "My name is Arlen. Arlen Shail. I've lived here in this farmhouse for the past thirty years. The house is 'bout two miles from the closest town. It's just a little ol' town with one of those Mickey D's in it and about one little fire station.

"Anyways, I was just relaxing here, in my house after taking care of the horse in the barn. I was just about to turn the tele off when a heard a loud banging at the door.

"When I had been out with the horse, the snow had been making a blizzard of itself. By now, the snow was nearly three feet deep. I was sure wondering who or what was looking for me at that time of night, bein' about eleven o'clock and all. So I got up, walked over to the door, and opened it.

"You were there lying with your back in the snow. Your whole face was near blue and I could easily see icicles forming in your hair.

"I couldn't just let you stay there so I picked you up, looked around once more to see if anyone else was out there, and I brought you inside and sat you on the sofa in the livin' room. From there I spent 'bout one hour trying to warm ya back up."

"Wait a second," Travis began. "You found me at the door alone? There were no tracks on the ground?"

"It was dark," Arlen answered. "But I'm pretty sure that there weren't any."

"So how'd I get here then?" Travis asked.

"You mean you don't know?"

"No. I have no idea how I got here," Travis stated. "I was out sitting under a tree earlier yesterday and I fell asleep. When I woke, the snow had covered me and I was nearly frozen. I thought I heard a voice, but I passed out before I could find out who it was." Travis left out the part where the deer with the shimmering eyes came up to him and gave him the dream.

"Hmmm… Well, I don't know what to tell ya," Arlen replied. "I guess it's just a mystery. I'm the only one who lives within a two-mile radius of here so I'm not sure whose voice ya coulda heard."

Travis took his hands and rubbed them up and down his face. It was then that he realized how dirty and greasy he was. "If you don't mind me asking," Travis began, "do you have a shower I could use?"

Arlen chuckled. "I was wonderin' when you were going to ask that. You smell as if you slept in the horse's stall for the past week. And that's sayin' something since I don't spend a lot of time pickin' it out." He got up and pointed to the hallway. "Down the hall, farthest to the left. There are towels in the bathroom. After you undress, set your clothes outside of the door. I'll take them and give 'em a washin' that they so badly need. I'll leave you some clothes outside of the bathroom when you're finished."

"Thanks," Travis replied as he got out of his seat and walked down the hall to the bathroom. He shut the door and quickly undressed. Then he set his clothes outside of the room and turned on the warm water in the shower. *Finally,* he thought to himself, *my luck seems to be turning around.*

After Travis finished his shower, he dried himself off and peeked outside of the bathroom door to find a clean pair of jeans and a gray sweatshirt.

Filled with warmth and relief after he put the new clothes on, Travis walked out of the bathroom and into the hallway. Of course, the clothes were a bit baggy on him but at this point, he did not care. Clean clothes were a blessing enough as it was.

Travis called for Arlen but there was no response. He looked in the living room and kitchen but he still could not find him. *He's probably just outside,* Travis thought to himself.

However, instead of going to look for Arlen outside, Travis thought that it might be better to relax for a while and watch some television.

He turned on the tube and flipped through the channels by pressing the buttons on the side of the screen. Finally, he came to a show he thought he might enjoy. He retreated to the sofa.

Before Travis new it, his eyelids grew too heavy and he fell into a peaceful sleep.

STORIES

The next couple days were filled with rest and stories for Travis and Arlen. Travis told Arlen all about where he had come from and his previous life but excluded the part of the abuse from his step-dad.

Arlen told Travis stories about his life as a younger man. Many stories included crazy pranks, exciting parties, and getting into trouble.

Arlen told a story once of how he had attempted to trick a girl by telling her that his parents were millionaires. However, his plan hadn't turned out so well.

"What happened next?" Travis had asked

"Well, I'll just say that I haven't had a girl look at me since," he ended with a chuckle.

Travis commented, "Seems like you got yourself into tons of trouble way back when."

"You're right about that, Travis. Just remember, when you get older, girls hate to be wrong—especially when they are tricked into thinking something," Arlen smiled.

Travis just nodded.

He felt like he had forgotten something and it was bugging him. His eyes unconsciously drifted to the window and he stared blankly into space. Outside the ground was still covered in a blanket of snow. The sky was a clear blue and the sun was shining brightly. He could just hear the winter birds twittering in their trees.

Travis got up out of the chair he was sitting and went over to get a better look out the window. High in the sky, a hawk was flying. *Wait a second, a hawk! Sarora! I completely forgot!*

"Er, Arlen?" Travis asked, turning to the older man.

"Yes, Travis?" came the reply. Arlen had his head buried in a newspaper.

"I was wondering if it would be okay if I could go outside," Travis said.

"Well," Arlen began as he folded the paper and sat it down on the kitchen table. "Only if you're feelin' up to it, then yeah, I guess it would be okay."

"Thanks Arlen!" Travis called as he darted out of the room.

"Wait a sec!" Arlen called down the hall, "You need a coat and some other winter things!"

As soon as Travis had been outfitted with a coat, gloves, snow pants, and a hat, he set outside to look for Sarora.

The woods was not far from Arlen's home. The home was situated in a corner of a clearing where two sides were shrouded by forest and the other two were open to long plains.

Travis walked briskly into the woods, prepared for a long walk if need be. In his right coat pocket was his pocketknife and in the other the compass. As always when Travis walked in the woods, he marked every few trees with his pocketknife in order to keep track of his path.

As Travis walked through the forest of oaks, maples, and pines, he looked for any sign of Sarora. The snow thickly covered the ground so he had to lift his feet up high to walk. However, this method of walking became tiring quickly. But Travis did not care. He just wanted to find Sarora and make sure that she was okay.

Travis began to call out his friend's name. "Sarora! Where are you? It's me, Travis!" But for the first hour, there was no reply.

Travis decided to take a little break and rest awhile. As he sat, Travis tilted his head back to rest against the tree and he began to close his eyes …

He snapped back awake, remembering what happened the last time he fell asleep outside. He quickly forced himself to stand back up and keep moving.

"Sarora!" he shouted repeatedly, now becoming worried that he was lost or that something bad could have happened to her.

Travis took a deep breath. The icy air bit at his lungs as he inhaled and exhaled. The sun had already passed the center of the sky and was beginning to retreat. *Just one more call this way,* Travis told himself. *If there is no response, I'll head back to Arlen's.*

Travis walked farther in the direction he thought would lead to the hollow rock. He made one last call, "Sarora!"

No response. With a sigh, Travis turned and began to head back to Arlen's house.

Travis stopped in his tracks. He thought he had heard a noise. He looked behind him but saw nothing so he kept walking.

"Travis …" the voice called. Once more, he looked back. He thought he saw something moving through the trees.

"Sarora?" Travis almost whispered to himself. A figure began to appear among the trees. Now he could make out a bird-like head and a cat-like body.

"Travis!" Now he knew it had to be her.

"Sarora!" Travis called in excitement and began to run to her.

Sarora ran at Travis at full speed. They collided with each other and Travis wrapped his arms around her neck and together they laughed.

Once their laughing had settled, Sarora finally spoke. "I thought I lost you."

Travis pulled himself away just a bit. "What do you mean?"

Sarora's eyes held an emotion she had never shown to Travis. "I thought you were going to freeze. When I found you, you were fading away."

"You're the one who found me?"

"You never do know, do you, Empty Head?" A "gryphon smile" broke out on Sarora's face.

"How did you find me?" Travis asked.

"Well," Sarora began, "once the sun had begun to set, I decided that I should go and look for you. But just as I headed out, there was a giant snowstorm that came out of nowhere—literally, *nowhere*. I kept trying to go and find you but the storm held me back.

"Once the storm had started to clear, I went out once again. I thought I heard something the way you had headed. As I went out, something strange happened. This deer leapt out in front of me. I tried to scare it away, but it wouldn't move. Finally, I asked it, just for the sake of asking, 'You wouldn't happen to know where Travis is, would you?' And you know what? It answered me! It nodded its head once, turned away from me, and began to walk away. So I followed it.

"The snow was still blowing on the wind but I followed the deer. Finally, I thought I heard something ahead of us. I walked toward the noise and I saw you freezing half to death on the ground.

"I tried to wake you but you wouldn't come to, so I carried you on my back until I reached that farm house a little ways from here. I sat you down and banged on the door until I heard someone coming. Quickly, I turned and covered up my tracks, when I flew off so not to leave any evidence that I had been there.

"I came back to the hollow rock and I sat there for the past four days. And since you hadn't come to see me again, I thought that you hadn't made it and that I had failed to save you," Sarora ended with a deep look of sadness in her eyes.

Travis didn't know what to say. For the past few days, he had been curled up warm and cozy in Arlen's home without even remembering to come and find Sarora.

"I'm sorry, Sarora," Travis finally found the right words to begin with, "I was just so wrapped up at being with, you know, another person, and at that, a person who didn't want to bring any harm to me, that I … well, I kinda forgot that you were here. I'm so sorry."

Sarora wrapped her head around Travis's shoulder. "I forgive you," she assured him.

"You … you do?" Travis asked, surprised.

"Of course I do. Why wouldn't I?"

"Sarora, are you okay?" Travis asked.

Sarora pulled her head back again and answered with a question. "Why would you even ask that? Of course I'm okay. Why wouldn't I be?"

Travis sat down on the ground. "I don't know," he said. "Today you just seem … different."

"It's probably just the occasion," Sarora replied. "I … I really haven't had a friend to talk to in a while. And the thought of losing you really made me feel sick inside." Sarora shook her head and put a gryphon-like smile on her face. "I'm just glad you're safe, Empty Head."

"Well, at least you haven't forgotten my pet name," Travis smirked.

Sarora's eyes twinkled and she turned away from Travis and looked over her shoulder at him. "Come on, I'll show you back to the hollow cave."

Travis opened his mouth to explain to Sarora that he could not stay in the rock, but he thought otherwise and tagged along.

EXPECT THIS

Sarora eagerly led the way back to the hollow rock, trying to get as much information as possible about what Travis had been up to.

"So what was it like where you stayed? Who lives there?" Sarora asked.

"The house was really nice. Arlen, that's the older man who lives there, loves to tell stories of all sorts. Especially ones about when he grew up. It's definitely not like what I had at my home." Travis grinned happily at first but then his smile went away. He had never told Sarora about his step-dad's cruelty.

Sarora stopped and looked at Travis quizzically. "What do you mean by 'definitely not like your home'?"

"Nothing," Travis replied, looking down to avoid Sarora's gaze.

No one spoke for a few seconds but Sarora finally replied, "All right then. We'd better keep going. We're almost there." She then turned and kept walking on with Travis close behind.

"Here we are!" Sarora declared once they could see the hollow rock.

Travis squinted his eyes as bright sunlight reflected off the snow in the small clearing. The hollow rock rested in the warmth-giving sun.

Together, Sarora and Travis walked into the homely boulder together. Travis could see that nearly everything he had in there was as he had left it. His backpack was up against the wall and beside the badger pelt. The small fire pit was situated in the middle of the rock. Charcoaled wood was scattered inside the pit and the rocks that circled it were flecked with black.

Travis began the fire with a flick of his palm (the task was becoming increasingly easy). As the flame flickered to life, Travis and Sarora sat down to talk for a while. It was just like at home in Sarora's old den, only better because of the relief of not having to deal with his step-father.

Travis inhaled deeply and closed his eyes, taking in all the scents of the outdoors. This was his kind of living—trees surrounding him, blue sky above him, a fire flaring, and a close friend beside him. Nothing could get much better than this.

"This is unreal …" Travis mumbled, his eyes still closed.

Sarora, who had been in the middle of a whole other conversation, stopped talking and looked at Travis quizzically. "The fact that I caught a moose while you were livin' the life is unreal?" she asked him.

Travis, now just realizing that he had not been paying any attention to what Sarora was saying, snapped back to reality and replied, "Sorry, I wasn't listening, I was just thinking about what's going on, you know? Like here and now …" He suddenly remembered what Sarora had just asked. "You caught a moose while I was with Arlen?" he asked in shock.

"Got ya," Sarora chuckled. "I knew you weren't paying any attention. Sievan could have run through here and attacked and you still wouldn't have noticed while in your dream state."

Travis shook his head, feeling quite stupid. But he still had to smile; Sarora did have a way of making him laugh.

"Good one," he replied as he continued to smile.

"Hey, anytime you need to return from your orbit around the galaxy, let me know. I will know how to bring you back to earth."

Travis chuckled a little. "Yeah, let's hope that it will always be this way."

"I hate to burst your bubble and all," Sarora began, "but fate has many ideas in mind for everyone. One day you can soar, the next you could sink."

Travis looked at her, puzzled. "Where did you ever hear that?"

"From your soon-to-be mentor," Sarora replied. "He has a way of ... well ... making metaphors." She once again flashed her gryphon-like grin.

"That'll be interesting."

"More than you know," Sarora chuckled. "Just, F.Y.I, when we get to Firmara, uh ... how do I say this ... my master will probably pull me aside and uh ... speak a few 'interesting metaphors' to me so ... as a heads up, you may want to cover your ears."

Travis shifted his position so that he sat up, Indian-style. "Why? You did something you weren't supposed to?"

"Something like that ..." Sarora trailed off.

"What'd you do?"

"Let's just say, don't ever disobey him if you value your life."

Startled, Travis asked, "Why? Is he that strict?"

"It's more because he's looking out for us and wants us to be safe. He's … like a stern father, looking out for you but won't let you get away with anything. You know?"

"Not entirely …" Travis replied.

Now it was Sarora's turn to look at Travis quizzically. "And what do you mean by that?" she asked.

Travis really wanted to tell Sarora about his step-dad. He figured that it would be nice to actually tell someone about all the secrets that had been bugging him for so long. Yet he did not know where to start.

"Well … it's kind of a long story."

"Hmm …"

"I'll tell you a little, but then I should probably head back." Sarora merely nodded.

"You know, of course, that I had a home."

"Yes, yes I saw it," Sarora replied. "Stop beating around the bush and get to the point."

Travis nodded and stared down into his lap. "Well, I lived there with one other person, my step-dad." He took a deep breath before continuing. "My step-dad used to be nice, until my mom passed away. After she died, my step-dad locked me in my room and only let me out to go to school or to use the bathroom.

"A couple years ago, I finally learned how to pick the lock on both my window and my bedroom door without step-dad ever noticing. That's how I was able to sneak out and visit you. And that's also why I was always on a strict schedule.

If I wasn't home before my step-dad got there, I wouldn't put it past him to whip out his twelve gauge and start shooting around the forest until he found me or I returned.

"That's all there is to it. That's why I was always in a lousy mood when I came to visit. But I knew that you would always be there, to brighten up my day."

Sarora's eyes had steadily grown larger in surprise while she listened to Travis's speech. "But what about your real father?" she asked. "What ever happened to him?"

"Don't know." Travis replied, finally looking back up. "Mom says he passed away, but I've always had this inner feeling that he might still be out there." He finished with an inward sigh.

"You know," Sarora began, "they say that if you truly believe in something, it may come to be true."

Travis gave a grim smile. "Yeah, but if that were really true, I'd still be at home with both a dad and a mom." He looked at his feet again.

"Never say never," Sarora replied as she got up to sit beside him. "The sun will die when you believe it is not warm."

"Let me guess," Travis said, looking up again. "Another quote from your master?"

"Nope," Sarora answered. "I made that one up on my own." Again, she gave another "gryphon smile," her eyes twinkling.

And once again, Travis grinned. Then he stood up and wiped the snow from his gloves and his snowpants. "Care to walk me home?" he asked, looking to her.

Sarora stood up, shook herself, and nodded. "Sure, but

only to the edge of the woods. I don't want your friend Arlen to catch me." And together, the two walked out of the hollow rock and back to Arlen's cozy home.

A BAD CONSCIENCE

"So, how was your day?" Arlen asked when both he and Travis were seated at the kitchen table. Travis had arrived home about an hour before and had been sent to the shower to warm himself. Now that he was warm and dry, they were feasting on some chicken drumsticks and mashed potatoes.

"Great. How was yours?" Travis asked, looking up from his food.

"Good, but I'd at least like to know what you were doing outside all afternoon," Arlen answered back. "It couldn't have been all that boring," he added as he put a spoonful of mashed potatoes in his mouth.

"Well …" Travis quickly tried to think of a way to tell some of the truth without exposing Sarora. "I went out into the woods and found the camp where I had been staying before."

Arlen swallowed his food, wiped his mouth with his napkin and asked, "Really? What's it like at your camp?" His blue eyes looked at Travis.

"Well …" Travis began again. "It's in this cave sort of rock and in the middle I made a little fire pit."

Arlen kept his gaze. "That couldn't have been your only source of heat?"

"No …" Travis started again. "I … I used a badger hide

as a blanket."

Arlen's eyes went from curious to surprised. "A badger hide? Where did you get that?"

This time, Travis was really stumped. How should he put his wording exactly? "I have this staff and I sharpened one of its ends and used it to kill the badger," he replied cautiously, wondering if he had said the right thing.

"Hmm," Arlen responded. His lips pursed closer together and he continued to look surprised. He looked down at his food and said, "You'll have to show me how to make one of those staff thingies sometime. You never know, it might prove useful around the farm." He shoved another spoonful of potatoes into his mouth.

"Yeah, sure, I will," Travis replied, relief sweeping over him when Arlen did not pursue the subject any more. *That was too close,* he thought as he picked up a drumstick and began to dig in.

Two weeks later, December was well under way. Travis visited Sarora every day and together they would play in the snow. There were two reasons they had not left again for Firmara: Sarora's wing and the fact that it was the beginning of a cold winter.

One dark night, Arlen went into town in his old, rusty pickup truck to buy some more groceries. He told Travis to go ahead and do whatever he wanted as long as he stayed out of the attic upstairs. His only excuse for the "no attic" rule was that he was afraid that the boards were too loose and would give way.

Travis tried to entertain himself with the television but it was not keeping his attention. Since they only got the basic channels, he would not classify the weather lady as "entertaining."

As he continued to flip back and forth from the weather channel to the news, Travis decided that he was getting nowhere. So he grabbed the flashlight that was on the stand in the living room and walked upstairs to see if he could find anything to do.

As he walked through the upstairs hallway, Travis noticed the three empty, unused rooms. He peeked inside each of them, only to find that they were being used for storage and cluttered with cardboard boxes.

As he neared the end of the hallway, Travis noticed the pull rope for the stairway to the attic. It was within arm's reach, and he knew that if he really wanted to go upstairs, all he had to do was reach up a little and pull on the rope …

No, Travis told himself as he turned away from the attic and walked back down the hallway to the stairs. But there was this little voice that seemed to whisper tempting thoughts in his ear.

Arlen would never find out … it whispered to him. *All you have to do is pull down the rope and walk up the stairs…*

No, that's wrong, Travis told the voice. *Arlen trusts me to know right from wrong. I … I can't break that trust,* he said as he struggled to overcome the voice.

But it wouldn't be all that bad … Just walk up the stairs, take a quick peek, and come right back down … It's that simple …

"Mmmm …" Travis moaned. "But it's not right," he said as he turned one-eighty again and walked back to the rope, his flashlight still in hand.

Come on ... the voice encouraged. *That's it... Just pull that rope...* Travis reached out and pulled the rope.

He looked up into the hole, but it was too hard to make out anything even with his flashlight. So, as quietly as possible, Travis walked up the creaking attic stairs.

When he reached the top, Travis shined the flashlight all around him as he turned in a circle. Dust was flying around in the dark, eerie room. The attic was somewhat like the unused rooms downstairs. Almost every inch was covered with dust-covered cardboard boxes of every size.

Slowly, Travis walked around the room, peeking in all the boxes. One box in particular grabbed his attention. Inside of it were pictures. Travis pulled out the one on top and stuffed his flashlight under his chin. Using both hands, Travis wiped the dust off it.

In the picture was a much younger Arlen with his blue eyes shining through the gray and white. To his right stood a boy that looked like he could possibly be Arlen's brother. Both of them wore worn-out jean overalls and plaid shirts. They were smiling, having fun with each other, each holding an arm around the other's shoulder.

That's Arlen for sure, Travis thought as he smiled. *Nobody has a bigger grin than he does.*

Travis set down the picture and picked up the next one in the box.

Inside the frame was another picture, but this time, it didn't look like a photograph. Instead, it looked like a sketch of an animal. But not just any animal—it looked like a gryphon!

Travis stood, gazing at the picture. For all he knew, it could have been an exact replica of Sarora. It was so life-like. Travis quietly ran his hand down the sketch, mesmerized by the beautiful drawing ...

"What are you doing up here?"

Travis spun around and dropped the flashlight in surprise as the attic lights turned on. Next to the stairway stood Arlen, a completely different man then Travis was used to seeing. His face was reddening and his usual smile was now a frown. Arlen's eyes were a blazing blue and his arms were crossed across his chest. Travis took in a deep gulp. This would not end like his little voice had said.

"Well?" Arlen asked again.

"I ... uh ... I ..." Travis stammered.

"You deliberately came up here after I told you not to," Arlen snapped at Travis as he walked closer to him and snatched the picture of the gryphon out of his hands. "This is why I did not want you up here!" He spoke angrily as he shook the photo frame at Travis.

"I thought I could trust you to listen to me." Arlen stopped shaking the sketch as he looked down at his feet, his voice now filled with more grief than anger.

"Arlen, I—"

"Just," Arlen stated exhaustedly as he pointed to the stairs and stepped out of the way, "just go downstairs and get to your room."

Travis gave up trying to talk to Arlen. Instead, he somberly avoided Arlen's hot gaze, and walked to the stairs with his head lowered.

Boy, Travis thought to himself as he reached his room

and planted his face in the pillow on the bed, *I've really messed things up this time.*

Travis slept uneasily all night. The guilt of disobeying Arlen kept eating at him like a ravenous wolf. *What you did was very wrong...* the voice that had first tempted him into breaking the rules chastised him.

Oh, shut up, Travis told the voice while his face was still planted in his pillow. This voice was going to be his Achilles' heel forever. *Note to self,* Travis thought, *Ask Sarora if she knows any 'magical' ways to fire your horrible conscience.*

Grudgingly, Travis made his way down the stairs to the kitchen. He would have to face Arlen's disapproving look sooner or later.

When he got to the kitchen, Arlen was already sitting at the table, eating a bowl of cereal and reading the newspaper. Even when Travis walked in, Arlen did not look up at him once. Quietly, he walked over to the cupboards and randomly pulled out a cereal box, a bowl, and removed the milk from the rusty refrigerator. After his bowl was filled to his satisfaction, Travis walked over to the table and sat down to eat.

For the first few minutes, Travis and Arlen ate in silence. The only sound to be heard was the fridge that was trying to cool itself down while sounding exactly like an airplane taking off. Outside the window, the winter birds were out and about, trying to find food.

Travis and Arlen both spoke at once.

"Arlen, I—"

"Travis, I—"

They each stopped. Taking a deep breath, Arlen spoke

again, "Okay, you first."

Gulping once and sending out a silent prayer, Travis responded, "Arlen, I'm really sorry about last night. I know you told me not to go upstairs, but I couldn't help myself. I was just too curious to see what could come from it." Travis looked up to see Arlen looking back at him. "I'm sorry."

"No, Travis," Arlen began. "I'm the one who should be sorry. If I hadn't mentioned anything at all in the first place, you wouldn't have been so tempted to go in the attic. I'm sorry I tempted you by telling you not to go up there and I'm sorry that I overreacted last night. Will you please forgive me?"

Travis was astounded that Arlen would ask for his forgiveness. He knew that it was entirely his fault. He also knew that he should still be the only one begging for forgiveness, not Arlen.

"Arlen," Travis began, "you should be the one forgiving me because what *I* did was wrong. It's not your fault that I was tempted."

Arlen reached out one hand and set it on Travis's. His light blue eyes that had been filled with fire the night before were a sad, pleading ice blue. "Please, Travis," Arlen began once more, "Just say 'I forgive you.' I long to hear those words."

Travis could not resist the pleading look on Arlen's face. He stared back into his eyes and said, "Okay, Arlen. I forgive you."

"Thank you, Travis. I forgive you, too," Arlen replied, his usual smile returning to his face and his blue eyes beginning to twinkle happily once more. Then he stood up, pushed his chair in, and picked up what was left of his bowl of cereal and sat it in the kitchen sink.

After taking care of his dishes, he looked back to Travis and said, "Now that we have this all sorted out, feel free to do whatever you would like. I'll be out, cleaning the barn."

As he turned to walk out, Travis asked, "Need any help cleaning the barn?"

"No thanks," Arlen replied with smile. "I can handle it myself." Then he turned and walked into the hallway and out the door to the cold winter's day.

Travis took his time finishing his breakfast, lost in thought. He almost felt like he had been in a long, confusing dream, but everything had been real. *Wait until I tell this to Sarora,* he thought to himself as he got up out of his seat and took his bowl to the sink. *Actually, she might not be that surprised. Especially after we met again after I got caught in the snowstorm.*

Travis smiled on the outside as well as on the inside as he had a random realization: *People are weird.* Of course, Sarora was not a person, but to Travis she felt like one.

Quickly, Travis gathered his snow clothes and put them on, starting with his thinner snow pants and ending with his warm gloves. As he walked to the door, he grabbed his compass and jackknife, because he figured that he would visit Sarora later.

The chilly air nipped at Travis's face as soon as he stepped outside. December was definitely a great time of the year, but Travis still was praying for spring. Although he would miss the actual presence of a real human, an actual one that is non-magical, he knew that Arlen would understand. At least, he hoped that Arlen would understand.

The sky was icy blue with only a few clouds. The ground was still covered in at least four inches of snow and so were the trees. Everything looked like a Christmas winter wonderland with the glittering, fine white powder covering it.

Close to Arlen's old, white farmhouse towered a large, red barn. It had a black-gray roof, white-rimmed windows and a giant door that slid to the side to open. Even with its paint chipping from its sides, it looked to be in great condition.

Inside the barn, Travis could hear Arlen working away. It sounded like he was replacing a board or something to a stall side but he couldn't be sure. Travis almost thought about checking to see exactly what Arlen was up to, but he did not want to walk in to find some other great secret that Arlen might be hiding that would cause their friendship to break.

The woods were fairly quiet but of course it was winter. Only a few animals dared to stay during the cold months. Travis walked briskly into the woods with a quick look behind him to make sure that no one was watching. As he paced himself to the hollow rock, he thought of exactly how he was going to explain everything to Sarora.

"I'm gonna get an earful of something all right," he mumbled to himself as he spotted the large rock, hidden between the trees.

A PEEK AT ARLEN'S PAST

"What do you make of it?" Travis asked Sarora after he had finished the tale of the past events.

Sarora gazed at the floor, lost in thought. After a few seconds, she looked up and responded, "I'll tell you what I think. I think you are at the top of the list of the stupidest people in the world!"

Travis let out an exasperated sigh. "I know that! But I was talking about the highly accurate picture of a gryphon that Arlen had hiding up in his attic."

"What about it?" Sarora asked. "Does there need to be a reason that a person likes to draw magical creatures?"

"No," Travis replied. "I just thought that it was kinda weird that he would need to hide something like that from me."

"Maybe he just didn't feel like having you see it," Sarora suggested.

"Or maybe there is some deep, dark secret connection between the gryphon sketch and the picture of Arlen and the other man," Travis suggested.

This time, Sarora let out an exasperated sigh and asked, "Even if there was, what would you like me to do about it?"

"Well," Travis began. "You said it yourself. I'm on top of the stupid list so I was going to ask you to just think on it a little and see if you can figure anything out. I was just thinking how strange it was that a small-town farmer like him would actually be into drawing things like that."

"Alright," Sarora sighed, finally giving in. "I'll think on it, but don't expect any answers."

"Thank you," Travis smiled and breathed an inward sigh of relief. He had been afraid that she would not accept his offer at all.

Sarora shook her head. "Just, whatever you do, stay on Arlen's good side and don't go looking for any evidence because trouble seems to try and walk hand in hand with you." She flashed her gryphon-like "smile" and her eyes twinkled. Travis guessed that she was referring both to how he always seemed to get into a predicament and the voice that had been leading him into trouble.

"I'll try my best."

"You'd better," Sarora replied. "Especially if you want to train as an Acer's apprentice." Sarora stood up and walked to the front of the rock. "Days fly by," she commented as she looked at the sun that was not to far from setting. "You'd better get going. Unless you'd like to spend the night out here and become the first human popsicle."

"Hey, I almost made that possible," Travis joked as he stood up and walked over to stand beside her.

"Yeah, thanks to me, you were never able to accomplish it." Sarora looked at Travis. He was almost sure that he could see a smirk-like grin in her eyes.

He smiled back in reply and then looked down and zipped up the rest of his winter coat. "I'll be headin' off then," Travis stated as he patted Sarora's shoulder as he now always did when he left.

"Be careful!" Sarora called after him as Travis began his walk back to Arlen's home.

"You too! And keep thinking!" he called back to her over his shoulder and then continued on his way.

The reflections of the TV screen shone through the window as Travis walked inside the house to see Arlen sitting on the couch, watching an old Christmas special.

"How was your day?" Arlen asked without turning his head away from the screen.

"Good. How was yours?" Travis asked in reply as he shook off his boots and began to unwrap himself.

"Same ol'. Fix one thing and another breaks."

"I heard you slaving away in the barn," Travis stated. "What were you working on?"

"Horse got fidgety last night and put a nice hole in the side of her stall. Course it was nothing that I couldn't handle."

Travis rubbed his hands together as he walked into the living room after throwing his wet snow clothes down into the basement. "What ya watching?" he asked.

"A poor little reindeer getting picked on because he has a built-in light bulb on the end of his face," Arlen said.

"Oh, I remember that show," Travis replied as he sat down next to Arlen on the sofa. "My mom and I used to watch it every Christmas before I went to bed …" Travis trailed off at the thought of that warm, stale memory.

Arlen looked from the screen to Travis. "Something bothering you?" he asked him.

"No, why?" Travis asked.

"Cause you just seemed down when you talked about

your memory there."

"I … I guess, you know, that with it being around the holidays, it just makes you miss your family even more."

Arlen looked away from Travis. "I know that feelin'. One day you could really care less to have the memory in your head an' another it becomes your pillow and comfort zone," he said, then sighed.

Travis looked at Arlen with curiosity. "Arlen?"

"Yes?"

"If you don't mind me asking, who was that other person in that old picture with you upstairs? You know, the one where the two of you hung an arm around each other?"

Everything went silent. Even though the television was still on, it seemed to make no noise at all. Arlen kept a steady gaze on the screen, or was he just staring into space? Travis wasn't sure at all.

Travis finally decided to speak instead of waiting for Arlen. "You know you don't have to tell me if you don't want to. It is your past, not mine …"

Arlen took in a deep breath. "No, you have the right to be curious and find out," he said as he turned his head back to face Travis. "The boy in the picture with me was my younger brother, James. I was about sixteen when that photo was taken and James was fifteen." His eyes began to mist over at the thought of the memory.

"That photograph was taken during the harvesting week," Arlen continued. "My dad really didn't like the whole idea of new motorized technology so we used man labor to harvest everything. And, we are proud to say that we did it with smiles on our faces." Arlen finished with a little chuckle, half to himself.

Travis smiled back. "So, what ever happened to James?"

Arlen's smile vanished as quickly as it had appeared. He looked away from Travis once more, his eyes losing their sparkle. And once again, everything went silent.

Arlen finally broke the hush. "I wouldn't know."

"Why not?" Travis asked, wanting to know what was the matter.

Arlen looked at Travis with watery, sad, regretful blue eyes. "Because I left." He spoke sadly as he let out a faint sigh.

Travis looked down at his hands, which rested in his lap. What had Arlen meant by "left"? His question was soon answered.

"Travis," Arlen began again. Travis lifted his face so that he could look at Arlen again. "I hope you never turn out to be like me. I was never the sharpest knife in the drawer.

"See, back then, even though James and I were the best of friends, I always found myself jealous of him. He always got good grades in school and our parents seemed to like him more. Although he had hidden a secret for the last couple years …" Arlen trailed off then quickly began again.

"But anyway, no matter how hard I tried, trouble always followed close behind me. I got into fights at school so that the injuries hurt enough to keep me up all night, which in turn would make me very tired the next day, which would lead me to fall asleep in class and then I would get bad grades, and find myself in another fight because the kids picked on me because I was the only one failing gym. I could have done so much more for myself by simply ignoring the taunts of my peers." Arlen placed his hand on Travis's shoulder and continued. "Travis, if there is one thing that I have learned in my lifetime, it would be these two things—cherish what you have now, and never let your anger get the best of you."

"So, you left because you felt like no one cared?" Travis asked.

"Sorta. I left because no one really thought that I cared. The first chance I got, I packed my things and left a note for James to tell my parents what had happened. I haven't seen them since I was seventeen. And for me, that's a lifetime." Arlen stared deep into Travis's eyes. The look made Travis feel a little uncomfortable.

"Travis, can you promise me something?" Arlen asked suddenly in a solemn tone.

Travis tried to hide the questioning look from his eyes. "Sure. What is it?" he asked.

Arlen looked even deeper at Travis. "Travis, promise me that in the years to come, if you come to a fork in the road, never leave your friends. Because when times get rough, friends are about the only thing you can have."

Travis tried to understand the emotion in Arlen's eyes. Was it something like regret? Sadness? Travis could not be one hundred percent sure.

It took Travis a minute to realize that he needed to respond. He thought about what Arlen was asking for another second and then responded, "I promise Arlen."

"And that's all I could ever ask of you," Arlen replied, taking his hand off Travis's shoulder. A smile replaced the serious look on his face.

GIFTS AND WISHES

Travis slept better that night knowing the truth about the first picture. He also felt better knowing that Arlen trusted him once again. The evil conscience that had spoken to him two nights ago was now completely silent. *Good riddance!* Travis thought to himself as he crawled out of bed and slipped into some clean clothes.

Christmas was now only two days away. Arlen and Travis had spent much of their time hanging up lights, wreaths, and any other decorations they could find. A few days before they had gone out to the edge of the woods and cut down a small pine tree, which now filled the corner of the living room and was covered in popcorn strings, lights, and garland. At the very top sat a humble, silver star.

Today, Travis and Arlen had planned to take a drive into town to get some needed groceries. So they got up early, ate cereal for breakfast, and then jumped in Arlen's old, rusty, blue pickup truck.

The town was fairly small. There was a post office, a bank, a McDonald's, and a couple stores, including a pharmacy and the grocery store. Everything looked old and worn out except for the Mickey D's which looked somewhat new. The buildings were made out of bricks and some were even made of wood. Over the door of the post office hung an old deer skull. It no longer held the white shade of a bone—it was an aged yellow-brown, showing that it was very well preserved even though it was old.

Arlen parked his rusty truck outside of the bank and he and Travis walked over to the grocery store. Once there, Arlen handed Travis a twenty dollar bill.

"Here," he said, "consider this an early Christmas gift. Go and find something to spoil yourself rotten with." And he left for the grocery aisles with a pleased smile.

With the money in hand, Travis felt spoiled. Ever since his mom had died, he hadn't ever been given a true gift. Excitedly he ran up and down the toy aisles. Every little trinket caught his eye.

Then a thought crossed his mind: He hadn't thanked Arlen at all. However, instead of thanking him with words, Travis came up with a better idea. Taking his twenty dollars, he went over to the tool department and a familiar object caught his eye. It wasn't the most advanced or nicest of its kind, but it was still a gift that he could afford and that Arlen might enjoy.

Picking up the item, Travis took it to the checkout counter and paid for it with the money Arlen had given to him. *Arlen is going to love this!* Travis thought.

On Christmas Eve, Travis went out to visit Sarora while Arlen unpacked the truck. Arlen had left most of his supplies that he had bought the day before inside the old Ford. However, not wanting Arlen to see his gift ahead of time, Travis had taken the liberty of hiding it away in his room.

Travis and Sarora were sitting quietly together, just admiring the sunny winter day. Every once in awhile, Travis would sneak a quick glance at Sarora. He wanted to ask her a question that he had been pondering since the day they left his home, but he had never asked because he was afraid that Sarora would not reply. She had been so much fun to talk to that he really did not want to risk getting the cold shoulder from her.

She must have noticed his anxiousness because she asked, "Yes, Travis?"

Travis felt his face grow warm at the embarrassment of being caught. "I, uh, well, I, uh ..." Travis stammered after he turned to face Sarora.

"Spit it out before I slap it out!" Sarora humorously retorted as she looked over at Travis.

"Well, I was wondering, if it would be okay if I could possibly look at the Crystal of Courage again, since well, ya know, I haven't looked at it since the day I touched it ..." Travis said, dragging out the question.

Sarora's expression went from inquisitive to serious. Both were silent for several moments before Sarora finally replied in a nod. She stood and moved to the back of the hollow rock. From there, she dug a small hole open and, using her talons, pulled out the small sack that held the Crystal of Courage. She picked up the sack using her beak, walked over to Travis, and sat it in his lap.

Before he opened the sack, Travis inquired, "Didn't this used to be in my backpack?"

Sarora nodded. "I took it out when I ate the majority of the granola bars. That was the main reason I dug into your pack anyway."

Travis nodded and looked at the small bag in his lap. It

was made of some sort of tan cloth that felt rough to the touch.

Before he was able to open the cloth, Sarora reminded him, "Just don't touch the crystal itself with your bare skin. If you do, it'll react again and Sievan will be here quickly."

Travis looked up at her with a smirk on his face, "Oh yeah, guess there's no pressure at all at looking at this thing." And then he looked back down at the sack and began to unwrap the crystal.

The Crystal of Courage was a shiny, sphere-like, red orb. In the light, Travis could easily see his reflection. Without lifting his head to look at Sarora, Travis asked, "Why do they call it a crystal if it is a sphere?"

"They call it a crystal because when you have finished your training and are an Acer, the crystal changes form to look like a diamond-shaped crystal," Sarora explained in a matter-of-fact manner.

Travis slowly nodded in understanding as he swept his gaze up and down the flawless sphere-crystal. The longer Travis looked at it the more he wondered, *How is it really going to help me?*

The rest of Christmas Eve was a blast. After visiting Sarora, Travis had gone back to Arlen's home and together they had watched Christmas specials and drank hot chocolate until they were on a sugar high. With smiles on their faces, they had said goodnight to each other and went to bed. *How could life be any better?* Travis wondered to himself as he drifted into a peaceful sleep.

Travis woke early Christmas morning. He didn't expect to get any gifts of any sort although he had planned a present for Arlen.

As he walked down the stairs, the smell of his favorite breakfast foods reached him—donuts and chocolate chip muffins. As he walked into the kitchen, Arlen turned around with a silver tray full of donuts and muffins. "Merry Christmas, Travis!"

Travis felt a large grin grow on his face. "Merry Christmas, Arlen!" he replied joyfully as they walked into the living room to watch the Christmas Day Parade and feast on their delicious breakfast.

After breakfast, Travis grabbed Arlen's unwrapped gift from his room. When he returned, he held out his gift for Arlen.

"This is for you so I can show you how I made that staff," Travis explained simply. The tool that he held in his hand was a small pocketknife, vaguely similar to Travis's.

Arlen stared at the gift for a long time before either of them spoke. Travis was worried that Arlen was unhappy with his gift. The thought grew worse when Travis saw a tear run down Arlen's cheek.

Wanting to break the silence, Travis spoke. "I know it's not much, but ..." he broke off when Arlen looked up. What he saw in Arlen's eyes was happiness. His blue eyes welled with emotion.

"Travis," Arlen finally spoke, "this is all I could ever ask for and more. Thank you." He reached out to Travis and gave him a big hug.

"You're welcome ..." Travis said under his breath.

Later, Travis visited Sarora in the hollow rock. The day was bright and cheery and the sun shone through the clear sky. Outside of the barn, the horse was digging deep into the snow for its meal.

Travis and Sarora greeted each other merrily. Even though they didn't exchange gifts, they shared each other's company and stories of the past.

After a long while, Travis asked to be excused so that he could have dinner with Arlen. Sarora smiled and let him go, wishing him a good evening and a merry Christmas.

Dinner with Arlen was a great time. Arlen and Travis feasted on medium-rare steaks, corn, and mashed potatoes while Arlen shared many of his "When I was a boy…" stories.

This Christmas came close to being as happy as any he'd had with his mom. *If I can't have any family, I'm glad that I can at least have good friends,* Travis thought that night as he crawled into bed.

THE TRUTH ABOUT JAMES

January and February flew by so fast that Travis felt that the time since Christmas couldn't have been more than a couple days ago. In fact, the last couple of months hadn't had any eventful days. However, that feeling wouldn't last for long.

Travis slipped on a jean jacket as he walked out the door to visit Sarora. Arlen's horse was watching Travis leave and she softly nickered to him. Travis smiled and walked over to her. "Hey there, girl, how 'ya doing today?" he asked her as he patted her on the neck.

Arlen's mare was a quiet, young-looking, dark bay horse with a perfect white star on her forehead. In the sunlight, her chocolate-colored fur looked like it was leopard-printed.

"Travis, we need to go." Sarora's sudden statement caught Travis off guard. They were both sitting in the hollow rock talking to each other.

"Why? Can't we just stay here?" he asked her. Travis had come to love his easygoing life with Arlen—no school, no real work, no more hunting, and best of all, no step-dad. A new question formed in Travis's head that he had not considered before: Had step-dad been looking for him?

Sarora stared so hard into Travis's eyes that he thought she would be able to saw him in half. "Travis, while you may be sitting here, having the time of your life, there are people out there, innocent people, who are being hurt because they stand against evil."

Travis really didn't want to buy into any of this. "I have a simple way for them to solve this then."

"Please share," Sarora said sarcastically.

"How about they stop fighting against the evil and join together, then, maybe, just maybe, they won't die." Travis used his fingers as quotations around the last word.

"Travis, this isn't a laughing matter!" Sarora shouted at him, her eyes blazing with fury. Strangely, the wind outside seemed to be blowing faster.

"I know it isn't!" Travis yelled back at her. "I meant, like, everybody could work together to talk it out."

"Don't you think someone already tried that?" Sarora spat. "There are innocent creatures standing against Lord Trazon, risking their lives for what they know not! While my master and friend are training and struggling to grow stronger, you sit here and think of yourself!"

Travis tried to utter an excuse but Sarora interrupted him. "Don't think that I don't know that you enjoy having a kind person to talk to, but for once could you at least lend a hand at helping someone!" The wind outside began to howl.

"Helping someone?" Travis stated quietly, his eyes narrowing, "Helping someone! I've helped you, haven't I? If it wasn't for me, you would have lost that wing and could have killed yourself trying to get back to your home! So don't going shooting off at me that I haven't helped someone because I've been taking care of you!" The small fire they had built blazed and the wind began to howl even louder.

Sarora didn't speak at all to Travis at first—she only continued to stare through her narrowed, anger-burning eyes. "If I had died," Sarora finally began in a quiet but upset voice, "no one would have known the difference."

Even though Travis was still wound up from their spat, his emotions went to inquisitive. "What do you mean?" he asked.

"It's not important right now," Sarora sighed, beginning to settle down. The wind outside became quiet again and the fire began to fade away. "What is important is that my wing is nearly fully healed and spring is dawning. We should leave as soon as we can."

Travis looked down at his feet and nodded in agreement, suddenly feeling ashamed of himself. "Yeah, you're right." He paused for a second before quietly saying, "Sorry."

Sarora nodded her head as well and looked away from Travis. "You know what you have to do then."

"I don't know who is going to take it harder though, me or Arlen."

"Travis, if Arlen is truly the person that you say he is, then don't worry about it. He'll understand," Sarora replied calmly.

Travis stood up and stretched his legs and arms. "Tomorrow then?" he asked.

Sarora nodded again. "Tomorrow is great. You need me to walk you back?" she asked.

Travis smiled as he picked up his backpack and staff so that Sarora wouldn't have to remember them the next day. "No thanks, I'm good. If I can't find my way back to the house by now, I'm a lost cause."

Sarora gave a smiled back and said, "Whistle to me when you're ready, I'll hear and come."

The way back seemed to take forever. Travis had spent the whole walk trying to think of what to tell Arlen. He decided that the best way was probably to just come out and tell him without beating around the bush.

Once he was back, Travis saw that Arlen was outside on the porch of his home, working on the stick that Travis had given him along with the pocketknife three months ago at Christmas.

Arlen heard Travis and looked up to see him. Arlen's smile went to a questioning look when he saw the backpack and staff. "Well," Arlen began, setting down the pocketknife and branch. "What'cha got there?" he asked.

"This is my staff that I told you about." Travis said as he reached Arlen and handed it to him to examine.

"So this means you're leaving?" Arlen asked suddenly, catching Travis off guard.

"Yeah, how did you know?" his eyes widened in surprise.

"Call it old man's intuition but I kinda figured that once the weather got better that you'd be taking off." Arlen looked up from the staff to Travis.

"I was going to tell you," Travis started, "I really wish I could stay but I have to go. If it was my decision, I would stay but ..."

Arlen cut him off. "Don't worry about it, Travis. I understand. You leaving in the morning?"

"Yeah," Travis nodded and the idea of leaving finally began to sink in. *I probably won't ever see Arlen again.*

"In that case then, let's get some dinner and hit the hay early so you can get up before the crack of chickens." He ended with a smile. And that's exactly what they did the rest of the evening.

Travis woke up early the next morning, dreading his departure. He wished he had more time with Arlen but he knew that he had to go. They had spent too much time here, three months to be exact.

Travis walked down the stairs. He wore the white T-shirt and blue jeans that he had worn when he had first met Arlen. It felt weird to be wearing his old clothes again.

In the kitchen, Arlen was sitting down, waiting for Travis with a cup of coffee in his hands. Next to him on the table sat Travis's backpack. "Hope you don't mind but I stocked you up with a loaf of bread and some other small foods," he said to Travis quietly as if to make sure that it was okay.

Travis smiled. "Thanks, Arlen." Then his gaze drifted to the window as he sat down to talk with Arlen before he would have to leave.

The sun was just beginning to peak above the horizon. The few clouds that were in the sky turned pink and orange as the light hit them. The sight made Travis forget about leaving, but only for a second.

Arlen brought Travis back to the present. "Travis, before you go, I'd like to give you a late Christmas present," he said as he stood up.

Travis looked back to Arlen in surprise, "Oh, no, Arlen, you don't have to do that," Travis replied as he stood up as well.

Arlen looked at Travis with his deep blue eyes. "All the

more reason that I want to."

Arlen led Travis outside and into the barn. Travis had only been in the barn once before to carry hay out to the horse. The inside was old and musty. The beams had holes in them where the bugs had made their homes. There were two horse stalls, one in which Arlen's horse stood. In between them stood a large chest.

In the farthest corner of the barn was a pile of hay for bedding and, next to it, the wheelbarrow.

Arlen turned around and flicked on the barn light so they could see. Startled, the horse let out a panicked whinny and stomped her hooves on the floor.

"S'all right, girl." Arlen walked up to the horse and stroked her forehead. Then, he quietly walked over to the chest, opened it, and pulled out a picture frame.

"Come, sit with me," Arlen told Travis as he closed the chest and sat down on top of it. Filled with curiosity, Travis moved closer and sat down on the chest next to Arlen.

For the first few seconds, Arlen was silent. He rubbed his hand on the back of the frame, not yet showing it to Travis. Finally, he spoke.

"Travis, how much have I told you about my brother James?" he asked, not looking up.

This question took Travis off guard once again. "Not a whole lot. Just that he's your younger brother and that you haven't seen each other in a while." Travis paused for a second. "Why?" he asked.

Arlen took a deep breath and looked up at Travis. "Please forgive me for noticing but when I put food in your backpack for you, I saw the tan sack and opened it up."

Travis looked at Arlen. "I know, I know. I shouldn't have, but I got carried away with my curiosity." Arlen stopped talking for a moment and placed his free hand on one of Travis's legs. "I saw the crystal, Travis."

"I … I don't know what you mean," Travis stammered, looking down at his lap and trying his best to lie.

"Travis, I know what that crystal is capable of. Don't try and lie to me." Arlen spoke to Travis with a serious tone. Travis looked up at Arlen; his blue eyes had lost their serenity.

Travis gave up. "All right, fine. That's my crystal; it's the Crystal of Courage."

"Well, you don't say," Arlen gave a grin, "the Crystal of Courage." Then Arlen got serious again.

Travis spoke before Arlen. "Wait a minute, what's this got to do with James?" Arlen looked deep into Travis's eyes and spoke.

"Travis, James was an Acer."

"What?!?" Travis exclaimed. "How-Who-What-How'd he? I mean, how's that even possible?"

"Well, Travis, to tell you the truth, when James and I were growing up, we didn't grow up in the U.S. That's for sure."

Now Travis was confused, "Well, where did ya grow up then? Mexico? Canada?"

"Firmara," Arlen answered simply. "Yup. You know that picture of me and James? That was taken after we were relocated to a small farm in the U.S."

"Relocated? Why?"

"Trazon burned our village down looking for James." Arlen's face was downcast. "The second Trazon had heard of a sighting he had set off for our village to destroy him."

"Why, though?" Travis asked, mystified. "Was James really that big of a threat?"

"To Trazon, everyone is a threat. He didn't want to risk even an Acer's apprentice taking him down." Arlen took in a deep breath. "I'll tell you what, Travis, whatever your future holds, life won't be easy, and that's a guarantee."

Travis nodded to show that he understood. "Arlen, if you don't mind me asking, what was James' spirit animal?" Travis asked, his curiosity still as big as ever.

Arlen smiled once again. "Well, that brings us back to this," he said, holding out the picture frame for Travis to take. "This is a sketch of my brother's spirit animal."

Travis took the frame and flipped it over. Inside was the same sketch that Travis had found the night he had ventured into the attic. Travis looked at Arlen. "James had the gryphon?"

"Yes," Arlen nodded. "He was the Ice Gryphon."

"Ice Gryphon? So he had the power to control ice?" Travis asked.

"Yep, and was his animal spirit ever beautiful. It was different from most gryphons that you would think of. Instead of having a golden-brown coat, it was a shimmering white."

"A white gryphon? So what was it a mix of exactly, a house cat and a seagull?"

Arlen chuckled, "No, no, no. He was a snow leopard and a white hawk. He was white, had cloudy gray-black spots, and a golden beak."

"What was his name?"

"Xue," Arlen replied. "He was the last of his kind, the last known gryphon."

Now Travis was really curious, "The last gryphon?" he asked out loud. *But that doesn't make any sense. Sarora is a gryphon, so Xue couldn't have been the last.* Then a thought struck him, *What if Arlen just doesn't know about Sarora? Maybe that's why he thinks that Xue was the last.*

"It's a shame he was the last," Arlen continued. "Gryphons were very intelligent creatures. And like I said before, they were magnificently beautiful. I only wish they could have lived on. But the thing is, with an Acer's 'spirit' animal, they are animal spirits."

"Meaning …?" Travis asked.

"Meaning that they aren't really alive," Arlen explained. "When a spirit animal belongs to an Acer, they have already died but they live on through a spirit form to help in any way they can."

"So, Xue had already died?"

"Yes, Xue passed before James was born. He died trying to save his eggs from a poacher. Since his mate had died even before then, he was the only one who stood a chance, but unfortunately, he wasn't able to."

But wait a second! If Sarora is my spirit animal, has she already died? No, that can't be. So if Sarora isn't dead, does that mean that the worst is still to come?

Travis tried to hand back the picture of Xue but Arlen refused, saying, "You keep it. It is no longer of use to me."

"Arlen, there is something I'd like to show you," Travis said to the old man after a couple minutes of silent pondering. He had come to a conclusion and he knew that it was the right thing to do.

"Sure," Arlen replied, "what is it?"

Travis stood and wiped the dust off his pants. "Well, you have to get up and go outside with me to see it."

Arlen looked at Travis quizzically. "What are you gettin' at, Travis?"

"You'll see." Travis smiled as he helped Arlen up and led him outside. Now the day was beginning to warm up. The sun was just finishing its ascent above the trees. Only a few wispy cirrus clouds floated across the sky. The grass was already growing back and all of the winter's snow had vanished.

Travis led Arlen away from the barn and into the large field that sat next to his yard. "So, what am I seeing here?" Arlen asked.

"You'll see," Travis said again, and then put two fingers in his mouth and whistled.

Seconds passed and nothing happened. Only the birds could be heard twittering in the trees of the woods.

"Uh, Travis?" Arlen broke the silence.

"Yeah?"

"I still don't see anything."

"Just wait another second. Maybe if we're quiet, we can hear her."

"Hear who?"

"You'll see," Travis once again answered Arlen. Travis looked at the edge of the woods, expecting to see her, but she still wasn't there. Travis whistled again. A cry came from the sky and Travis looked up. Over top of the trees, Travis could see an outline flying toward them.

"What ... Travis, who is that?" Arlen asked in a nervous surprise.

"Don't worry," Travis replied reassuringly, "she's my friend."

The figure grew larger and larger as it came closer and began to descend from the sky. "Hey! Over here!" Travis called to Sarora. After a couple more seconds, Sarora was upon them. She flew right over the tops of their heads and landed on the other side of them.

"I ... I can't believe it," Arlen stammered as Sarora turned and cautiously walked up to them.

Travis could just about read Sarora's eyes, *Really, Travis? Really?* they asked him. He mouthed, "I'll explain later," and Sarora just nodded.

Arlen walked slowly up to Sarora. "What is her name?" he asked Travis as if Sarora couldn't understand him. Travis at first waited for Sarora to reply, but she didn't. She merely stood there and gestured at Travis by using her eyes.

"Her name is Sarora," Travis finally replied, figuring that Sarora didn't feel like talking to Arlen.

"Sarora ..." Arlen repeated. "How fitting," he observed as he walked closer to her. A couple feet from Sarora, Arlen stopped and asked, "Sarora, may I have permission to look at your wings?"

At first Sarora narrowed her eyes as if unsure of how to answer. Finally, she nodded slowly and she let out her folded wings for him to examine.

Arlen first walked up to her uninjured wing and Sarora let him hold it. Travis walked closer up behind Arlen, carefully watching him stroke his right hand down the feathers of Sarora's left wing.

"Sarora's a very healthy young gryphon." Arlen commented to Travis as he walked around the front of Sarora to her other wing.

"Yes, very healthy beak, strong legs and nice clean wings—" He stopped short as he saw Sarora's scarred wing. "How did this happen?" he asked.

Travis looked to Sarora once again to speak but she only looked back at him and nodded. Travis took it as a gesture for him to explain what had happened to her.

"She got into a fight," Travis began to explain.

"A fight? A fight with what?" Arlen asked anxiously, still examining Sarora's wing carefully.

"A fight with a dargryph."

Arlen's head snapped around quickly to look at Travis. "A dargryph?" he repeated.

Travis nodded.

"What was its name?" Arlen asked.

"His name is Sievan," Travis answered.

"*Is* Sievan? You mean he isn't dead?"

"No, afraid not," Travis replied. "I assume you know about dargryphs then?" he asked.

Arlen nodded. "James fought one once. It had a tiger's body, a scorpion's tail, and the wings of a raven. Luckily, he was able to kill it or it could've easily killed him."

"A scorpion's tail!" Travis exclaimed. "Yeah, I guess he was pretty lucky to survive."

Arlen nodded and then changed the subject. "That must have been a nasty cut. Looks pretty well healed now but it would be best if she didn't fly with it quite yet. There is still a chance that she could open it back up so you'll want to keep an eye on it."

"But if we can't fly, we'll have a difficult time getting around from place to place. I'll get to worn out from walking and Sarora might be spotted if we take it nice and easy," Travis protested.

Taking his hand off Sarora's wing, Arlen replied, "Well, you dragged me out of the barn so fast I wasn't able to give you present number two."

"Number two?" Travis echoed. Hadn't Arlen already given him enough?

Arlen nodded and began to lead the way. "Follow me back to the barn. There'll be a solution for your problem."

Sarora shot a quizzical glance at Travis, who just shrugged his shoulders. He wasn't sure either what the gift was.

At the barn, Arlen asked Travis and Sarora to wait outside for a moment. After a few seconds, Arlen led his horse out of the barn using a lead rope.

"Travis, I don't believe I've ever truly introduced you to my mare before."

Introduced? Travis thought.

"Travis, this is Shadra. She's a very special horse."

Travis thought he heard Sarora gasp. Arlen must not have heard because he went on talking. "Shadra was my brother's horse back in Firmara."

"Back in Firmara?" Travis asked. "But isn't that impossible? Shadra would have to be over fifty years old!"

"Actually, she about one hundred and fifty-three but, who's counting?" Arlen looked from the horse to Travis and gave a big grin.

"One hundred and fifty-three!" Travis exclaimed and looked to Sarora, expecting a shocked expression. However, Sarora nodded to show him that she believed that Shadra was that old.

"Yes," Arlen kept up his smile. "She was James's horse, and before belonging to him, she belonged to a countless number of famous Acers."

"But how?" Travis asked. "How has Shadra been able to live this long?"

"Shadra's not just any horse, Travis," Arlen began. "Shadra is one of four horses that were enhanced by the first Acers. She understands any human language, can run for countless miles without wearing, and is immortal as long as she is not killed by an iron sword."

"Amazing," Travis said softly as he walked closer to Shadra. Now that he knew more about her, he could just about see a twinkle of personality in the mare's eyes that almost seemed to form words, *I am old, but stronger and wiser than any other,* they told him.

Arlen stood next to Travis and gently stroked Shadra's neck. "Travis, I want you to ride her. She has been sitting and wasting away for the past forty or more years. It's time that she got back on the job."

Travis looked at Arlen and saw a warm emotion that he wasn't familiar with. "I ... I don't know, Arlen," Travis began, letting his unsure feelings show. "I'm not sure if I'm ready for this. It's a big responsibility and—"

Arlen cut him off by handing Travis Shadra's lead rope. "Travis, I know you're ready just because you say that you aren't. You've been taking such good care of Sarora that I know I can fully trust you with caring for Shadra."

Travis looked at Shadra, staring into her deep, mystery-filled eyes. They seemed so calm, so trusting … "Okay, Arlen," Travis said, turning back to the old man and smiling. "Thanks, I'll do my best to care for her."

Arlen's grin seemed to warm the whole area. "Thank you, Travis. This would've meant a lot to James." Arlen walked into the barn for a moment and then brought out a saddle with several saddlebags.

"This ought to help," he said as he strapped the girth around Shadra's stomach and double-checked the rest of the straps on the saddlebags. Giving Shadra one last pat, Arlen looked to Travis. "You're all set then." He smiled, but Travis could tell that Arlen wasn't feeling exactly what he showed on his face.

"Not quite," Travis began again.

Arlen looked at Travis. "What do you mean, 'not quite'?"

Travis opened his backpack, reached inside, and pulled out a small, round item. "Arlen, I want you to also have this. It's very dear and close to me but I no longer have any need of it. I wouldn't want it getting ruined or lost."

Arlen took the compass from Travis's hand. "Very dear to you? Are you sure that you want to give it away, just like that?"

Travis nodded. "I won't really have a need for a compass in Firmara, now that I have Sarora."

"Well then, thank you, Travis." Arlen smiled again. "I'll be sure to take good care of it."

Travis bit back another reply. He wanted to confide in Arlen, to tell him about his mother and step-father. He wanted to tell him that his mother had given the compass to him, saying that it had been hers when she was a little girl. But instead he held all of the thoughts in his heart, wishing to treasure them rather than to share.

"Thanks, Arlen," Travis thanked his friend. He looked down at his feet and then back up at Arlen as he searched for the right words. "I'll try to come back as soon as I can. And when I can, I'll come back, for good."

Arlen's sad smile faded and was replaced by a more happy expression. As a tear trickled down his face, Arlen came forward and nearly lifted Travis off the ground as he gave him a tight hug.

"Thank *you*, Travis. That would be wonderful." Arlen finally let go of Travis and backed away from him. "Just, don't hurry through what needs to be done just for me. And I hope that the next time we meet, Trazon will be just a story used to scare children."

Yeah, in my dreams, Travis thought as he remembered Sarora telling him about Trazon's evil powers. "I'll do my best." Travis smiled at Arlen, trying to shake off the foreboding feeling.

Changing the subject, Arlen asked, "You need help getting on?" It took Travis a moment to realize that he was talking about helping him get on Shadra.

"Uh, yeah, sure, thanks." Quietly, Travis stepped closer to Shadra so that his right shoulder was closest to her. Attentively, Travis put his hands on the horn of the saddle and his left foot in the left stirrup.

Arlen helped by coaching him on where and how to sit in the saddle and how to use his hands to guide him through.

Once he was all set, Travis turned to look at Arlen. "Thanks again," Travis told him, "for everything. Without you, I wouldn't be standing here."

"Travis?" Arlen called.

"Yeah?"

"I got one last question for you."

"Shoot," Travis gave him permission.

"Wasn't it Sarora that had really saved your life?" Arlen asked.

Travis thought back to the freak snowstorm. "Yeah, but she brought me to you. If you hadn't been here, I would've froze anyway."

"I'm not referring to the storm," Arlen said. Travis looked from him to Sarora, who had wandered a ways off—she seemed not to be paying any attention to what they were talking about.

Travis knew that Sarora had saved him from a number of things: Sievan, starvation, and the storm. What else could Arlen be talking about?

"You'd better be off then," Arlen said, snapping Travis from his thoughts and back to the present time. Travis once again looked back at Arlen, who had taken a few steps back. "You don't need to steer Shadra. She'll know where to go," he explained and then curled his pinky and the finger next to it in on his right hand and placed that hand on his heart.

"Keep your mind focused, your reflexes sharp, and be prepared for the task ahead," Arlen recited to Travis, who remembered Sarora saying the same thing to him the first time they had met. He wanted to ask Arlen more about it but figured that it wasn't the right time or place.

Sarora walked to Arlen and inclined her head in a formal nod. "Farewell, Sarora, may destiny bring our paths together to meet once again." Sarora rested her head on Arlen's shoulder as if to agree with him.

"You ready?" Travis asked Sarora once she had said goodbye to Arlen. Sarora nodded and stood next to Travis and Shadra.

"All right, Shadra. We're headed for Firmara and we need to get there fast, understand?"

Shadra vigorously nodded her head up and down and began to use her front hoof to count. Then, without any other sign, Shadra darted off at a full gallop that nearly wiped Travis off of the saddle.

Travis looked behind at Arlen who was quickly disappearing from his sight. "Goodbye, Arlen. Take care!" Arlen called back from where he sat on Shadra. Arlen was the only true friend he had ever had (other than Sarora). He knew that he had to come back someday, not just for himself, but also for Arlen's sake.

"I'll be back," Travis spoke his vow aloud. "Arlen, I will return, whether or not it kills me." And he meant every word of it as they sped off into the growing day.

ON THE ROAD AGAIN

Travis was covered in sweat and his rear ached from sitting so long in Shadra's saddle. Not far in front of them, Sarora continued to move at a jogging pace but for some reason, she didn't seem as tired as Travis felt.

After leaving Arlen, the group had galloped for about an hour and a half straight before Shadra needed to slow to a walk. Even though she was strong, Travis hadn't expected her to run hours on hand. He had to let her take her time; she could easily hurt herself running that hard after sitting around for fifty years without any real exercise.

Several hours they had spent on the move, trying to keep out of sight and follow the path to, well, however they would get to Firmara. Many times they had to be careful where they had walked because the ground was covered in roots. The woods were covered in all sorts of trees and blooming bushes. Everything in nature had begun to finally wake from its winter slumber.

Finally, after the long day, the sun had started to sink and now the sky was tinted with pinks and oranges. The day, though ending, was still clear and, when Travis looked to the darkest side of the sky, he could see the stars beginning to show.

"Hey, Sarora?" Travis called up to the gryphon.

"Yeah?" Sarora turned around and waited for him to catch up to her.

"Shouldn't we stop for the night?" he asked. "It's getting pretty late." Travis yawned.

Sarora looked into the fading sunlight and then turned back to Travis. "I suppose. But I'd like to get an early start tomorrow," she paused and then added, "unlike today."

Travis had to admit that they had gotten off to a late start. "Right," he smiled as they searched for a place to hang their hats for the night, "unlike today."

Travis woke the next morning when Sarora prodded his side with her talons. The sun was already beginning to peak through the trees. Outside, Shadra stood, looking inside the hollow tree that Travis had spent the night in. Since only one could fit in the tree, Travis got the spot while Shadra remained outside and Sarora had slept on one of the tree's branches.

"Five more minutes ..." Travis mumbled as he turned away from Sarora and the bright sun.

"No," Sarora stated plainly to him as she removed the warm badger hide that was covering Travis. "You'll get up now. We can pick up breakfast for you as we move."

Travis sat up and tried to shield the sun's light from his eyes. Once Sarora saw that he was getting up, she turned and walked out of the small tree.

Rubbing his eyes, Travis tried to wake up and get ready to go. He stood up and stretched, grabbed his backpack and staff, and went outside to saddle up Shadra.

The unlikely group was on the road a few minutes later, starting at their usual fast speed. While Travis rode Shadra,

Sarora went off to find food.

Listening to the steady rhythm of Shadra's hooves beat against the ground, Travis fell into a daze-like trance. For the first hour, he looked around at nature and almost, just almost, felt at peace.

Sarora returned about two hours after she had left. In her jaws, she carried three rabbits by their scruffs. Travis asked Shadra to slow to a quiet walk so that Sarora could keep up with them on their way.

"Here you go," Sarora's words were muffled by the rabbit fur in her mouth. She dropped one on Travis's lap and placed the other two in a saddlebag as they continued at a steady pace.

With his free hand, Travis gingerly lifted the rabbit with two fingers, "and you'd like me to eat this how?"

"Hey," Sarora smirked, "I caught it- you cook it. You're smart enough to figure that out, right?" And she trotted forward and left Travis to his rabbit.

"Okay, umm …" Travis spun the rabbit around to look at it thoroughly. "Let's try this," he thought aloud in an optimistic voice. He focused his energy and sent fire out of his hands and down on the rabbit. Instantly, the rabbit's fur caught on fire.

"Ah!" Travis screamed in surprise and he dropped the rabbit, which was extinguished by the wet ground. Sarora turned to see what he had done and Shadra stopped to give them time to pick up the rabbit.

"Gee," Sarora said in a "why" kind of matter, "I thought that you might be actually bright enough to figure that one out." She couldn't help letting out a laugh before she bent down, sniffed the rabbit, and swallowed it whole. Travis winced at the sight.

"Mmm …" Sarora said, bringing her head up to face Travis. "Tastes better without fur. Thoroughly cooked, but could be better without the ears, eyes, tail, and pretty much any other part that really isn't good, quality meat."

"How could you eat that?" Travis put all his disgust on his face.

"Like I just did," Sarora replied simply. "So, just to recap, remove the hide from an animal before disintegrating it into charcoal."

"Wait, recap?" Travis asked. "When did you remind me of this before?"

"I didn't," Sarora gave him a "gryphon smile," "but I would hope that your conscience would have." And she trotted up ahead as they continued on their way.

Travis leaned down and patted Shadra's neck. "I've known her for over six months and I still don't get her. Do you?" he asked the horse, who had flicked her ears back to listen to him.

In response, Shadra shook her head, although Travis wasn't sure if she was saying, "No, not at all," or if she had just been shaking a fly off herself.

Smiling at the thought, Travis figured that the rabbits would best be saved for later, and he reached back behind him into his backpack and grabbed a couple slices of bread, figuring that it was better than nothing.

The days flew by but the miles didn't. After each day, Travis felt as if it wouldn't be long until they reached Firmara, but then Sarora would tell him that they had a full day's travel to go.

This afternoon, the sky was blue but Travis could only see small glimmers of it through the treetop canopy. The weather was fair enough, but the humidity was starting to get to Travis. Yet none of the weather they had experienced seemed to affect Sarora.

Once again, Travis was covered head to toe in sweat. Underneath the saddle, Travis was positive that Shadra was drenched, too. In front, Sarora was leading the way, and, once again, Travis couldn't help but notice that she was not tired at all.

"Are we almost there yet?" Travis asked tiredly. He felt his energy draining, even though he was riding Shadra.

Sarora turned around and paced back to walk next to Shadra, "Close, far, that part doesn't matter. We'll get there eventually." Sarora spoke in a "wise" manner.

"And by eventually you mean you have no clue when we'll get there?"

"Precisely," Sarora replied with her "gryphon smile," "so sit back and enjoy the ride."

They continued walking for a few minutes before Travis finally asked, "Sarora, aren't you tired?"

"What do you consider tired?" she asked him without taking her eyes off the invisible path they were following.

"Um, tired is …" Travis started, "tired is, uh … tired is when you begin to feel, uh, worn out?" He tried to put together a sentence that unfortunately sounded like a question.

"Worn out?" Sarora asked rhetorically. "You don't know worn out. If you had a pair of wings and tried flying, then you may just graze upon that knowledge."

"Well, maybe if you were human, you'd wish you had wings so that you wouldn't have to walk everywhere," Travis countered back, his anger strangely beginning to rise. "I'm pretty sure you'd find out the true meaning of worn out."

Sarora stopped in her tracks and kept her gaze away from Travis. Shadra, seeing that Sarora had stopped, halted as well and turned to the gryphon.

At first, everything was silent once again. Travis was a little confused. He hadn't meant to say anything offensive to Sarora and he couldn't risk losing her as a friend.

"Sarora, I—" Travis started.

"You go on ahead," Sarora stopped him mid-sentence. "I need to be alone for a while."

"We could just stop for the day," Travis suggested. "Give us time to have a day of rest."

Sarora flicked her tail dismissively. "Do whatever floats your boat." And she silently padded away.

Travis jumped off Shadra. The second he got off the saddle, he felt his sore legs screaming at him.

Like a loyal dog, Shadra followed Travis to a clearing not far from where they had stopped. The clearing was covered in short, dry grass and was bordered by a small stream.

Travis sat by the stream and splashed water over his face to cool himself. At the bottom of the stream sat smooth stones, some of which were quite large. Taking a liking to one, Travis picked it up and placed it in his pack. Though it was a little heavy, he figured that it shouldn't weight him down much.

With his face wet, Travis turned to Shadra and told her, "Go ahead and go where your heart desires. Just come back when I whistle." In response, Shadra nodded her head a couple times and walked away from him into the forest in search of food more delicious than grass.

Travis leaned back against an oak tree to take a rest. Maybe they could get further in their journey tomorrow.

Travis woke a couple hours later. He must have dozed off waiting for Sarora to come back. As he rubbed his eyes and looked around, he felt something, and it wasn't good.

Sarora still hadn't returned and, even though he had no idea what time it was, he figured she must have been gone for at least three hours. Even though he knew that Sarora sometimes enjoyed being alone, he never would believe that she would intend to be gone for this long.

Travis stood slowly and stretched a little. It took him a minute to realize that everything was silent. Travis listened. Strangely, the birds were silent, the frogs were silent, and even the wind seemed to be stilled.

Travis walked quietly around the clearing, listening for any sign of Sarora. However, the only sounds he could hear were his feet crushing leaves and branches.

Travis stopped walking to listen for any other sounds. Nothing. There was nothing at all to hear.

Suddenly, out of the corner of his eye, he spotted a shape running toward him. As the shape grew larger, he began to here the rustling of branches and leaves as Sarora came closer.

"Hey, Sarora!" Travis called out to his friend. "Where have you been?"

"Travis!" Sarora's call back came franticly. "Grab the

backpack! Hurry!"

For minute, Travis stared at Sarora blankly. "What's the matter?" he called to her as she continued to run closer.

"Travis!" Sarora called back, agitated. "Now!"

Seeing that Sarora really meant it, Travis went to his backpack, zipped it shut, grabbed it and his staff, carried them in his hands, and waited for Sarora.

Just as Sarora reached the clearing, a dark shadow leapt at her and knocked her to the ground. Sarora struggled to get up but the medium-sized shadow pinned her down.

"Travis!" Sarora cried, "Get Shadra and run! We can't stay here!"

"But what about you?" Travis asked, "I can't leave you behind!"

"Yes! You must!" Sarora argued as she continued to flap her wings and flail her legs in a helpless attempt to get free.

Travis nodded, but as he turned to run away, a shadow jumped in front of his path, snarling. Travis let out a small yelp of surprise. The animal in front of him sent shivers down his spine.

"You will not be leaving anytime soon," the deep voice growled at him. Travis spun around. The voice that had spoken to him was not who he had wanted to see.

AN UNUSUAL ENEMY

Travis stared nervously at the creature in front of him. It was a wolverine.

The creature had a broad head, small beady eyes, dark brown fur, a light mask, and two stripes down the side of its body. Its short legs held wide feet with long, dangerous-looking claws that could easily cut through Travis's skin.

There was more than one. There were three holding Sarora down, one standing by to keep an eye on her, two standing guard behind Travis, and the one that had spoken and was standing in front of Travis. Travis thought this one might possibly be the ring leader.

The leader of the wolverines was slightly larger than the rest and he had a small, open nick on his left ear. Its body was about half of the length of Sarora. Travis figured that the lead wolverine easily weighed around fifty pounds, or possibly more.

Travis stood post still, watching the large creature in front of him with large, round eyes. His brain screamed "run" but his legs were frozen in place. The question was not how he could get away from the wolverines but if he could get away from them.

The alpha wolverine laughed, evil in its voice. "This is the boy who we have come to retrieve?" he asked rhetorically.

126

"He's not even a threat to an ant hill!"

Travis felt anger begin to burn within him. *Don't,* he told himself. *Don't let him get the best of you. You can't show him your fear.*

The wolverine turned to Sarora. "This is what you were trying to hide from us? How pathetic! Even for a low-life like you!" He let out another booming, dark laugh.

A thunderous growl came from deep in Sarora's throat. "If you say he's no threat, Gore, then why all the back-up guards?" she challenged him. "Too afraid to take on a thirteen-year-old boy?" When Gore did not respond quickly, Travis saw a small flash of triumph flicker in her eyes.

"If I were you, I would start speaking for myself," the large wolverine retorted. "You're not even trying that hard to escape from us, especially not like last time." He walked over and leaned his head in so that he and Sarora were only a hairbreadth apart. "Donigan starting to get the best of you, is he?" he spoke just loudly enough so that Travis could hear.

Sarora flinched ever so slightly that Travis almost doubted that she had moved at all, however, Gore must have noticed. A large, dark smile formed on the evil wolverine's horrifying face, "At least I'm fourth in power, under Donigan and Sievan. You're just an outcast, Sarora." His voice sent a chill down Travis's spine.

Sarora seemed to regain her composure as she said, "At least I'm not nicknamed the 'Skunk-bear'." She once again smiled.

Even Gore's friends chuckled at that and looked to each other, giving their comrades a that-was-a-good-one look.

"SILENCE!" Gore boomed. "She's talking about you as

well!" The other wolverines immediately went silent once more and an apologetic look formed on their downcast faces.

Trying to ignore Sarora's latest comment, Gore turned to face Travis. "What do you say, boy?" he asked him in a sly tone. "You can give us the crystal and let us take you to Firmara ourselves, or else."

Travis looked to Sarora, who locked gazes with him. Travis looked back to Gore and stated to him, "I'll choose or else. It sounds a lot more promising." Travis smiled at the thought of mimicking Sarora's retort to Sievan.

Gore narrowed his eyes at Travis. "Don't play coy with me, boy," he chided. "You don't even know what or else means."

"Well," Travis began, "maybe if you tell me in the next hundred years, I'll find out." Travis smirked innocently as the other wolverines laughed and he began to see pure anger rising in Gore's face. Travis looked across the clearing to Sarora and found that she was smiling with confidence as well.

"SILENCE!" Gore boomed like before and the other wolverines silenced, their faces looking down at their large paws in shame.

"You won't be so easy to make a decision when I tell you." Gore turned his head away from his silenced soldiers to face Travis.

Travis was now really beginning to realize how serious Gore was. He frowned and narrowed his eyes at the wolverine. "Tell me then," Travis demanded. "What does your 'or else' mean?"

Gore cleared his throat.

"You can come with us quietly or we can give you a demonstration on how cunning our killing techniques are." Gore smirked in evil delight once more. "And we'll use her," he added, thrusting his snout Sarora's way to indicate her as the possible victim.

All of Travis's confidence disappeared in horror at the thought. His head snapped to look at Sarora.

"Travis! Don't listen to them!" she called desperately. "I'll be fine! Don't give them the crystal!"

Travis looked at his backpack that he held by the strap. What was the right thing to do? He could give in and let the dark creatures take him to see the dark lord or he could see Sarora die and then be taken to the dark lord. Either way, it looked as if he was out of luck.

Everyone and everything was still and silent while Travis tried his hardest to make a decision. Finally, he reached into his pack, pulled out the sack that held the stone, looked up at Gore and said, "Fine, you win." And tossed the sack to Gore.

"Travis, no!" Sarora cried to him, but it was too late. Travis no longer held the small sack in his hands.

Gore, who had not expected or intended to have the case thrown at him, was taken off guard, and the sack slammed him in the forehead, leaving him in dazed. After that, everything seemed to move fast.

With a forced effort, Travis threw his spear-like staff at one of the wolverines that held Sarora captive. To his surprise, it barely missed Sarora, speared the shocked creature right through, and killed it instantly. Sarora's words echoed in his mind, *We do not kill for joy or for sport, we kill to live.* And he felt he finally began to understand the true meaning of her words.

Quickly, while Gore and the other wolverines were still dazed, Travis ran past the leader and yanked his staff free of the still-warm cadaver.

The other two guards only just seemed to realize what Travis had done and began to growl. However, with one less heavy body on top of her, Sarora flipped over onto her back and the evil talking creatures followed. Without difficulty, Sarora pushed her legs under the dazed wolverines, and she pushed them high up into the air where they collided with a large tree branch that knocked them back down to earth. Quickly, Sarora rolled out of the way as they landed with one large, simultaneous thud on the ground. The fall killed one and knocked the air out of the other.

Travis heard more growling and looked to the other couple of guards that were standing beside their leader. Gore was beginning to wake from his trance. The large wolverine stood on all four once more, shook his massive head, and turned to focus on the sack.

"Travis!" Sarora yelled, bringing Travis out of his worried thoughts. "Get the crystal and let's go!" She no sooner ended her cry when Gore's filthy paws reached the sack and he began to try to remove its contents.

"There's no time for that!" Travis told her and caught her off guard when he leapt on top of her back and tried to scramble into sitting position.

"Travis!" Sarora protested. "We can't leave without—"

"There's no time for that! We have to leave. Now!" he demanded to her when he noticed that Gore had seen the inside of the sack. His face turned to Travis and Sarora and they could see his eyes burning with fury.

"Hurry!" he ordered the remaining soldiers. "Get them!"

"Sarora ..." Travis began as the creatures sped toward them.

"But we can't—"

"NOW!" Travis screamed, the monsters gaining on them. This time, Sarora did not argue. She ran toward the wolverines, who yelped in surprise at the charging gryphon. Gore, however, did not flinch and kept running at his rolling gait.

Just at the last second, when Travis thought they were going to crash, Sarora used her back leg and launched them into the air, her wings snapping open. As they ascended, Sarora worked hard to maneuver out of the way of the branches.

As they reached the treetops, Travis looked over Sarora's side at three standing wolverines. Even though they were now several yards in the air, Travis picked Gore out of the group; the wolverine's cursing rampage easily gave him away.

"You'll be sorry!" Gore cried out. "I'll get you some day and even a pity potion won't save you then!" His cries began to fade away the farther they got away from the clearing.

Travis let out a sigh of relief. "Phew, glad that's over."

"Well, I'm not!" Sarora spat at her rider, "Now because you had to play that dumb little trick, it has possibly cost us our chance at victory!" she howled in anger and despair. "You are such a thick-headed, no-brained, stubborn fool—"

Sarora's rant was cut off when Travis pulled a familiar item out of his backpack. "Ha—how did you ...?"

Travis laughed when Sarora couldn't figure out the puzzle. In his hand, Travis held the Crystal of Courage, which was wrapped in the bread bag.

"Now, what were you saying about me?" Travis asked rhetorically.

"I was saying—" Sarora started in an angered tone and stopped before continuing in a quieter, more intrigued way. "I was saying that you actually had me fooled." She said, her tone showing Travis that she was genuinely surprised.

"It was easy," Travis began. "While I still seemed to be deciding, I slid my hand through a hole I had left when I partially zipped up the bag. I then took the bread bag, dumped in the crystal, and placed one of my new best friends in the sack."

"And who would that new best friend be?" Sarora asked.

"Heavy rocks," Travis replied with a smile and then burst out laughing, quickly followed by Sarora.

Once the laughing had quieted down, Sarora spoke. "I have to admit Travis, I am both very perplexed and astounded that of all people, you could pull that off in a matter of seconds."

"Well," Travis began, trying to sound full of knowledge, "you know what they say."

"Yeah," Sarora stopped him before he could continue, "don't judge a book by its cover." This time, only she burst out laughing.

"Wait," Travis was confused, "I don't get it."

Sarora continued laughing as she spoke, "That's exactly what I mean!" And, although Travis still didn't get the joke, they both laughed and laughed as Sarora flew on, getting them closer and closer to Firmara.

NEARLY THERE

Travis and Sarora flew the rest of that day, making sure they stayed in a one single direction. Most of the time they had spent talking about things like how Sarora had met the wolverines.

"So you must go way back with Gore then?" Travis had asked.

"Well," Sarora had started, "I wouldn't say *way* back. I got in a fight with him once outside of a city in Firmara. Thankfully, I had a friend there to back me up, or I would've been toast."

"So when did you know that they were after us today?" Travis asked.

Sarora chuckled a little. "I figured that out when they jumped out from behind some bushes and tried to put a bag over my head. I really hadn't seen them coming at all."

"So you managed to escape and run from them then?" he asked.

Sarora nodded. "I was able to escape only after I had screeched. That's why it was so quiet when I found you."

"Wait, wouldn't I have heard you?"

"If you had been asleep, you probably did but don't remember it because it could have paralyzed you as you slept," Sarora explained.

"Okay, I think I get it," Travis replied, trying to remember if he had heard anything at all.

"Well, I should hope you get it," Sarora replied. "How much simpler could I have put that?" And she had laughed once more.

Travis and Sarora landed that night in a tight clearing. The sky was filled with both stars and wispy cirrus clouds. Surprisingly, Sarora's wing had held up and wasn't bothering her at all.

When they landed, Sarora advised Travis, "You'd better whistle for Shadra so she can catch up over night."

Travis's eyes grew wide and he slapped his hand on his forehead. "Oh, shoot, I forgot! How's she supposed to hear me now? We are several miles away!"

"Technically we covered around fifty-three," Sarora replied, matter of factly.

"But she won't be able to hear me, will she?" Travis asked.

"If she can't," Sarora began, "then I'm a rabbit. Now whistle and let's settle in for the night." Then she began to find a comfortable place to rest.

Travis doubtingly placed two fingers in his mouth and let out a long, loud whistle. *If Sarora's not a rabbit, then I'm a mouse for doubting,* he thought as he found a comfortable place to rest his head for the night.

The next morning, Travis woke as light streamed into his eyes. It was a little while after dawn and the day was warming up quickly.

Slowly, Travis rubbed his eyes and looked around at his surroundings. Sarora was awake, naturally. She seemed to get up a long time before him. She was sitting in the sun, her eyes closed. From her throat, Travis could hear a sort of humming that sounded like "Oouummmmm …" *Meditating?* Travis guessed. Is this what she did in the morning when he slept in?

Travis stood up, a yawn escaping his mouth as he stretched. "Good morning," Travis stifled another yawn as spoke to Sarora. Instead of speaking, she flicked a feathery ear back in reply.

Travis walked over to where he had set his backpack on the ground and opened it up. Travis grabbed the last piece of bread and ate it slowly, trying to savor it. It was beginning to grow stale, but food was food.

After Travis finished, he picked up his staff to discover that the entire point was covered in a thick, dried, coat of wolverine blood.

"Gross," Travis mumbled as Sarora stood up, shook herself, and walked over to Travis. "Good morning," she finally spoke.

Travis suddenly remembered calling Shadra last night. "Have you seen Shadra yet?" he asked her.

Sarora shook her head, "No, but don't worry. She'll catch up eventually. In the meantime, why don't we continue walking, we only have about ten miles to go."

Travis was astounded, "If we were that close, why didn't we keep flying toward it last night?" he thought for a moment and then replied with Sarora, "Shadra."

"Plus," Sarora continued, "it'll take plenty of energy to get there."

"What do you mean?" Travis asked. "We've spent plenty of energy getting here already!"

"You'll see." Sarora replied with a smirk on her, well, beak. She stretched her front legs before speaking again. "Let's be on our way. But this time, you don't get a free ride," she added as Travis had begun to come closer to Sarora, preparing to get on her back.

"Fine," Travis agreed. "Maybe it'll do me some good to stretch out my legs." And they began the rest of their journey to Firmara.

The sun burned in the sky, even the trees couldn't give Travis enough shade. They had been walking for about an hour and now they were nearly to where Sarora said that Firmara would be.

Travis was curious, however, because before he had met Sarora, he had never learned of a place called Firmara in school. So how were they going to be magically there? Was it a hidden society? Was it as big as the United States or was it a smaller, struggling island? Even though the questions poked at Travis constantly, he didn't ask Sarora because he wanted to be surprised, not that he wasn't about every second of every day now.

As they walked slowly but steadily, Travis kicked a pebble along their path, trying to find a way to entertain himself. Sarora walked silently and only ever made a single noise when she cursed the bugs that were swarming around her face. "Dang flies …" she would murmur as she shook her bird-like head.

Suddenly, Travis began to hear a pounding off in the distance. Both he and Sarora looked back in time to see Shadra rocket toward them.

"Whoa!" Travis let out a shocked yell as Shadra stopped

in front of him, just a few inches from plowing him over.

Shadra exhaled an exhausted breath of steamy air in Travis's face. He cringed as the hot and sticky air blew across his face. "Nice to see you too." Travis finally patted her on the nose as a greeting. He then looked to Sarora. "You're still a gryphon I guess then," he replied jokingly.

"And you're still a doubtful, annoying boy," Sarora gave her "gryphon smile." "Go ahead, hop on her. We've only got a couple miles to go."

Travis heaved himself onto Shadra's back. Her tack was still sitting on her where he had left it. "I promise I'll get that off you as soon as I can," he told her with a pat on her shoulder. He could feel her sweat seeping through the saddle and sitting everywhere on top of her.

Sarora lead the way. Her head was held high as she seemed to search for any sign of this "magical land" they had been heading for. Shadra padded as silently as horsely possible, closely behind her. Travis was almost positive that she knew exactly what was going on and he could almost feel her chomping at the bit to keep moving faster.

Finally, after what had seemed to have taken forever, Sarora stopped in front of a large oak tree. It had just begun to sprout leaves once again and the tip of the branches and twigs were budding. The tree was the main fixture in the center of a small clearing, which was covered in tall, green grass. The whole place seemed serene. The wind gently blew a wind across Travis's back and the small leaves rustled softly like a wind chime. Everything in nature seemed at peace. But yet, Travis wasn't.

"So," he began quietly, "are we in Firmara? Have we

crossed the border yet?" Only Shadra seemed to flick her ears back in response to Travis's questions.

It was so quiet that Travis could hear Sarora's calm, steady breathing. "Whatever you do, don't pull out a weapon," she said as she approached the large oak tree.

"I don't get it," Travis said. "Why not? What is going on?" Sarora did not respond and her pace had not slowed, showing Travis that the time for questions was over.

The silence continued as Sarora came closer to the tree; her whole body seemed to strain for every sign of movement or sound. Everything was quiet, until Sarora took a step that placed her a badger length from the tree.

A DAY WITH WOLVES

Out of the shadows leapt a dog, its fangs bared and a roar resounding from its throat. Sarora didn't even flinch. Instead, she simply ducked her head away from the large dog's attack, leaving it to fly over her.

As soon as the dog hit the ground, it spun around and leapt at Sarora again, its fangs a glistening white against its long, black fur coat. This time, Sarora reared and grabbed hold of its front paws with her talons, stopping it mid-attack.

To Travis's surprise, the dog didn't try to escape her grasp. Instead, it stood along with Sarora in a reared position, its massive paws just touching the ground to hold it up.

Thinking that Sarora was going to need help in this combat, Travis reached for his staff in the hoop on the top of his backpack. As soon as his hand touched the wood, another dog came out of the shadows, only this time it was right next to Travis instead of Sarora. "Don't touch your weapon if you value your life," it growled menacingly. This dog had a freckled gray coat, black-tipped ears, and a whiter underbelly. Its yellow eyes dug into Travis like a dagger. He quickly snapped his hand down away from his staff, not wanting to provoke a fight with the large beast.

Travis looked back to Sarora and the large, black dog, finally realizing that they weren't dogs at all, but wolves—

large, ferocious, bloodthirsty wolves.

Sarora and the black wolf were still in reared position, their eyes staring at the others. Sarora's wings were spread out fiercely behind her and the wolf's fur prickled with defiance.

After what had seemed like an eternity of stillness and growls, the large, black wolf dropped to all fours, quickly followed by Sarora. Its growl ceased and its teeth disappeared behind its lips. Now, instead of revealing hostility, its amber eyes communicated an apologetic look. Finally, it spoke.

"Sarora," the dark wolf began and bowed his head in respect, "my apologies, honorable apprentice. We were informed, by one of our spies, that you hadn't survived the fight with the dargryph. Forgive me for doubting that you weren't still alive." His eyes looked up pleadingly at Sarora.

Travis looked to Sarora. "Honorable apprentice? What is he talking about?" he asked from his perch atop Shadra.

"Silence!" the gray wolf commanded me. "How dare you be speaking directly to her without permission!" he growled.

"Timur," Sarora spoke to the growling wolf. "It is all right. He has every right to speak to me directly." When the wolf looked at Sarora confused, she explained, "The last has accepted him."

The gray wolf's eyes widened as he looked from Sarora to Travis, "My apologies, waiting apprentice. I did not know that you were the one."

Travis looked to Sarora, who looked back at him. She seemed to mouth, "Forgive him" but it was hard to tell. Travis stared at her through narrowed eyes as if to say, "Are you sure?" which prompted a small nod.

Travis looked back to Timur, "That's all right. I was not informed that there would be wolves guarding the way to Firmara." He looked to Sarora with upset burning in his eyes.

"I apologize for that, Travis," Sarora began, "but I figured that there was really no need to tell you that Firmara was guarded. I figured with what I've told you that you would've figured that out."

Travis nodded, understanding. With the brains that he sometimes used correctly, he knew that the knowledge was really a no-brainer.

Sarora turned back to the black wolf. "There is no need for you to apologize, Oberon. I hadn't even expected to return again. I assume then that all of the land believes me to be dead?" she asked him.

Oberon looked up to her and nodded. "All except for the Midnight Lord, I'm sure. But yes, all peasants that had once seen you or heard of you now believe you to be dead," he said, adding after a short pause, "even your master."

To Travis's surprise, Sarora nodded and answered, "Good. The less people who know I survived, the better. It'll make it easier to hide without them constantly searching for me."

"Would you like one of my pack members to run ahead and give a message to your master?" Oberon asked.

Sarora shook her head. "Thanks, but no. I'd like for him to first see me alive rather than to hear it first."

Oberon nodded. "Then it is so. Will you be needing an escort to the camp then, Sarora?" he asked her.

Again, Sarora shook her head. "Once again, no, thank you. I'd only be putting us all in danger if we traveled with more than we are. But I would like to see a map to where it is though, if you have one."

Oberon nodded again. "Yes, of course." He turned and let out a lonely, howling call. Quickly, a brown wolf padded out of the shadows with a map in its mouth. With his head lowered, he dropped the map at Sarora's feet and backed away into the trees once more, but without turning.

"Thank you," Sarora told Oberon as she uncurled the map to show the land of Firmara. From where he was, Travis couldn't clearly see the chart so he gently urged Shadra to take a few steps closer.

"Here," Oberon pointed at a small section of woodland with his large paw, "is where your last camp was. And here," he moved his massive paw across the page not too far to a large plain next to the woods, "is where they are staying approximately now. That's what I heard a couple weeks ago." He finished looking up at Sarora.

"Hmm," she thought aloud, "it's about a four-day's journey, wouldn't you say?" she asked Oberon.

The black wolf nodded. "It's about that by foot. But if you were to fly there, you could cut your time in half."

"It would, but I don't want to get too far ahead of the horse so that she isn't able to stay on track with us. Because when we get there, I don't want to have to call her from such a large amount of distance. It's too risky," she concluded.

"I see," Oberon observed. "What if you walk a day and give her a fair amount of distance with you, then you fly for about a day and a half. It would give his horse a chance to keep up and not get lost." He recommended another idea.

Sarora nodded back. "That sounds reasonable." She

agreed and then looked to Travis. "What do you think?" she asked him.

Travis, who had been wrapped into listening to the conversation, almost forgot that he himself was standing there, "Uh, I don't know. Whatever you think best is good with me," he said reawakening from his focused state.

Sarora looked harder at Travis. "It's up to you," she told him. "What do you think is the right way to travel this distance?" she asked him, looking for a clearer answer.

Travis thought a moment and then replied, "I like the last option. It'll allow Shadra to keep up with us and get us there in almost half the time, like you said."

Sarora nodded again. "Good." She turned to Oberon and told him, "We'll leave as soon as possible."

Oberon looked back at her. "Why don't you stay with us for lunch, Sarora?"

"Well," Sarora began, "we wouldn't want to be a bother-"

Oberon cut her off mid-sentence, "Oh, no, no, no. It would be our honor," he said with a small bow at the end.

Sarora looked to Travis and he nodded, beginning to notice how his stomach was as empty as a hollow log. Sarora turned back to the dark wolf. "Then we will be delighted to join you for a meal, Captain Oberon."

Oberon gave what Travis thought to be a smile. "Then allow Timur and myself to lead you to our humble camp for a small feast." He called to his companion, who had been standing at the back of the group, to come and walk alongside the group. Without hesitating, Timur trotted to Shadra's right side and Oberon began to lead the group to the wolves' makeshift camp.

The whole walk, Oberon and Sarora chatted with each other and walked side by side. This left Timur and Travis to keep each other company.

"So you're going to be an Acer then, huh?" Timur asked Travis as Shadra padded next to him.

Travis nodded. "Yeah."

Timur gave a wolf's smile. "Then I assume you've already had plenty of adventures then?" he asked.

Travis grinned. "More than I need but yeah, we've had some interesting times. I wouldn't fully call them adventures."

"Oh really?" Timur asked. "Why not?"

"Well we really hadn't gone anywhere for the past few months." When Timur looked at him quizzically, Travis briefly explained, "Bad weather."

"Oh." Timur understood.

There was a short silence before Travis asked, "So, what exactly do you do then?" he asked the gray and white wolf.

"I'm second in command among the wolf legion," Timur replied. "I help Oberon keep track of information, help to train pups, and take control of the group when Oberon is away."

"Hmm," Travis thought politely, "that's cool."

Timur chuckled, "Well, I'm glad you think so. I spend a lot of time sitting around here doing nothing because there is little information, not many pups, and Oberon is usually always on guard."

"Oh, sorry," Travis replied quietly.

Timur chuckled again. "Don't be. It's not the most exciting or safest job, but it's what I do best. And the rewards are great." He finished with a smile and his head held high.

The camp wasn't too far away from the oak tree, maybe only two-tenths of a mile. As they reached it, Travis jumped off Shadra and let her roam free through the woods, reminding her to come when he whistled.

The camp was held in a medium-sized clearing, about the size of a few outdoor pools. At the edges of the clearing stood tepees, each with its own special designs painted on the sides.

Outside of each tepee were different things. One tepee had a fire hole sitting in front of it with a rack of weapons, including swords, which sat with their silver blades hiding in leather sheaths. Other tepees had fireplaces outside. Most had posts that dangled a cauldron of some sort above the flickering flames.

As they walked along, Travis spotted wolves emerging from almost everywhere to get a good look at the group. A couple of wolves came out of the woods, another came out of his tepee and sat by a boiling cauldron. A group of younger wolves were practicing battle skills outside of a dark brown tepee. They stopped the second one spotted Sarora and Travis. The larger one leaned over and whispered into his friend's ear, who nodded and they continued to stare.

Other wolves of all shapes, sizes, and colors eyed them suspiciously, as Oberon led them to the other end of the clearing where a large, white tepee was situated. On top of the tepee were strange characters, written in red paint, which seemed to spell something out but, since it wasn't English, Travis had no clue what it said.

When they reached the large tepee, Oberon motioned for them to sit on a large, patterned rug just outside of the tepee. Once Travis and Sarora were seated, Oberon turned around and the wolves instinctively gathered in a large cluster to hear what he had to say.

The group of wolves wasn't necessarily quiet, or thrilled. In fact, some of the older-looking wolves shot angry, burning glances toward the newcomers. Some even barked their feelings louder than Travis felt they needed to: "What are *they* doing here?" "We don't need no help!" "Why would Oberon bring such bad luck into the camp?" Their hostile calls echoed among the trees as they continued their rant.

"Silence!" Oberon's stern and controlling bark silenced them all at once. "These are our guests and you must show them some respect!" he glared at his soldiers angrily. "I know not all of you like the idea and some of you may have good reason not to. But times change and the new age brings us hope! Now return to your duties. Don't worry about the strangers, they are friends." He finished with a glare that both frightened and commanded.

Most of the wolves grudgingly began to return to what they had been doing before. Others let out a low growl of defiance before sulking away.

Oberon turned to Travis and Sarora. "My apologies. They are not all a welcoming type. You know what I mean, right, Sarora?"

Sarora nodded. She did not seem to have been fazed by the outbreak. "Of course. I completely understand what they are feeling," she replied.

After speaking with Sarora, Oberon let out a whine and then a couple of barks. Quickly, two wolves, one brown and the other white, carried to them a cauldron, still hanging from a pole. After they had sat the cauldron in the middle of the rug, another wolf carried a bowl that held several smaller replicas of it inside.

Quietly, Oberon and Timur passed a bowl to each Travis and Sarora and they filled them with a broth that smelled of freshly cooked beef. The smell made Travis's mouth water.

"What are you waiting for?" Oberon asked. "Dig in." And he began to lap up his bowl of broth. Luckily, instead of having to slurp up his meal like the other three, Travis was given a spoon by the same wolf that had brought the bowls.

The meal was delicious. The broth soothed Travis's dry throat and removed any trace of hunger from his stomach. The juicy beef only added to his delight. A question lingered in his mind: *How did the wolves make this?* He pondered this but never asked.

While they ate, Sarora and Oberon swapped stories about the past few months. For a while, Travis listened intently to what Sarora remembered of their journey. Eventually, though, Travis grew bored of the details and Timur seemed to as well. So Travis began his own line of questions for the wolf.

"Hey, Timur?" he began.

"Yes?"

"What do all the drawings and writings mean on the tops of the tepees?" Travis asked.

"Well," Timur started, "the drawings mostly depict the stories of the wolves that had first slept in that tepee. They tell of how they used to raid from the Midnight Lord and both their trials and tribulations."

"Am I correct in saying that the Midnight Lord is what you call Lord Trazon?" Travis guessed.

Timur flinched a little at the mentioning of Trazon's name. "Yes, that is what we call him and what we will always refer to him as." He looked from side to side and then leaned in closer to Travis and whispered to him, "It is in your best interest to call him that around every creature. Some of us have been influenced by the Midnight Lord so much that we cannot even speak of his name," he looked side to side again to make sure no one was listening, "or its meaning."

Travis didn't want to ask any more questions about Trazon. He could tell by the fear and panic in Timur's eyes that it was best to keep any thought of the man unsaid.

Timur cleared his throat and then continued. "As I was also going to mention, those wolves in the highest three ranks have their names painted on the front of the tepee in honor and respect toward them."

"What do they write it in?" Travis asked.

"They write it in a form called *Firsoma*. It is an ancient writing of Firmara that is no longer spoken—at least, not by normal people. It is, though, a current idea for wolves and other animals working on the good side to learn to read, write, and speak it so that we would be able to talk with others from far away without the Midnight Lord being able to read our every word," Timur explained.

"So," Travis began, "on this white tepee, does it read *Oberon?*"

Timur nodded. "The first three characters say 'Oberon' while the others describe him as 'The Dark's Light.'"

Travis asked, puzzled, "Dark's Light?"

Timur nodded again. "Yes. Wolves refer him to a light in the darkness. He was the first wolf of his kind to stay on the good side."

"Of his kind meaning …"

"Meaning most of the wolves here are arctic, gray, or timber while he is, in fact, what you humans would call a 'Mackenzie Valley Wolf.'"

"What's the difference between him and the other wolves, though?" Travis asked. "He looks the same as the others to me."

"He looks *similar*," Timur corrected him. "Oberon's kind is the largest known living of all of the wolf species in both Firmara and the world. Not only that, but it is rumored in Firmara that only Mackenzie Valley Wolves have the ability to have magical powers."

Travis's eyes widened. "Really?" he asked. "How?"

Timur let out a long and heavy sigh. "For a soon-to-be-apprentice you have more questions than the night sky has stars. For right now, I'll just say ask your master. It's not my full right to tell you."

Travis looked down at his hands, slightly disappointed. "Okay, I'll ask him." He remembered one more question he wanted to ask. "Timur? One last question. What does Sarora's name mean and does everyone have a meaning to their name?"

Timur chuckled again. "For as bright of a fellow as you seem, your math isn't correct. But I'll answer both questions anyway." He leaned in closer to speak so that Sarora and Oberon would not hear them while they chatted.

"Sarora's name actually is derived from a word in Firsoma

meaning, 'Running with Winds,'" the wolf explained.

"That name *does* suit her …" Travis spoke under his breath, remembering Arlen mentioning something about Sarora's name.

"What was that?" Timur asked.

"Nothing. You were saying?"

Timur nodded and continued. "As for your second question, not all people in Firmara have names that actually mean something. Sure, some people have names that relate to an action or character but it doesn't usually relate to anything that has to do with the nature of that person."

"That's kinda confusing." Travis scratched his head.

"Yes," Timur smiled. "It can get very confusing. However, I'm like Sarora and my name does have meaning to it. My name that you call me means Iron."

"But doesn't that only describe you?"

Timur shook his head. "My full name is Al Timur Sonj, which in Firsoma, means 'Courage Stronger than Iron.'"

"That's a nice name," Travis complimented the gray wolf.

"Thank you," Timur said. "My parents gave me the name when I was a pup."

Suddenly, Sarora stood up and stretched, interrupting Travis from his conversation with Timur. "I hate to leave you all so quickly but it is best that the two of us get going."

Oberon nodded. "Of course. You need me to walk you back to the oak?" he asked courteously.

"Thanks, but no thanks," Sarora said, turning down yet another offer. "I should still remember the password and it'd be best that we even approach the gateway undetected. We don't want you to have Gore or Sievan nipping at your heels in record time."

Oberon and Timur smiled. "We appreciate that. If you truly must go then ..." he backed a few paces away from Travis and Sarora. Then, Oberon and Timur spoke in unison the words that Travis had now heard three times, "Keep your mind focused, your reflexes sharp, and be prepared for the task ahead," they said simultaneously as they dipped their head in a farewell.

"And you," Sarora said, dipping her head in respect to the commander wolf and then turned to Travis. "Let's go." Travis nodded and walked behind Sarora, out of the camp. And even though his back was turned, Travis could feel gleaming eyes staring with hate at his back.

FIRMARA

Once they had reached the oak, Travis let out a loud whistle to call Shadra back. Within a minute, the dark bay mare was at their side, her breathing deep and quick as she tried to catch her breath.

Travis patted her on the shoulder and said, "Good girl," before turning back to look at the large oak once more. There was nothing special about the tree, at least outwardly. It looked just like all the other oaks Travis had seen. It was quite tall, its leaves fell off every fall so he knew that it was deciduous, its bark was brown and very rough, and its leaves had pointed edges. So what was really the big deal about this tree?

Sarora stepped in front of Travis and placed the tip of her beak on the tree. That's when Travis expected something to happen, but nothing did. Then he thought, *Well, did you really think that after they had talking wolves guarding Firmara, that there would be no other defenses?* He thought for another moment and then nodded to himself, Yes, I would have.

Travis opened his mouth to ask but was cut short when Sarora spoke,

"Darkness rises, light falls,
Bad omens heard, all hope thought lost…
…But then there shall come,

One who is Courageous, one who is Just, and one who is
Wise,
That shall bring the darkness to its demise."

Suddenly, the ground began to shake violently. Sarora slowly took a step back to watch the tree as a piercing light shot through the trunk, forcing Travis to hold his hand to his forehead to block some of the illumination.

Finally, the light began to dim. Travis removed his hand from his forehead and looked at the "ordinary" oak in astonishment. He could see straight through it! Not only that, but on the other side of the oak was an entirely different world.

Sarora looked back to Travis, "You ready?" she asked him.

Travis was still looking past Sarora and through the tree. "As I'll ever be," he replied to her, his voice little more than a whisper.

"Don't worry," Sarora told him. "It's just like walking through a door. But make sure that you keep your thoughts focused on something from the side of the Acer's." She paused for a minute and then added, "Like me. When you step through here, only focus your mind on me. If you stray to think about Sievan or Gore, the gate will snap shut, possibly leaving one half of you in this dimension and the other in Firmara."

Travis nodded. "Okay." Then he realized what she had said, "Wait, Firmara's not on earth?"

Sarora nodded, "That's part of the meaning of *dimension*," she teased him lightly. "Now, let's go." And she walked forward into the tree. The last thing Travis saw of her was her lion tail.

Taking a deep breath, Travis closed his eyes, stepped forward and, with silent prayer, he focused on Sarora and began to step through.

Okay, I'm thinking about Sarora. Yeah, that's it. The gryphon, golden-brown feathers, black-tipped beak, birdlike talons … Suddenly, an image of Sievan popped into his head.

No! Travis fought back the thought. *Sarora, gryphon, makes a lot a smart remarks …* Finally, Travis felt both of his feet on the ground. Cautiously, he opened one eye, and then the other, and he was amazed by what he saw.

From where Travis stood, he could see nearly everything. Sarora and he stood up high on a hill that overlooked what seemed to be the whole land. Vast woodlands stretched as far as the eye could see straight out ahead of them and below them in all directions.

The sun still hung over the tops of the trees, making them glow a light green. A few clouds drifted through the sky and when Travis looked to stare at it, the sky was an unbelievable shade of blue: pureness and calmness was what the land seemed to hold.

"Beautiful, isn't it?" Sarora woke Travis from his thoughts once again, her voice in a content, dream-like state.

"Yes," Travis replied. "It certainly is."

Sarora blinked and let out a long sigh. "That's what makes it all the more worse."

For the first time since they arrived, Travis looked at Sarora. "What do you mean?"

"I mean it's all the more worse because this is about the

only slice of land that Trazon hasn't cast his dark powers over. That's why everything seems so," she paused for a moment, looking for the right word, "serene."

From behind Travis, he heard Shadra clop through the gateway to stand behind them. She let out a low nicker and nipped Travis's shirt. Travis turned his head around to look at her. Her eyes looked from Travis to the land of Firmara, as if she was begging to keep going.

Travis gave in with a sigh. "All right, let's keep moving." He then hopped on Shadra's back into the saddle and, with one more look back at his previous life through the oak, gave Shadra a little kick and yelled, "Let's go!"

Sarora let out a screech-like roar and leapt into the air, her wings snapping out after she had dropped a few feet toward the bottom of the hill. The wind under her wings lifted her high above the hill and, with ease, she flew on.

Shadra began to run at full speed, the same speed at which Sarora flew up. "Whoa!" Travis yelled nervously as Shadra sped dangerously down the hill, the excitement lifting Travis's heart. *This is my new home!* he thought, overcome with excitement as the odd group moved into the woods, the oak's gateway closing behind them.

Travis groaned as once again the sunlight woke him up. Without opening his eyes, Travis sat up, stretched his arms high, and wiped the sleep from the corners of his eyes. With a small yawn, he opened his eyes and stood, stretching once more. "Can't the sun take a day off?" he asked Sarora when he spotted her walking toward him with a freshly killed rabbit in her mouth.

Sarora sat the rabbit down on the ground, "Technically,

if the sun took a day off, we'd all freeze to death. But that's only technically, right?" she gave Travis a joking smirk.

Travis smiled as he tried to squint the light out of his eyes. "Yeah, technically. Technically I guess then that we want it on."

Sarora gave a "gryphon smile." "Come on," she told him. I'm going to take you to get a meal, something other than this rabbit." She noticed the questioning look on his face. "Hey, this is all I could find and I need to eat, too." She flicked her tail to tell him to follow her.

Travis sleepily walked, trying to fight back another yawn. "If you're eating that, then what am I eating?" he asked her.

"This," Sarora replied and moved out of the way to reveal a raspberry bush.

Travis's eyes lit up, "Mmmm ..." He moved closer to the bush, plucked a berry, and plopped it into his mouth. "I haven't had one of these since Mom was around."

"I know you'd like to savor them, but eat quickly," Sarora told him. "I'd like to get going." She turned and began to walk on. "Call Shadra as soon as you're ready. I'm going to walk ahead. Shadra will know where to go."

Travis looked away from her and began to indulge himself with the raspberries. After the hunger disappeared from his stomach, Travis stood, wiped his mouth with the back of his hand, and whistled for Shadra.

The mare found Travis in about a minute and as soon as Travis was on, she bolted in Sarora's direction. In about ten minutes, they caught up with the gryphon. "Took you long enough," Sarora teased. "I thought the berries had begun to eat you." She chuckled a little more and they walked together.

After an hour of silence, Travis asked, "How far are we traveling exactly?"

Sarora thought for a moment before replying, "About twenty more miles today if we can and then I'll fly you about forty tomorrow. Sound good?" she asked him.

Travis nodded, "Yeah, the faster the better."

"Exactly what I was thinking," Sarora replied happily. There was a pause before she said, "You must be able to understand."

"Understand what?" Travis asked. His mind had just begun to wander.

"What it's like not to be able to see your friends for such a long while."

Travis looked away from Sarora and to his hands that rested on his lap. "Well, not necessarily friends, but family," he replied to her.

"Hmm, family for me too …" Sarora replied as though she were thinking to herself aloud. Travis didn't pursue the comment, afraid of the friendly conversation turning into another fight.

"Travis?" Sarora asked after a moment of silence.

"Yeah?"

"What's it like to have a family?" Seeing his puzzled look she added, "I mean, what was it like with you and your parents?"

"Well," Travis began to think back to his days at the farmhouse, "I can't tell you anything about Dad because I never knew him."

"Oh," Sarora replied quietly. "I'm sorry."

Trying to fight back his emotions, Travis said, "No, don't worry about it. At least I still had Mom." His sadness began to fade as he thought of all the good times he had with her. "My mom was great. Well, she spoiled me rotten, I got a lot of things I wanted, but not because I whined, but maybe rather because it was to try and make up for not having a father."

Travis smiled and chuckled a little. "I remember she used to play with me out in the yard. Sometimes, she even helped me to make mud cakes."

"Mud cakes?" Sarora repeated.

"Yeah, I'd take the water hose, spray the dirt in the back of our yard, and we'd sit there for a couple of hours, patting it, shaping it, and baking it in the sun."

"The best times that I had with her though, had to be story time," Travis continued.

"Travis, exactly how old were you then?" Sarora looked concerned.

"When she told me stories and we made mud cakes?" he asked. Sarora nodded.

"I was about six during mud-cake time, but story time lasted until I was nine, when she passed away." His cheerfulness seemed to begin to fade at the mention of his mother's death.

Sarora must have seen how he felt because she quickly cut in. "You don't have to continue if you don't want to."

Travis shook his head, biting back the gloom. "No, it's okay, I'm fine," he replied.

Sarora nodded, though she still looked a little unsure. "What stories did she tell you then?" she asked.

"Many," Travis replied, his smile returning once more. "There were many, many stories that she told me. Too many to count."

"Okay then, what was your favorite one?" Sarora asked, narrowing down her question.

"Well, my favorite had to be about the young king."

Sarora looked to him, her eyes full of interest. "Young king?" Travis nodded. "So what did this young king do?" she asked him.

"Well, my mom always told me that he was a young boy from a while ago. She said that he had wanted to make himself known and make a difference in the lives of others.

"Eventually, he became an apprentice and learned how to call upon his own magical powers. With his great training, he was able to save a whole kingdom from its evil ruler.

"Then, seeing his worth, the Kingdom proclaimed him the new king and he lead for many years. For some reason, though, he went missing and never returned to his rightful place as king." Travis took a breath, "Mom says though that he must have gone home to his family, but she told me no one really knows the whole story."

Travis looked back at Sarora's eyes to find that they were no longer filled with interest, but more a questioning curiosity. "Hmm," she told him, "that's some story." She looked away from his gaze to face the invisible path again.

"What about you?" Travis asked a minute later. "What is your family like?"

Sarora stopped walking, looked to Travis, and then looked away. "I really don't feel comfortable talking about that," she told him, her voice almost a whisper.

"Why?" Travis asked. "I told you what I knew about my mom, why can't you tell me at least about your parents?" he pursued her this time.

"Don't, Travis," Sarora replied—her voice full of emotion unlike it had ever been. "I don't want to talk about it."

Travis wasn't going to let the question be denied. "You don't tell me a lot, so why not at least this time tell me about your family? You must have parents."

"Travis!" Sarora turned back to face him and he was shocked by what he saw: tears. Sarora was never emotional like this. Her eyes held sadness and anger, "I don't want to, please stop!" she snapped her head away from his gaze and began to charge forward, leaving Travis and Shadra in her dust.

Realizing what he had done, Travis gave Shadra a gentle kick and called for his friend, "Wait, Sarora! I'm sorry!"

Shadra ran hard and fast to try and catch up with the gryphon. Travis was surprised, he had not known that Sarora could run this fast. He kept calling for her, but she had disappeared from his sight.

"Sarora!" Travis called as loudly as he could. "Come back! I didn't mean it!" *How is it that I am always getting us into a fight?*

Shadra soon became worn and Travis slowed her down to a walk. "Where did she go?" Travis asked the mare. Shadra shook her mane as if to say, "How should I know? You're the one who pushed her to this, so you figure it out!" He was almost sure that was exactly what she had tried to say.

The sun in the sky began to sink below the trees and the light grew dimmer as Travis continued to search. After about two hours, he'd about given up hope.

When he thought all hope had been lost, Travis thought he heard a noise. He squinted his eyes, looking for any sign of the gryphon. "Sarora?" he whispered, "Is that you?" The noise came again. It sounded like a shuffling of feet. Who could it be?

Suddenly, behind Travis a figure leapt out. "Ahhh!" The person let out a loud war cry. Instantly, Shadra spooked and bucked Travis off. No sooner had Travis hit the ground than Shadra was gone.

ONE-ON-ONE SKIRMISH

The figure, unfazed by the retreating horse, attacked Travis again. Travis moved out of the way just in time. His eyes searched the ground and he spotted his staff, which must have fallen off of Shadra when he did. Travis reached for it and held it up just in time to defend himself as the figure attacked again.

His attacker was just a little taller than he was and must have been close in age. He figured it was a boy, but he couldn't see any other details other than he was cloaked in black and the hood of his cloak shadowed his face.

Travis's attacker was using a slim sword but luckily, for Travis, it wasn't strong enough to split through the staff. The sword's silver glare struck fear into Travis's heart.

Both of them groaned and grunted as they rolled and fought for control. Eventually, the boy jumped off Travis, giving Travis time to stand, only to be punched in the face.

"Ah!" Travis yelled at the pain. Travis rubbed his right cheek where his attacker had struck. Turning back to the fight, Travis jabbed the pointed end of the staff at the boy, who easily jumped out of its way. The boy then leapt back at Travis, his sword swiping at Travis's neck. His eyes wide in terror, Travis dropped to the ground, avoiding the sword by an inch.

Wrong move. The attacker then brought his sword downward at Travis's heart. As quickly as possible, Travis rolled out of the way of the sword's strike.

When there finally was a lapse in the repeated strikes, Travis stood up as fast as possible and once again locked gazes and weapons with his opponent.

The boy finally spoke. "What are you doing here?"

Travis struggle to hold his stance. "Me? What about you? I was only looking for a friend."

"Likely story," Travis could see his mouth formed into a sneer. Both boys hopped back a couple steps and then lunged at each other again, locking their weapons once more.

"I'm sorry if I trespassed," Travis told him, wanting to stop the fight. "If you'll let me, I'll leave now and never come back."

"That's what they all ask for," the boy sneered again and then added, "before I slit their throats ..." Travis felt his heart plummet: he wasn't going to win this fight and he knew it.

Seeing Travis's fear must have given the boy more confidence and strength, and he shoved Travis backward. Travis stumbled and fell with a thud. He looked up to see the boy coming at him once more, his sword held high and coming down on Travis's throat.

Travis closed his eyes, expecting the worse but it never came. A screech halted the boy and they both looked to see Sarora running at them. "Get away from him!" she roared menacingly at the boy.

Travis searched the boy's face for fear. Instead, he detected annoyance.

Sarora was soon upon them. "I said get away, Stephen!" she reared up over them and finally the boy retreated a few steps.

"This was *my* fight, Sarora." Stephen replied angrily. "I could have beat him too if you wouldn't have barged in—"

"Stephen! What use would it have been to kill him?" she spat. "You could have killed us all!"

"So?" Stephen retorted. "I don't care who he is! And if he's with you, then it's all the more reason to get rid of him!" Stephen looked to Travis but he was still talking to Sarora, "You know, put him out of his misery." He sneered again, arrogantly.

"Just leave!" Sarora's fur stood on end, her eyes blazed with anger. "Don't you have candy to steal from some scared four-year-old?" She turned to Travis. "Come on, let's go."

"It'd be in your best interest to look for me instead of her next time you need help, kid." Stephen called after them, "I'm at least human and smart!" his voice began to fade away as they continued to walk on. Sarora ignored Stephen's last retort and both of them refrained from talking to each other until they were out of earshot.

Sarora stopped and turned to Travis. "What were you doing picking a fight with a rouge like him?" she demanded.

Travis put his hand on his bruised cheek, feeling the hotness. "I was still looking for you when he came up behind us, scared Shadra away and picked a fight with me," he tried to explain to Sarora.

"If you ever see him again, don't be afraid to kill him. You wouldn't hurt my feelings by doing so."

"Kill him?" Travis asked, his face giving a "seriously?"

expression. "How am I supposed to do that? If you hadn't come, I'd be wishing that I had a head!"

"That crystal forgot to give you brains," Sarora sighed sarcastically. "Instead, it gave you fire that you never think of how to use the right way."

Travis looked down as his feet. "Shoot. I guess I forgot about that."

Sarora sighed. "Well, at least you're not dead and the worst injury you have is that giant, purple bruise on your cheek."

Everything went silent for a moment as they continued to walk. Finally, Travis apologized. "Sarora, I'm so sorry. I didn't mean to … I wasn't thinking."

Sarora silenced him with a glare that quickly softened. "Don't mention it." Travis opened his mouth to speak but Sarora stopped him. "Really, don't mention it. Let's forget about the whole thing. We've lost a little time so it won't be hard to get back on schedule." She continued to lead Travis along the invisible path.

That night they settled in under the clear sky and listened to the bugs and birds as everything went to sleep. Shadra had found them not long after they had found their camp site for the night. Luckily, Shadra wasn't hurt and none of the items had been lost.

After they had eaten their fill and said goodnight to one another, Travis rested his head on his backpack, laid on his back, and stared into the night sky.

Mom, he prayed to her, *If you can hear me, know that I miss you but I'm fine. Sarora and Arlen are my new family.* And he fell fast asleep into a peaceful dream, and it was like his mother had heard him, for she was in every part of his dreams.

THE ACER AND HIS APPREN-TICE

The wind whistled under Sarora's wings as she flew on. The sky had brought storms, forcing them to fly above the clouds, and making it difficult for them to keep track of where they were going.

Above the gray clouds, everything was peaceful. Travis and Sarora enjoyed themselves as they flew steadily and silently through the air. Travis was finally getting used to the feeling of flying—the way the air seemed to suck you upward as Sarora ascended, and the rush he felt when she dropped hundreds of feet at a time. Flying was nothing like riding Shadra—it was much more exciting.

Eventually, Sarora grew tired of flying in a straight line and the undertainty about where they were. "Hold on tight," she told Travis as she folded her wings in and plummeted to the earth.

"Whoa!" Travis cried in excitement. They were going down so fast that his hands were now the only thing that held him onto Sarora as the rest of his body flew through the air like a streamer.

The clouds drenched Travis and Sarora as they dived into them. After three seconds of nothing but white wetness, they reached the height where they could see the ground. The storm had seemed to have passed and the skies ahead of them were bright blue.

Sarora leveled herself by snapping her wings out once more and coming out of her steep dive. "Ah ..." she sighed, "much better."

The wind slowly began to dry off Travis as they flew on. It was refreshing to have water to cleanse some of his body, considering that he really hadn't taken a proper shower since they left Arlen's home. *Boy, I must smell bad,* he thought as he scrunched his nose up.

The sun was more than halfway across the sky so Travis figured it to be around noon or one o'clock but he wasn't sure. "Sarora?"

"Yeah, that's my name, don't wear it out. What?" she asked him as she smiled.

"How much farther?"

"I'll let you know when we're there."

"But we traveled all day today and most of the day yesterday so we must be close," Travis observed. Two days had passed since Travis's fight with Stephen and since then, they hadn't seen hide nor hair of that reckless teen.

"Very good, Travis," Sarora praised him like a little kid. "You can now count days!"

"Sarora," Travis complained.

"Oh, lighten up. It's not that much farther."

"But my rear is sore," he complained again.

"Well, my back isn't one hundred percent so, if you wouldn't mind, give my ears a rest and chill!"

Travis gave up and sat back down on Sarora's back. Below

them, the woodlands never seemed to end, parted only by an occasional small river. Could plains really exist in this vast land of trees? That seemed nearly impossible.

"Huhhh …" Travis sighed as he found himself back in the land of boredom, where everything was dull and plain. *Where had all the excitement gone?* Travis wondered inside himself as Sarora kept a sharp eye out for any signs of getting closer.

"Travis!"

Sarora's cry of excitement woke him a couple hours after he had fallen asleep. They were still high in the air. Travis sat up and rubbed his eyes, squinting in the bright sunshine. "What? What is it?" he asked, drowsiness still filling him.

"We're here! We're here!" she chanted like an excited child. Travis's eyes snapped open all the way. On the horizon he could see the plains that had been marked out on the map.

They had flown all day yesterday, thinking that they would be there soon only to stop for the night because they were both worn out. Now, three days after the fight with Stephen, they were finally there.

"Really?" Travis was becoming revved up at the sight of their journey's end.

Sarora nodded vigorously. "Really! I can see the plains!" She turned her gaze from the horizon back to Travis. "Once we're over the plains, let me know if you see anyone at all. It might be them!" she cried cheerfully as she went a little lower to the ground.

Travis nodded. A huge grin had formed on his face. "I can't wait!"

Sarora's wings began to beat faster and faster as they

closed in on the area. Now Travis could see the form of the plains. Just like the woods, the plains seemed to stretch forever. Instead of tall green trees, all Travis could see was the golden flat plains that seemed to shimmer as the wind blew over them.

As soon as they were only a few hundred yards above the plains, Sarora excitedly looked back and forth, trying to find her friends. They were just over the clearings that turned into the plains when Travis spotted a figure sitting on a boulder.

"Sarora!" Travis cried eagerly, "Look over there!" He pointed toward the boulder with his finger.

Sarora snapped her head around and stared at the fixture for only a second before yelling even more excitedly, "It's him! It's him, Travis!" Sarora came lower to the ground so they could see the figure more clearly. He seemed to be sitting on the boulder, whittling something in his hands and he had not seemed to have noticed them at all.

Too excited to contain herself, Sarora let out a long, excited screech. The boy's head snapped up. Travis could just see words form on his mouth. "Sarora?"

"Zack!" Sarora cried with joy as she dove down quicker.

"Sarora!" the boy cried back excitedly and waved both of his hands.

Sarora came out of her drop only a few feet from the ground. It was too quick for her, however, to stop right there, her speed flying them over top of Zack's head and landing them a few yards past him.

Once on ground, Travis hopped off Sarora. As she sped at Zack, her whole body seemed to quiver with excitement.

Travis doggedly followed behind her, trying to catch up.

Zack was a little taller than Travis. He had blonde hair, bright blue eyes, a skin that would have naturally been light but was now tanned, and he wore a sand-colored tunic and brown leggings. Travis guessed he was about fourteen, but, once again, he couldn't be sure.

Zack opened his arms wide and gave Sarora a hug as she stopped just short of running into the boy.

"Zack!"

"Sarora!" They cried together and laughed with joy. Travis stood about seven feet behind Sarora, not wanting to interrupt.

As soon as they broke apart, Zack spoke. "I ... I thought you were dead! Master told me to believe it and that's what he believes! I'm so glad you're alive!"

"Zack, I'm so sorry I left!" Sarora rested her head on his shoulder as if she were giving another hug. "It's just, well, maybe because I left, things in the future are looking brighter."

Zack took a step back. "What do you mean?" he asked, and then spotted Travis standing behind Sarora.

Travis could see the uncertainty in Zack's cold, blue eyes and he was sure it was reflected in his own expression. "Sarora, who is that?" Zack asked the gryphon, his eyes still on Travis.

Sarora turned so that she could look at both of them. She beckoned to Travis with a flick of her tail and he stepped forward nervously. "Zack, this is Travis."

"Hello," Travis greeted the older boy uncertainly, "nice to meet you."

"Excuse me for my rudeness but, what are you doing here?" Zack asked Travis, though the question was meant for Sarora to answer.

Sarora looked to Zack, "I'd like to explain everything at once. Could we see Master Racht please? Then I promise that everything will be told."

Zack still looked uncertainly at Travis as if he was expecting him to attack at any second. "Uh, sure. But if Master gets mad, I'm not taking blame." He looked away from Travis back to Sarora.

Sarora nodded. "I am fine with that. Besides, I'm pretty sure he's not going to be mad at Travis, but rather at me."

Zack looked back at both of them and then turned back a little ways towards the woods. "Okay, follow me." And he lead them away from the boulder.

Travis followed slowly behind Sarora, not wanting to get near Zack. He felt uncomfortable around strangers. He wasn't afraid that Zack would hurt him or anything, but he still didn't want to get too close. So, instead of conversing with him, Travis decided to walk silently at the back of the group.

Zack glanced back at the other two every once in awhile, but never spoke. Even Sarora seemed fidgety. *What's going through her head right now?* Travis wondered.

Finally, in the distance, Travis spotted a large tent. *Why are they living in such a large tent when they are trying to hide from everyone? Wouldn't their location and living quarters be like lighting a signal fire?* Travis wondered.

Zack walked quicker ahead of them and walked into the tent. Travis heard his voice from the inside of the tent while he and Sarora stood outside. "Master, someone's here to see you."

"Who is it this time?" an exhausted voice said. "Not the wolf patrol again, I suppose?"

"No, but it's someone you should see."

"Call them inside then."

"One of them would have a hard time getting inside."

Travis heard a chair scoot backwards and a hand slam on wood as the Master stood up from where he had been sitting. "What are you trying to pull, Zack?" he asked and Travis heard both of them walk to the entrance. Zack walked out of the tent and Travis saw another man's shape begin to follow him out. The master continued on, "Why couldn't you tell whoever it is that I'm busy—" he said, stopping mid-sentence as he spotted Sarora. "Sarora?" he asked, puzzled.

Sarora bowed her head. "Yes, master, I've returned."

Master Racht was a man in his sixties, with gray hair reaching his shoulders and a long, curly beard. He wore a green robe that was decorated with a magical creature pattern in gold thread at the rims of the sleeves and at the bottom.

Master Racht's eyes looked over Sarora, as if he couldn't believe what he was seeing. He took a step forward and gently touched the side of Sarora's head. His eyes lit up in recognition. "Indeed, you have returned. We may still all live."

Sarora nodded. "I know for sure now that we will live." Master Racht looked at her questioningly just as Zack had. "The last of the prophecy has arrived," she explained to him.

Master Racht's eye grew wide. Sarora moved out of the

way to reveal Travis, who was feeling uncomfortable in the old man's gaze. Once again, Master Racht's eyes flashed with understanding. "So he is the last?" he asked Sarora, who nodded.

"Come, boy," Master Racht spoke to Travis. Hesitantly, Travis stepped forward until he was right in front of him. Master Racht looked him over and then asked, "And what would your name be, young lad?"

Travis gulped and then spoke. "My name is Travis. Travis Wegner."

"Hmm," Racht said. "Your name is just as appropriate as the names of these two are." He motioned for them to come inside. "Let's all get in. We all have some sharing to do." Zack followed right behind Master Racht, followed by Sarora, and then Travis.

The inside of the tent was large. There were four rooms: the middle quarters served as a study, and three bedrooms were at the north, east, and west sides of the tent. In the study, there was only one bookshelf, filled with scrolls and tattered old books. There was also a desk, which Travis guessed that Master Racht had been sitting there when they had arrived.

There were three oil lamps, one outside of each bedroom, and one candle on the corner of the desk. Everything else seemed plain, and yet, to Travis, it was cool. He had not seen a tent like this ever before. The only one he had seen, in fact, was one that was being sold at a department store.

Master Racht sat at his desk and motioned for the rest of them to sit down. Travis and Zack sat on small cushions on the ground and Sarora sat half-in, half-out because there wasn't enough room for her to maneuver inside.

"So," Master Racht began, "we need explanations, from both of you." He looked from Sarora to Travis and back. "Especially you, Sarora. Don't think that the joy of the fact that you're still alive is going to save you from a punishment, no matter how glad I am that you left and brought Travis back with you." He gave a small grin and then looked to Travis. "Why don't we start with you? Tell us, Travis, how you came to be the holder of the Crystal of Courage."

EXPLANATIONS

Travis gulped before starting to tell his story. "Well, I'm thirteen years old and I lived with my step-dad for the past four years. I met Sarora one morning after a storm, when I went for a walk. I had to sneak out of the house when my step-dad was at work. I found Sarora in a hole made by an uprooted tree. First, she tried to convince me that I'd met my death by meeting her."

"Oh really?" Master Racht looked at Sarora. "I didn't know that you could ever be so tough. When did you become so less, well, Sarora-like?" he asked her.

"I … I was trying to intimidate him. I was hurt and I needed to find a way to heal. So I kinda backed Travis between a rock and a hard place so that he would suggest helping my wing to heal," Sarora rambled on with her explanation.

"Wing wound?" Master Racht asked. "When did this happen? I knew you weren't an A-plus flyer but I never expected a wound to come out of this."

"I'll explain when it's my turn if that's okay with you, Master Racht. I'd like you to get the full picture when I explain my reasons."

Master Racht nodded to Sarora and then looked back to Travis. "Please continue."

"As I was saying," Travis began and explained the rest of his tale from the time he and Sarora first met until he touched the crystal. "So, that's how it all got started."

"Uh-huh," Master Racht said, stroking his beard. Then he turned to Sarora. "Now, I presume you have some good excuse for leaving us in the middle of a battle, Sarora?"

"Middle of a battle?" Travis looked at Sarora, puzzled. "You never told me about this."

Sarora looked at her feet. "I felt that I only needed to explain myself to Zack and Master Racht. I'm sorry if I offended you," Sarora apologized, completely out of her normal character, or, at least, the character that he was used to seeing.

"Please begin," Master Racht broke the awkward silence.

Sarora nodded. "It all started at the battle. I was upset that you wouldn't let me fight and instead you had assigned me to protect the crystal. I felt that I could be of more use so I went against your wishes.

"When I felt it was safe to come out, I left the crystal hidden in a tree trunk. Quickly, I found myself in a fray and I fought alongside Oberon's pack. However, we soon found ourselves defeated when Sievan showed up. He told me to surrender to live, but of course, I wouldn't give in to him. The wolves distracted him to save my life, sacrificing theirs.

"I quickly went back to where the crystal was, only to find it missing. Zack surprised me when he crept up behind me and was holding the crystal. I asked for it back but he wouldn't give it to me, like a good friend would save his friend from disaster." She shot a grateful, but also apologetic glance, at Zack before continuing.

"But my decision was made and I wouldn't take no for an answer. That's when I screeched. It knocked Zack out cold as well as Sievan. While they were both unconscious, I grabbed the crystal and flew away, hoping to save the crystal from any destruction.

"However, luck was not on my side that night. A couple hours after I had passed through the gate to the other world, Sievan caught up to me, and so I was forced to fight for the crystal.

"We fought neck and neck and finally, I was able to slash through his wing. He was wounded enough that he wouldn't last much longer. I thought I had won but he made one last attempt to hurt me and caught me off guard. As he flew past me back toward the portal, he slashed through my wing.

"I kept flying even though I knew that it could be fatal. Finally, I could not take the pain any longer and I plummeted to the earth. Everything went black.

"The next day Travis found me in the den I had managed to crawl into while I was hurt. That's pretty much it in a nutshell."

Master Racht let out a long sigh. "Oh, Sarora. You may have much wisdom, but you're not helpful in times of quick need." He paused a second before continuing. "However, you did manage to find Travis. It does not right your reckless move, but it does clean some of the slate." He turned to Travis. "Now both of you must explain how you got here. I want to hear everything." So together, Travis and Sarora told Master Racht about their journey during the previous months.

Travis and Sarora finished their tale a couple hours later.

Though it had taken a long time to explain, the time had flown quickly. Travis and Sarora had taken turns explaining what had happened, though, for some reason, when it was Sarora's turn to tell about rescuing Travis from the snowstorm, she never mentioned Arlen. When Travis was about to interject, Sarora shot him a look that said, "No, there is no need to tell him of Arlen." He gave a very small nod and they continued with the story.

Once finished, Master Racht looked at the two of them and said, "If Sievan was that into getting rid of you, we best keep our activities quiet." He looked to Zack. "You just bought supplies yesterday, right?"

Zack nodded from where he sat listening to the tale. "Yes, we have enough to last three of us another couple weeks. Sarora, however, will have to try her hunting skills out around in the woods. Unless, you'd like me to hunt for her, Master."

Master Racht nodded. "That would probably be best. Tomorrow, Zack, you will go out hunting. And be sure to take Travis with you. It doesn't seem that his style of hunting has done him very well." He looked at Travis and smiled. Travis smiled back.

"With that settled," Master Racht continued, "let us, in celebration, have the day off from training and cook up some meat with a few spices."

Sarora gasped. "But, Master, you never used to share your spices with anyone!"

Master Racht smiled at her shock. "There is a first time for everything, dear one. Be sure to remember that. As for your punishment, tomorrow, you'll be stuck with plenty of tasks like flying me around from place to place to collect supplies and to clean up around here. I'm sure a good cart-pulling is in order as well."

A small groan escaped Sarora. "How'd I know that was coming?" she asked, jokingly.

"Because you saw Zack pull the cart the one time he was five minutes late for lessons," Master Racht said, continuing to smile. "And it tortured you just to watch him. Wait until you will do it."

Sarora bowed her head respectfully. "Yes, Master. From now on, I promise to listen to every one of your instructions, no matter how ridiculous they may seem at the time."

"And so you should," Master Racht told her. "You owe it to both Zack and I. Your disappearance crushed the last hope out of us. It hurt even more when we were told by a small wolf patrol that you had clashed with Sievan and fallen to almost certain doom."

"I know, Master Racht." Sarora had still not looked up from where she bowed her head. "I am truly sorry for what I have done and I ask that you would please forgive me."

Master Racht smiled. "Don't worry, young one. In my eyes, all is forgiven. And I'm sure that Zack is just glad enough to see you again that he may have forgiven you for leaving. However, I'm not so sure about the Fear Screech attack on him. That was unneeded and uncalled for."

Sarora looked to Zack. "Zack, you are the closest thing I have to family and I would hate to lose you. Will you please forgive me?" she asked. Travis, who sat and watched the whole scene feeling very awkward, continued to be surprised by Sarora's new behavior.

At first, Zack looked away from Sarora and at his hands. "I surely hope you know how much you hurt me, Sarora. And then when I heard that you were presumed dead, it nearly killed me." His voice at first was filled with anger, and then softness. "But now that I know you are alive, I don't care what you did. I'm just glad that my best friend is back." He smiled happily, joy brimming over between them.

Travis felt an unusual emotion burning within him. He was happy that everything seemed to be turning out okay, but something made him feel upset. He was shocked when he realized what it was: Jealousy? He tried to shake the feeling. He had no reason to be jealous that Sarora had a friendship with someone else as well as him. He guessed that he was just so used to having her all to himself that he didn't feel like sharing her.

Sarora's eyes lit with relief and happiness. "Thank you, Zack."

Zack hugged Sarora. "You're like my sister, Sarora. How could I not forgive you?"

Again, Travis felt the burning sensation but once more stomped it out. He'd just have to learn that Sarora could have more friends than him.

Once Zack and Sarora were seated again, Master Racht spoke. "Now, all we must do is leave the past in the past. The future is brighter when ghosts of past days are forgotten." He paused for a second before continuing. "Now, who is ready for some dinner?"

Dinner was fairly delicious. Even though it was a sparse meal, Travis enjoyed being able to find out a little more about Zack and Master Racht.

Zack supposedly had been an apprentice to Master Racht for the past three years. During that time, Zack and Sarora had been busy training for anything that may come in the future, such as a battle with Lord Trazon.

"It will be unavoidable," Master Racht had said to them. "One day there will be a battle. And the three of you will have to work together to save Firmara."

Travis barely thought about what he was saying. At the moment, he didn't feel like thinking about dark omens or bloody battles. He only wanted to think good thoughts.

After the dinner of chicken covered in delicious spices, Master Racht went on a walk and ordered Sarora to come with him. Meanwhile, Zack showed Travis around the tent.

"The room in the center there is Master Racht's," Zack explained. "He wishes for us to not go in there. In other words, it's forbidden." Then he pointed to the room on the right. "That's Sarora's room. It has an extra opening toward the outside so that she does not have to squeeze through the main entrance and the main quarters. And the last room is where I sleep, though I suspect that Master Racht will have us share rooms." Zack smiled and so did Travis. They were both glad to have someone around their own age to hang out with.

Zack led Travis into his room in the tent. It was a basic area: for the bed, there was a rolled-out mat on the floor with a pillow. On the floor was a candle with a holder similar to the one that had been sitting on Master Racht's desk. There was also an opening in the side of the tent that served as a window. The only strange thing about the room was that the floor was wooden. It just seemed strange that a traveler's tent would have a floor.

"I know it's not a lot," Zack began, "but it's enough for me."

Travis nodded, "It's not a fancy hotel, but it grows on you. The simplicity reminds me of my old home." Travis thought back to a few months ago. Back then, to him, Firmara had not existed, gryphons were mythical creatures, not magical, fun would be away from home, and the most exciting thing would be a sneak away out the window. Life was a little more complicated now but that's what made it so much better. The complications gave the fun times more meaning.

Master Racht and Sarora returned from their walk with an extra friend.

"No way …" Zack's voice trailed off as he spotted Shadra walking alongside. Master Racht rode on the bay mare.

Travis looked up and smiled at Zack. "Way. That's who I've been riding the past couple of weeks."

"What?" Zack looked at him in surprise. "How in Firmara did you find one of Master Racht's horses in another dimension?"

"Well, long story short, a person I befriended happened to have been keeping her at his place for a few decades and he gave her to me," Travis explained, trying to avoid talking about Arlen as much as possible.

Zack and Travis stood up and walked toward the three of them. Master Racht hopped off Shadra and handed her reins to Zack. "Here, why don't the two of you take her over to the others? That way she'll have someone to hang out with.

Zack nodded. "Okay." He turned to Travis. "You wanna come?"

"Sure!" Travis smiled. "Shadra's the only horse I've ever seen or ridden."

"In that case," Master Racht said, "she'll be the horse you use. Zack and I already have one."

"Come on!" Zack called to Travis. He had already begun to walk away. "Let's reunite her with her long lost friends!"

Travis and Zack reached the edge of the woods where the other horses were staying. Zack stopped and let out a low whistle. The sun was sinking in the sky but it would still be a little while before it would go down.

"Follow me," Zack ordered Travis as he lead him into the woods, followed by Shadra.

Not far into the woods, there was a small and three other horses. Shadra let out a whinny of excitement and Zack let go of her reins so she could join her friends.

"Here," Zack began, "I'll introduce you." He walked up to a large palomino gelding. "This is Mesha. He's my horse." Travis noticed how, just like Shadra, Mesha had a perfect star on his forehead.

"And this mouse-gray stallion over here is Abendega," Zack continued. "No one rides him right now but he's a brilliant fellow." He patted Abendega's side and moved to the next horse. Travis noticed how all the horses had a prefect star on their heads. *That's probably a special marking for the Acer's horses,* Travis figured as they moved on to the last horse.

"And here's Master Racht's pride and joy, Seraphi," Zack said, showing Travis the last horse, an almost completely white stallion. Unlike the others that had white stars, however, Seraphi's was a darker shade of gray.

"They're all beautiful," Travis finally managed to speak.

Zack nodded, "Yes, not to mention very intelligent. Seraphi can understand any word in any language. He's the one with the most brains of the bunch."

"Then they each have their own character really?" Travis asked.

Zack nodded again. "As a matter of fact, yeah. Like I said, Seraphi is the brains and then Mesha is the strong-willed, occasional clown, and Abendega is the talented one. He's able to jump about anything you ask him to."

"I'd say Shadra's the sensible one," Travis spoke up for his horse. "She's bright, well, brighter than me at least." He smiled and found Zack smiling back at him.

Travis and Zack sat talking to each other quietly in their room before they went to bed. Zack had been right—as soon as he and Travis had returned from their walk to the horses, Master Racht had told Travis that he would be rooming with Zack.

Zack had lent Travis a pair of his sleeping garments, which were really just a pair of shorts and something that resembled a muscle shirt. As the night stars came into view, the boys talked because both Master Racht and Sarora went to bed early.

"So you got the Crystal of Courage, huh?" Zack asked Travis, who nodded. "That's cool. I remember seeing my crystal for the first time. It felt like it had called me to it and Sarora keeps telling me that I should have seen my face when it lit up in my hands. She says I looked like a ghost had just scared the heck out of me." He chuckled.

"What's your crystal of?" Travis asked Zack, curiosity filling him.

"I own the Crystal of Justice," Zack replied. "And it's definitely meant for me. I'm a by-the-book kind of kid. If there's a rule, I follow it like a religion. As for being just, I feel like I know every rule in Firmara and as for anyone who breaks one of those rules, I feel the need to be just, you know?"

"I understand," Travis began, "but what's weird is that I don't feel all that courageous. I feel just like a normal kid."

"But you felt courage your whole journey," Zack explained. "You probably just didn't recognize when you felt it. I mean, you had to have courage to have made it this far."

"I guess so," Travis admitted. "But having courage doesn't mean that I wasn't ever scared. Like when Sievan attacked and the fight with Gore and his followers—it all scared me."

"But without fear, you are not human. Everyone feels fear at least once in their life."

"Speaking of fear," Travis said, "I was super freaked out when Sarora asked me to put my hand out and force my anger at a cloud and then flames shot out of my hand. Now that's what you call a surprise."

"Wait, you've already been able to use your powers?" Zack asked, surprised.

"Well, yeah. I thought it was normal that once you touched your crystal you could use your powers at any given time."

Zack shook his head, eyes wide. "I don't even know what my element is and I've been training for three years."

"Oh," Travis replied. "I didn't know that."

"Why didn't you or Sarora tell this to us earlier?" Zack asked.

"Well …" Travis thought back and remembered that in fact they hadn't shared that bit of information with them. "I guess we just forgot."

Zack smiled and sighed. "Sarora probably forgot on purpose, she does that a lot. You can never get every bit of information out of her."

Travis smiled and chuckled a little. "Yeah, don't we know that. She likes to tell you little bits of a story and then act like it's some show that's to be continued …"

Zack laughed. "That's Sarora all right." He looked out the small opening of the tent to see that the sky was as dark as it was going to get. "I guess we should hit the hay then. We'll want to be up early."

"Real quick, though, I have another question." Travis spoke before Zack could go to sleep.

Zack stifled a yawn. "Okay, what is it?"

"How are you and Master Racht able to hide a tent this large out in the open?"

Travis saw Zack smile. "That's a trick that Master Racht invented. Only those who have a pure heart can see it. In that case, Sievan, Gore, and even Lord Trazon himself cannot see or locate the tent."

Travis was in awe. "That is clever. Lord Trazon will never be able to find us. Unless he decides that being on the dark side isn't worth it and joins us," he joked.

Zack chuckled a little. "Fat chance of that," he let out another yawn. "All right then, let's get some sleep."

Travis nodded, stifling a yawn. "Okay, sounds good."

Zack turned to the candle that had been lighting their whole conversation and he gently blew it out. "Good night," he told Travis as both of them settled onto their mats.

"Good night," Travis replied and fell into an excited sleep.

LESSON NUMBER ONE

Travis intently followed behind Master Racht to the makeshift training grounds. The sky was blue and the sun warming. Today was Travis's first battle lesson and he was really excited.

Yesterday, Travis had accompanied Zack on a hunting trip. They each brought down a wild turkey—Zack using his bow and Travis finally able to use his staff correctly.

When they had returned, Sarora was too exhausted to talk. Master Racht had had her working hard all day and she looked like she would bite anyone who mentioned the pulling cart. Supposedly, she had a difficult time pulling it when Master Racht had filled it with sacks of oats and, when she finally did pull it, she accidentally tipped the cart over and the sacks ripped open. So, after pulling the cart, she had to go back and pick up every grain of oat that had been left on the ground.

Today, Sarora and Zack followed behind Travis and Master Racht to the training grounds where they would spar each other while Master Racht would instruct Travis on how to fight with weapons.

Travis observed his surroundings while they walked to where they would train. The ground here was mostly covered in dry grass and arid dirt. The golden parts of the plains were set around the grassy area, giving the land a polka-dotted pattern from high in the sky. Very few trees grew in the plains; the lack of shade and rain prevented them from thriving.

Finally, after a half-hour of walking, they arrived at the sandy ground where they would train. Sarora and Zack walked past Travis and Master Racht to a spot farther on where they would spar. Travis waved goodbye to them with his right hand because he held his pencil-like staff in his left.

Master Racht first motioned for Travis to have a seat on the edge of the sandy hallow. Once seated, Master Racht began. "All right then, today I will show you the common moves of the different elements so that when the time comes, you'll know which one to use."

"Master Racht?"

"Yes, Travis?"

"I-I already know my element." Travis stammered.

"You what?"

"I already know my element, sir. I found out the day I touched the crystal. I have the power of fire."

"That is quite peculiar, Travis." Master Racht seemed to shake himself from his shocked state. "There were only two others in the whole history of magic wielders who found out their element before the appointed time …" He seemed to lose himself in thought before returning to their conversation a few seconds later. "Well, then. I'll at least show you the earth pattern and then I'll show you fire. I would think you'd at least want to know how I use my forms."

"You have the power of earth?" Travis asked.

Master Racht nodded. "Yes. I have the element of earth

and my crystal is the Crystal of Knowledge." Master Racht then cleared his throat. "Anyways, let us continue. If I may, Travis, I would like to look at your makeshift staff."

Travis nodded. "Sure, of course," he said and handed his staff to Master Racht, who took it gently and swept his gaze all over it while he spoke to Travis. "This is a fairly good weapon, sturdy, strong, and obviously sharp enough at the end to kill or injure. You have any other plans for this then?" he asked.

Travis looked away from Master Racht for a couple seconds. "Well, I don't know about *plans,* but I was thinking about decorating it a little more."

"Oh really? How so?" Master Racht asked, his gaze still on the staff.

Gaining more confidence, Travis continued, "Oh, I don't know exactly, but I figured I'd take my jackknife and carve different shapes along the side."

"Really? Are you sure?"

Travis thought about it for another second and then spoke again, "Yeah, I'm pretty sure."

WACK!

"Ow!" Travis felt a throbbing on his head where Master Racht had whacked him with the side of the staff. "What was that for?" he asked, his voice filled with anger.

"This is a weapon, not a piece of pottery or furniture!" Master Racht yelled unexpectedly at Travis. "You put carvings on here and the only good thing that would come out of it would be that it would be a trinket to sit by your headstone. You would weaken the wood by adding your pretty little designs over it!"

Travis looked at his lap. "Sorry, Master," he apologized.

"You would have been if you'd have died because your staff couldn't hold its own against a sharpened sword," Master Racht chided him. "Now," he continued and handed the staff back to Travis, his tone becoming calm once again. "Let me show you the Earth Third. It's not the most complicated of the five earth forms but it'll give you an example of what all of the forms hold." He stood up and walked to the center of the sandy clearing, which was probably twenty-five feet in diameter.

He stood in the middle of the clearing, took a deep breath, and turned to his left, one hand at his side, and the right hand held at chest level. His left foot was on its ball, the other flat on the ground, and in a series of slicing punches, jabs, and fierce kicks, Master Racht was able to lift small patches of the earth out of the ground, which Travis figured to be about the equivalent of his own fire shot out of the hand.

Master Racht finished his form with a loud, "Ai!"

Travis gaped in amazement while Master Racht tried to catch his breath, "Wow! That was amazing!"

Master Racht took a deep breath, "I should hope so. Phew! That was a lot easier when I was your age. It gets harder when you pass forty but being my age ..." He smiled at Travis, wiping the sweat from his brow. "Now, stand up, Travis. I'll show you the first few moves of the Fire First."

Travis was drenched in sweat two hours later when they had finished. The sun was burning his used-to-be fair skin. Master Racht was meditating a few feet away, trying to stay cool. Zack and Sarora had finished sparring practice a half-hour ago and were probably now back at the tent, happily resting while Travis was only taking a break.

"I sense you are exhausted," Master Racht spoke from where he sat.

No, duh, Travis thought, though he tried his best to act polite. "Yes, Master."

"Come and sit with me."

Tiredly, Travis stood and moved over to where Master Racht was meditating, his eyes closed and his hands folded together in a prayer-like position. Travis sat next to him as quietly as possible and waited for more instructions.

"Close your eyes," Master Racht instructed quietly. "Imagine your breath flowing through your body—in, and out, in, and out."

Travis closed his eyes and tried to picture the air rushing through his mouth, down his throat, and then into his lungs and back out. Strangely, the method seemed to help him to relax. After a while, the heat seemed to disappear and Travis was lost in his mind, unaware of the time passing by.

In what had seemed to be a short period of time, Master Racht stood up by placing his left hand on Travis's shoulder for support. "We should be going now, Travis. It's getting late."

Travis slowly opened his eyes. To his surprise, the sun was just above the horizon. On the other side of the sky, stars began to appear as tiny, shimmering sparkles. Gradually, Travis stood up and began to follow Master Racht back to the tent.

"You did very well for your first day," Master Racht commented as they walked back.

"Oh, uh, thank you, Master," Travis stammered, unprepared for a conversation.

"Zack may have been training for three years now, however you're both easily matched in skill. It certainly won't take you long to catch up to his level."

Travis was taken off guard again. "Well, I don't know about that. I mean, he is pretty talented." He thought back to earlier that day. He had only seen glimpses of Sarora and Zack's pretend skirmish but he had seen plenty enough to know that picking a fight with Zack would be a death wish. Zack was fast, strong, and clever, most of which Travis was not.

Master Racht nodded. "That he is. But you have something special about you that I can't quite put my finger on. You remind me of someone, I just can't exactly remember who."

Travis just stared at his feet as they continued walking. He wanted just to be average, nothing special, not overly talented, and certainly, he didn't want to have a reputation at fighting well. He'd rather not do anything excellently than be praised for every move he made.

"I like you, Travis," Master Racht continued on, "you show great promise." He paused again, and out of the corner of Travis's eyes, he saw Master Racht's eyes widen. "And I think I know what goes best with your fire," he spoke quietly.

"Excuse me, Master," Travis asked, looking back at him, "but what exactly do you mean?"

"Don't worry about it. You'll find out when the time comes. Just like Zack, you'll each find it." He spoke to Travis, looking into his eyes with kindness and with somewhat of a foreboding feeling. What was Master Racht so worried about?

GOOD TIMES AND LAUGHS

Travis, Zack, and Sarora sat outside under about the only tree on the plains. They were hanging out together just having fun while they ate apples—a rare treat that Master Racht let Zack buy from the market in the town about ten miles away.

Today was their day off because it was Zack's fifteenth birthday. One month had passed since Sarora and Travis had left the woods next to Arlen's home. It was strange because Travis felt as if they had not been to Arlen's since about a week ago and yet he also felt that he had always lived in Firmara with Zack, Sarora, and Master Racht. It was strange but good feeling.

"Okay, okay," Travis continued to laugh at Sarora's joke as he tried to speak. "What do you call a dargryph with half a brain?"

"I don't know," Zack replied and looked to Sarora. "Do you?" Sarora shook her head.

"Extremely gifted!" Travis cried out and they all continued to laugh.

Later that night, Master Racht surprised them with a delicious fish dinner served with lemons. "It's not every day that an apprentice of mine turns fifteen!" he had explained when they all asked why.

After dinner, they sat outside and watched the sunset turn into stars. Master Racht went off for a small walk by himself, which was now becoming a regular event. Sarora relaxed a few yards away from Zack and Travis, who were sitting together, admiring the beautiful night.

"See that group of stars over there?" Zack asked Travis, pointing to a section of the sky.

"Yeah?"

"That's the water dragon."

"How do you know it's the water dragon?" Travis asked.

"It's a water dragon because of its long body. See? Its head is near the middle of the sky and its tail reaches to the horizon."

Travis nodded, "Oh, yeah, I see." Then Travis pointed over to more. "See that group of stars over there?"

"Where exactly?" Zack asked.

"It's over there. The one part of it is shaped like a square."

"Oh, yeah, now I see it. What's it called?"

"Where I'm from we call it the Big Dipper," Travis told Zack.

"You name constellations after silverware?" Zack asked, surprised.

"No, not all of them. We also have Leo, which looks like the shape of a lion, and Gemini, which are the twins of the sky," Travis explained.

"Huh," Zack observed, "we give all our constellations names from stories or legends of Acers."

"That's cool." Travis paused and then asked, "Is there one for Trazon?"

Zack shook his head. "No, he'll never earn enough

respect for something like that."

Travis nodded. "Yeah, you're probably right."

Zack chuckled. "I know I am."

They were silent for several more seconds before Travis spoke up again. "You're such a great person, Zack. I don't even know why I was ever jealous of the friendship that you and Sarora had." Travis's eyes grew large; this wasn't what he had wanted to say.

Zack's eyes became filled with an unnatural fury. "You were jealous that Sarora and I are friends?"

"Uh, well," Travis stammered, "At first I was but now I'm not. I mean, well, um, I guess I was just so used to her having me as an only friend for most of the trip that it, it was hard for me to understand that she could have more than one friend, that's all." Travis tried to explain, a pleading tone coming into his voice.

Zack looked away from Travis. "You have no reason to feel that way." He looked back at Travis. "Sarora and I have always been best friends and we always will be whether you like it or not." Zack stood up, and with a huff, he turned and walked away from Travis back into the tent.

"Zack, wait!" Travis stood up and called after his angered friend. Whether Zack heard him or not, he didn't respond.

"Great," Travis mumbled to himself, "I've really screwed things up this time."

The next day Master Racht was taking Zack out for some battle training while Sarora and Travis were going to practice on their own terms. Since last night, Zack still hadn't spoken to Travis and had seemed to try and avoid him as much as possible.

Sarora sat watching while Travis tried to remember and perform for her the Fire Second. The form itself was simple enough and yet, it pushed Travis hard to try to keep the movements flowing while focusing on his fire powers.

"You messed up again," Sarora commented from where she sat.

Travis stopped and looked to her with a complaining face. "What did I do wrong this time?" he asked, sick of the whole idea of training.

"You moved from the three fires to the 'Fire's Will' instead of three fires to 'Fire Fury,'" Sarora said to him and looked at him questioningly. "What's on your mind, Travis? You usually do a whole lot better than this. It's as if you're in a whole other realm," she observed.

Travis looked away from her gaze. "It's nothing. Here, I'll just start over again."

"Travis," Sarora stopped him just before he began the first move. "You've started over five times now, and I know you better than that. Something's bothering you, now what is it?"

Travis looked down at his feet and gave in. "You're right." He admitted and took a deep breath before continuing. "Zack won't speak to me."

Sarora looked at him, surprised, "What did you say to him?"

"I—" Travis started, trying to make sure that he wouldn't upset another friend. "I was kinda jealous when I saw how close you were to Zack. I just wasn't used to the thought that you had other friends like me."

"Travis," Sarora scolded him, "I'm surprised at you.

Even if you had to feel that way, why did you have to share those feelings with him?"

"Well, I didn't really mean to. We were just talking and then I mentioned how great of a person he was and then the rest just kind of slipped out," Travis explained, the whole sound of the explanation sounding absurd. Why had his brain not seized those thoughts and stopped them in time?

Sarora sighed. "Oh, Travis. You seem to be a magnet to catastrophes."

"What do you think I should do then?" Travis asked her, desperate to repair his friendship with Zack.

"I think you should give him another day or so to let him come back around," Sarora replied. "If he doesn't talk to you by then, you should confront him in another way. It won't be easy, though. Once Zack puts his mind to one thing, it's very difficult to bring him back out of his state."

"Sounds like someone else I know," Travis chuckled grimly and looked to Sarora.

"Who?" Sarora asked jestingly, "Me? Really?" she laughed as well. "Well, that's one thing you can figure out."

"What's that?"

"Stubborn personalities."

"Well," Travis began, "you know what they say-"

"Yeah, it takes one to know one." Sarora laughed. "Boy, did you just open yourself up for that one!"

"Hey!" Travis couldn't help but smile at himself. "Can't you pick on someone your own size?"

"You mean Sievan?" Sarora asked. She had stopped laughing.

Travis nodded, hoping that he hadn't provoked another

speech from her.

"Gladly!" Sarora replied and went into another fit of laughter. Once Sarora had regained control of herself, she spoke, "Okay, let's get back to our original order of business. Show me the Fire Second, correctly this time though."

"All right, all right," Travis replied, trying to get back into a strong mental zone. "This time I'll know what to do."

"Focus, Travis!" Master Racht woke Travis from his thoughts as they continued to spar without weapons.

"Sorry, Master," Travis apologized as he ducked out of Master Racht's next strike, a blow to the head. In return, Travis struck out with the second kick from the Fire First. Master Racht blocked his kick easily with a flick of his wrist. "Come, Travis, you can surely do better than that!" his master egged him on.

Letting out a loud "Kia!" Travis came at Master Racht, first a high kick, which forced his master to duck, followed by several low punches at his master's gut. While Master Racht was busy deflecting his other blows, Travis swung his right leg around, surprised to feel it hit its mark. Master Racht stumbled backward and Travis took the opportunity to knock his master off balance, forcing him to the ground.

Master Racht hit the ground with a thud and Travis smiled, this was the first time he had ever knocked Master Racht to the ground!

Master Racht let out a loud grunt. "Help me up, boy," he instructed Travis. Quickly, Travis grasped Master Racht's hand and pulled him up onto his feet. After wiping the dirt from his robe with a few swipes of his hands, Master Racht looked to Travis. "I must say, Travis, I am very impressed with your skills. I had never expected you to get this far this quick."

Travis felt his face grow hot. "Oh, um, thank you, Master," he replied.

"That'll be enough training for the day then," Master Racht stated. "You've earned a good, long rest."

"So soon?" Travis asked. He wasn't used to having such a short practice, he was used to working hard on his skills most all of the day.

Master Racht chuckled. "It's more for me rather than you. I haven't worked that hard to fight someone since I battled with Donigan."

"Master?"

"Yes, Travis?"

"I was just curious, but, who is Donigan?"

"Donigan is Sievan's partner," Master Racht explained, though he sounded as if he did it grudgingly. "They're a terrible duo."

"I didn't know Sievan had someone at his own level."

Master Racht nodded. "Yes, he most certainly does. Sievan as you may have noticed makes up part of Sarora's Achilles Heel, along with Donigan. But I can see that your worst enemy will be Donigan until the day he dies."

"If you don't mind me asking," Travis began, all the more curious. "why is that?"

"Your past and Donigan's share some of the same moments." Seeing the look on Travis's face, Master Racht continued, "You'll find out exactly what and why when the time comes. But for now, don't worry about it, take your time learning what you need to, the battles and secrets will all be revealed in the future." Master Racht looked away from Travis and to the sun in the sky. "Phew, it's already past noon," he looked to Travis. "Come on, let's get back so we can enjoy some lunch."

After lunch, Zack left without saying a word to Travis. It had been two days since his birthday and the misunderstanding and Zack was still not speaking to Travis. Deciding that this was the best opportunity that he would have, Travis quietly followed Zack, who walked out to the border of the woods. Either Zack didn't know he was being followed or he didn't really care because he didn't turn around to look at Travis.

Zack unknowingly led Travis along the path to where the horses stayed. It'd been about a week since Travis had visited Shadra. Most of his days were now booked with hardcore training with Master Racht.

As they reached the woods, Travis quickly ducked down in the weeds because Zack had turned around. Travis guessed that he was double-checking that he wasn't being followed. Travis watched carefully from where he lay on his stomach. It was hard to see through the tall, dry grass, but Travis could see Zack's every move. The blond-haired boy looked to his right, then to his left, and then to his right again before deciding that he wasn't being followed. Quickly and almost silently, Zack turned back around and ran full speed into the woods.

With only a moment's hesitation, Travis got up and swiftly followed behind Zack, trying to match the beat of his footsteps. It was very difficult to follow Zack quietly because of all the dry leaves and sticks that covered the ground. Not only that, but small groups of bushes and tight groups of trees also made it hard to follow him.

To Travis's surprise, it didn't seem that Zack was headed for the horses. They were way past the clearing where the horses spent most of their time grazing. *Where is he leading me?* Travis wondered as he maintained his jogging pace.

Finally, Zack stopped about five minutes after Travis had followed him through the forest. Quickly, Travis tried to halt himself. He did fairly okay but he heard a muffled crack of a small twig from under his feet. Travis prayed silently that Zack hadn't heard him as the older boy turned a corner, going out of Travis's sight.

Since Zack had stopped in the middle of a clearing this last time, Travis was slow to follow in his footsteps. He had come this far and getting caught was not on his agenda.

Slowly, Travis softly stepped into the clearing and looked all around for a glimpse of Zack. Cautiously, he spun himself in a steady circle, still not able to spot a sign of his friend.

A loud cry erupted from behind Travis, nearly making him jump out of his skin. He wasn't quick enough to dodge Zack's attack, so he was knocked to the ground to where Zack sat on top of him. Travis now realized that he must have climbed a tree, knowing that Travis had been following him.

"What are you doing here?" Zack demanded from where he had pinned Travis to the ground.

"So you're actually going to talk to me now?" Travis asked him, trying on force a smile. Zack wasn't too heavy but the pressure of him on Travis's stomach still hurt.

"Only because you can't mind your own business and

give me some space!" Zack spat at him, his blue eyes blazing. Travis flinched at Zack's unusual anger. "I was going to have a heart-to-heart talk with you until you began to act suspiciously. So I tried to follow quietly behind you to see what you were up to."

Zack glared angrily at Travis. "Why can't you keep your nose out of whatever I'm doing and go back to the tent?"

"Zack," Travis said, trying to put a friendly spin on the conversation. "I just wanted to speak to you. Since you've got me pinned down right now, why don't I start?" When Zack didn't respond Travis continued. "I'm sorry for ever feeling jealous of you and Sarora. As usual, I wasn't thinking clearly." Travis tried to chuckle a little. "Will you please forgive me now? I don't know what else to do," Travis pleaded.

Zack looked away for a moment and both were silent. The only sound was the birds. In the distance, Travis thought he heard the horses chasing each other in the large clearing not far behind them. But Travis didn't look away from Zack. He kept his gaze focused on his friend.

Finally, Zack looked back at Travis and stood up. His gaze began to soften. "Travis, I was the stupid one. I overreacted. Let's just call it even and move on, shall we?" he asked Travis, his arm outstretched to help Travis up.

Travis smiled back up at him and took Zack's hand. Once standing, Travis tried to wipe the dust from his jeans, which Master Racht had cut short to his knees so that he wouldn't be too warm in the summertime.

Zack looked Travis up and down. "Remind me next time I head into town to pick you up some normal clothes.

Whatever you're wearing isn't custom to any of the lands around here."

"You guys don't wear jeans?" Travis asked, looking at his pants.

"If that's what you call those," Zack pointed to his denim shorts, "then, yeah. It looks like someone softened a potato sack and died it blue." He couldn't help but chuckle and neither could Travis. It seemed that now the past would be forgotten.

"Come on," Travis told Zack, "let's go back to camp."

He began to walk away but Zack grabbed hold of his wrist. "What?" Travis asked. He was looking forward to a nice, long nap on his day off.

"You have the right to know what I was out here for," Zack told Travis, his eyes serious again. "But you have to swear not to tell anyone, especially not Master Racht or Sarora."

Travis was unsure whether or not to trust his friend but, he nodded, agreeing.

Zack gestured farther out into the woods. "Follow me then." He turned to lead the way, and this time, he knew Travis was following.

Travis followed Zack for what seemed to be another tenth of a mile before they stopped in front of an old willow tree that sat near a small, swampy pond. Mosquitoes buzzed around Travis and he smacked one that had tried to bite him.

"So," Travis began, annoyed by the lack of any real activity and the constant biting mosquitoes, "what did you want to show me?"

"Well," Zack began, "you know how Master Racht always says that the only animals we'll ever need are our horses and our spirit animals?"

"Yeah, so?" Travis had heard the same speech plenty enough times when he had only asked Master Racht once if they cared for other animals.

"Well, you'll just see." Zack looked away from Travis and let out three short whistles that sounded like a bird call. Across the small clearing, where the ground was dry, Travis spotted a head poke out from a hole under the root of a willow tree.

"Come here, Pran," Zack called gently to the animal. "There is someone I want you to meet."

Happily, the rest of the figure came out of the hole and trotted over to Zack. Once there, the animal made sure to give Zack a thorough face-licking. "Travis," Zack tried to start but was too busy laughing. "Travis," he tried again, "This is my dog, Pran."

"Um, hello, Pran." Travis spoke to the dog and he cautiously reached his hand out to pet the dog.

"Aroof!" Pran barked at Travis, making him jump.

Zack smiled. "It's okay. His breath is worse than his bite. Literally, that's how I named him. Pran means 'breath.' Too bad I don't know any other word in another laungage that means 'smells' or 'bad.'"

"I can't believe it," Travis murmured, half to himself.

"What? That he has bad breath?" Zack asked.

Travis shook his head. "No. That you, of all people, Zack, would disobey anything that Master Racht told you. *You,* Zack by the book!"

Zack chuckled. "Well, not everything is as it seems."

Pran was a medium-sized dog that had a reddish-colored back that gradually got lighter until it turned into a whitish-cream belly. Travis didn't know a lot about different dog breeds, but he was sure that Pran was some sort of an enlarged Shiba Inu. Pran's bright brown eyes were flickering with happiness and his tail that curved over the top of his back wagged enthusiastically.

Travis reached out again and stroked the top of Pran's head. Pran responded by jumping on Travis and giving him a thorough face licking.

Pran's breath really did stink! It smelled something of a combination between rotting fish, skunk cabbage, and animal excretions.

"Yuck! Pran! What have you been eating out here?" Travis asked the dog in disgust, though he couldn't help but laugh as the dog's tongue licked his face.

"Whatever he can find when he's hungry." Zack smiled and let out a small chuckle. "He's always been like that. I tried to feed him my food sometimes but he just won't take it. He's the strangest dog I've ever known."

"I wouldn't say strange," Travis began, trying to hold back a laugh, "but rather 'unique'?" Travis said, hand-gesturing quotation marks around the word "unique."

Zack laughed. "Yeah, I guess you could call him that. But other than his breath, he's the best dog ever. I couldn't ask for a better one." He scratched Pran behind one ear. "Errrrrr …" Pran groaned happily and his back foot began to thump the ground rapidly.

"Hmm," Travis observed, "half dog, quarter garbage can,

and quarter rabbit. That's a new one." And both he and Zack laughed. It was good to have both of them talking to each other once more.

PREPARATIONS

Travis watched Master Racht and Zack practice fight with the practice swords. It seemed as though they were evenly matched, until Master Racht would pull out the last quick move and beat Zack with it, as he did every time they were on the field.

"Come, Zack!" Master Racht taunted him, "you want to be an Acer soon, don't you? Then show me how an Acer *really* fights!"

Zack lunged again at Master Racht, who quickly batted away the blow from the sword. Just as many times before, Master Racht brought his back leg around, ready to finish off Zack. However, this time Zack remembered and grabbed Master Racht's swinging leg with both of his feet and spun, forcing Master Racht to the ground. Zack stood over top of Master Racht with the practice sword held to his master's neck.

Master Racht smiled as he grunted, "Finally, boy, you've done it. You are indeed ready."

Travis felt himself become more intent by their conversation, *Ready?* Travis wondered. *Ready for what?*

Zack helped Master Racht back up onto his feet. "Thank you, master," Zack bowed to him. "I do believe that I am ready for the task ahead."

It was eleven days since Travis and Zack had made up. Since then, as usual, days were full of training and hard work. Sarora and Zack never complained about their daily exercises, but Travis couldn't help uttering a complaint every now and again. Every day was pretty much the same, to the point that Travis almost wished there was danger lurking around a corner or at least something that would put excitement back into his life.

Travis followed Zack and Master Racht back to the tent. The day was just like each and every other—hot, dry, humid, and miserable. Travis began to wonder if Firmara ever had any other kind of weather. *What I would give for some precipitation now,* Travis thought as he continued to force his sweaty, aching legs to keep moving through the tall, dry grass that sliced small cuts into his skin.

It seemed to take forever to get back to the tent. As they arrived, Travis spotted Sarora lying in the shade of the tent. She had been given the day off since she had finally been able to complete what you could call a 'Gryphon's Form.' Travis didn't know exactly what it was because he could never pronounce it.

"Geez," Sarora began as Travis sat down, exhausted. "You look like something the cat dragged out from under the bed. How you holding up?"

"Don't you ever get tired?" Travis groaned.

Sarora nodded. "Well, sure I do. I'm just used to it."

"Oh yeah?" Travis asked. "And how long does it take to 'get used to it?'"

"I don't really know. Couple years probably."

"Great," Travis mumbled. "Two whole years of pain and

torture."

Sarora laughed. "It's not all bad. Wait until next year. Master Racht will probably let you go into town with Zack. That's when you'll have a great time."

"I hope you're not being sarcastic."

"No, I'm not. There's street performers, delicious foods, and even a small candy store."

"Really?" Travis's mood began to improve. "I didn't know that Firmara had candy stores."

Sarora nodded. "We have a lot of things that your world has."

"Except electronics and indoor plumbing," Travis responded with a grim smile.

Sarora laughed again. "Yeah, except for those things."

"I miss the indoor plumbing the most," Travis confessed.

"To tell you the truth, I don't even know what that is. Can you explain it to me again?" And Travis explained once again how there were pipes in the ground that carried water to sinks and toilets.

"Wow," Sarora observed, "that's amazing. I would have never thought that your realm could actually be that smart to invent something like that."

Travis inwardly smacked his head against a wall. *I'm glad I grew up where I did. Else I'd never have the knowledge that I have today.*

Suddenly, Travis remembered what Master Racht had said to Zack on the training field. "Oh, yeah. Sarora I wanted to ask you something."

"Okay, shoot." Sarora reached nearby and grabbed an apple that she must have found in the forest.

"I was wondering about something that Master Racht had said to Zack. He has told him that he was 'indeed ready.' What did he mean by that?"

Sarora's eyes grew wide and she began to choke on the apple. She went into a coughing fit and her eyes bulged as she tried to clear the apple from her airway.

"Sarora?" Travis asked, "Are ... are you okay."

Sarora finally gulped down the apple, gained her composure, and then nodded, "Yes, fine." Then she went back to their original conversation. "You said that Master Racht told Zack that he was ready?"

"Yeah, and Zack replied with something like, 'I indeed believe I am ready' or something like that. What were they talking about?"

"Travis!" Sarora exclaimed, "Master Racht is going to perform the Acer ceremony!"

"Which means …?" Travis began, not quite following her.

"Which means that Zack is going to be an Acer!" Sarora exclaimed excitedly. "Finally, after all these years!"

"Wait a second," Travis began, "so then, he'll finally find out his element?" Travis asked.

Sarora nodded vigorously. "Yes, and his spirit animal!"

"When does this happen then?" Travis asked.

"Usually on the apprentices fifteenth day of their fifteenth year!"

"Then that's ..." Travis looked away from Sarora, counting to himself.

"Four days from now!" they both exclaimed together, smiling.

214

"So you've heard, then?" a voice asked from behind. They both turned to see Zack standing next to them. In their excitement, they must have not heard him approaching. Sarora stood to congratulate her friend. "Yes! Oh, I'm so happy for you, Zack!" she came over and gave him what Travis guess was her form of hug.

"Thanks," Zack replied and then mumbled something into her ear, of which Travis only could pick up a couple words: "if only" and "different."

"Come on," Zack motioned for them to come back into the tent. "I was just coming inside to tell you two that dinner is ready." They followed him, smiling, even though Travis was curious to know what Zack had said to Sarora.

Zack was in bed early the night before the ceremony. Sarora had decided to retire early as well. However, Travis's excitement for Zack kept him awake. So quietly, Travis tiptoed out of the bedroom, out of the tent, and outdoors, where the night stars shone brightly in the sky.

Travis moved over to a small grass ridge that was a couple feet tall. Even though it was small, Travis still found this area to be his favorite spot, mainly because it gave a beautiful lookout view to the stars.

Travis had only been sitting for a couple minutes when he heard footsteps from behind. He turned to see Master Racht walking toward him. Before Travis spoke, Master Racht came and sat down at his right side. "Past your bedtime, isn't it?" Master Racht smiled.

Travis smiled back. "It's not past resting time in another place of this world."

"Yes," Master Racht agreed, "but all clocks follow one

time." He paused for a minute. "Are you nervous for Zack?"

Travis nodded. "A little."

Master Racht rested his hand on Travis's shoulder. "Don't worry about it, Travis. You know how talented Zack is. He'll do just fine, you'll see."

Travis nodded and looked to the stars. They were both silent for several moments before Master Racht asked, "Your birthday is coming soon, is it not?"

Travis nodded and looked back to him, "Yes, how did you know?"

Master Racht smiled. "I just had that feeling. To be exact, what day is it on?" Master Racht asked.

"The sixth of June." Travis replied, and he began to wonder what it would be like to have his first birthday away from home.

"Excuse me for one second then." Master Racht stood up, turned, and walked back to the tent. A minute later, he returned to Travis with a small package.

"Now, I know it is not your birthday for a couple weeks yet, but would you be willing to open your present now?"

Present? Travis wondered, but nodded and Master Racht handed him a brown package.

"Gee," Travis began, "I haven't received a gift at all for quite some time. Thank you, Master Racht."

"Don't thank me until you know what's inside." Master Racht chided him in a kind manor.

Travis smiled and turned back to the package. Carefully, he peeled back the tan paper wrapping. Inside was an old book. It had an elaborate brown cover, and in the middle of the book's cover was a gold seal that held a red ribbon

216

that kept the book locked. The gold seal had three animals on it: a dragon, a gryphon, and something that looked like a deer only it had one antler instead of two. They were all running in a circle, one at each other's end. In the middle of them was a star like that on the Acer's horses. Now Travis was almost completely sure that the five-pointed star was a sign of the Acers.

"That book will come in handy for you in the future," Master Racht explained, but continued on when he saw Travis looking for a way to open it. "I do have one request though—that you wait until I am no longer here when you open it."

Travis looked up to Master Racht, puzzled. "No longer here? Master, what do you mean?"

"Come now, Travis, you can't expect me to live forever. I'm an old man and my years are well numbered."

"You speak as if you know your departure time," Travis wondered aloud. "Does this knowledge involve your crystal?"

Master Racht smiled. "In some ways, yes." He paused before continuing more seriously. "But remember this, to have knowledge is to know things others don't, but to be wise is to know the difference between right from wrong. Always find wisdom before knowledge, for they are completely unrelated subjects."

Travis somewhat understood, but not all of it was clear. However, once again he refrained from asking a question about the response. Instead, he asked something different. "So when I need to open it, master, how will I do so? I don't see a slot for the key."

"That's easy," Master Racht said, reaching for the book.

While it was facing him, Master Racht steadily moved his hand about a half-inch over the gold seal Travis watched as the three animals moved their heads and began to run around the circumference of the seal, becoming a blur. The gold seal glowed slightly and all three animals jumped out of the seal, each a small, gold statue around an inch tall. All three were amazingly alive and moving, each having their own mind and personality.

"Whoa," Travis breathed as the ribbon fell from the seal and allowed the book to open.

"Is that an answer substantial for you, Travis?" Master Racht asked, closing the book once more and swiping his hand back across the book, to the left this time instead of the right.

All three animals quickly chased each other in a circle again, once more becoming a blur, and eventually landed back on the seal.

Master Racht handed the book back to Travis. "Like I said, make sure you only open this when my time has passed—even more in times of need. But beware, only use this book when you are alone. Anyone who you can't fully trust to keep a secret must not see the contents inside."

Travis nodded. "Thank you, master. I'll treasure this gift for as long as live."

Master Racht smiled. "As so you should. Now," he began, standing up, "I'm sure we'll have a long day tomorrow and I don't want even my least experienced apprentice to be drowsy for the ceremony." Travis looked up and saw his master smiling back down at him before he left and went back into the tent.

Travis waited a while before retiring for the night. He continued to sit on the ridge, looking back from the sky, to the book, and back to the sky again. He knew something was up with Master Racht, but he wasn't sure. Even though he had only known him for a month now, he felt just as attached to his master as he was to Arlen or Sarora. He realized how much his heart would ache to lose any one of his new friends, possibly even worse than losing his mom.

Travis studied the outside of the book carefully, a voice from the past drifting into his head: *He would never know…*

"Oh, no. I'm not listening to you," Travis scolded the voice as he tapped the side of his head. "You've gotten me into plenty enough trouble so stay out of this."

Deciding that it was time to get some rest, Travis stood and walked back into the tent, into the room that he shared with Zack. Quietly, he hid the book under his pillow and fell fast asleep, although his dreams were filled with thoughts, and one dream in particular was all too familiar.

Travis ran through the dark woods as fast as he could, although the creature he chased was dangerous. Ahead of him ran a shadowy figure, now clearer than ever before. It had a long, flowing tail and mane and its hooves beat the ground. Its coat was darker than the night itself.

Travis continued to keep up with the form until it turned on him. He tried to move out of the way and grab his staff, but his feet and arms seemed to be held in place. In a split second, the animal reared, and its hooves beat at Travis's head. Travis felt a short sting of pain before everything went pitch black.

THE CEREMONY

Travis woke with a start and the feeling of his dream slowly began to disappear. Absentmindedly, Travis's hand shot up to his head where the creature had struck him. To his surprise, the injury still stung and felt hot to the touch.

Travis looked out of the makeshift window. It was still early—only the sunlight reached above the plains. The sky looked clear for now, but Travis prayed that clouds would come in and help block some of the sun's harmful rays.

Travis quickly got out of bed and changed into his jeans and shirt (Zack had still not yet been able to buy new clothes for him in town), and walked out of his room and outside of Master Racht's. He had to tell him about his dream. It couldn't just be a coincidence that he had had it three times now, the next one always more vibrant than the last.

Travis tapped on the side of the tent, which only made a small wispy sound as his hand knocked against the cloth. "Master Racht?" he called quietly.

Travis heard Master Racht let out a groan from inside his room. "What is it, Travis? It's still a while before you *need* to be up."

"I need to share something with you."

"Can't it wait until later today?" Master Racht asked sleepily.

"Master, I don't know if it can wait. I think it may be really important."

Master Racht let out a long, groggy sigh. "It's either important or it isn't, so which is it?"

"It's important," Travis decided.

Master Racht let out another sigh. "Fine, then you may come in."

Come in? Travis wondered as he remembered the day he met Master Racht and Zack: *"The room in the center there is Master Racht's," Zack had explained. "Though he wishes for us to not go in there. In other words, it's forbidden."*

"Travis?" Master Racht called when Travis paused, "Are you coming?"

"Yes," Travis called back and stepped through the slit in the wall that acted as a barrier.

Master Racht's room was much like the one that Travis shared with Zack. It had a wood floor, plain walls (of course), and a cutout window. It was quite similar to the other room although Master Racht had a full bed that was lifted a couple feet off the ground and had a small canopy instead of a mat like those that he and Zack slept on.

In addition, Master Racht had a small dresser that sat next to his bed, and on it sat an oil lamp and a pair of spectacles that Master Racht used for reading.

Master Racht sat on the edge of his bed, and, as Travis should have known, he was still in his bathrobe. He rubbed his eyes and looked up sleepily at Travis as he entered. "So, tell me, Travis, what is so important that you have to wake me three hours earlier than I need to be awake?"

"I had a dream," Travis started.

Master Racht sighed. "Is that what this is all about? You had a bad dream?"

"No, no, no." Travis began again. "Well, yes, I had a dream, but I've had that dream two times before. And each time I have the dream, it becomes clearer." When Master Racht continued to gaze at him, interest finally entering his eyes, he continued. "It started just after I touched the crystal. And the time before tonight it happened when I met the buck in the woods, you know, the one with the starry eyes."

"Hmm," Master Racht observed, "and you're positive that it is the same one every time?" Travis nodded. "Then it must be trying to tell you something. Tell me about this dream," Master Racht ordered Travis.

Travis quickly explained his dream in the clearest way that he could. "Hmm," Master Racht said after Travis finished, "I don't know exactly what it means." Travis's heart sank. "But I think I may have some clue." Travis felt his hope begin to grow again. "I believe that your dream is foretelling a future event, one that you will not be able to escape."

"Then what should I do about it?" Travis asked, worried. He didn't want to face his future knowing that he was going to run into trouble.

"Did you not just hear me?" Master Racht started again. "No matter what you do, your destiny is laid out in front of you. I'll say just be prepared, for you never know when the last moment will be upon you." Travis understood; this was similar to the speech that Sarora had given to him about death.

Travis nodded. "Okay, and, thank you, Master."

"Don't mention it. And if you have the dream again, be sure to let me know. The more it happens the closer it'll become. Now, if you don't mind, I'd like to get a couple more hours of sleep before the ceremony."

Travis stood up. "Certainly, I'll be going then." And Travis turned and left Master Racht's room and went back to bed, leaving his clothes on.

The sun was warmly greeting Travis as he and Sarora reached the battlefield. It would be another few minutes before Zack and Master Racht would arrive, as was the custom for the ceremony.

Travis looked up to the sky. A few stray clouds were spread out everywhere, but still there was no sign of rain. *Well, at least it'll provide more shade,* Travis thought.

Sarora let out an excited sigh. "I'm so excited for Zack! He's wanted this ever since he touched his crystal and learned that this was his destiny."

Travis nodded. He was excited for Zack as well, but he was even more excited for the day *he* would become an Acer. "When do you think they will get here?" Travis asked.

Sarora shook her head. "I don't know. Not too much longer I should think."

There was a small lapse of silence before Travis asked, "So how does the ceremony work?"

"Well," Sarora began, "I don't know a whole lot about the ceremony. But what I do know is that it is split into two main parts—one today, and one later tonight. During the first ceremony, Zack will run through his first, second, third and fourth forms, then he will perform his fifth form, this time supposedly digging deep inside himself to find his element.

"After finding his element, Zack will find his spirit animal, but I don't know how they do that part. After the first part is done, Zack will sit for three hours alone, to strategize on how he will use his newfound powers to fight Master Racht in a fight using only magic, no weapons."

"Whoa, not a whole lot of work or anything," He said sarcastically.

Sarora put on a small "gryphon smile." "Yeah, no really. At least it's a little cooler out today. It'll be easier for him if the weather is 60 degrees instead of 90."

Travis nodded. "Yeah, be it luck or destiny, the day looks like it'll be a good one."

"Wow, I'm impressed."

Travis looked at Sarora quizzically. "About what?"

"Travis, can't you hear yourself?"

Travis smiled nervously. "What ... what do you mean?"

"You sound as if you've lived here all your life."

"I ... I do?" Travis stammered.

"Yeah." Sarora's eyes seemed to sparkle in a fond way. "You do."

Travis looked at his hands, feeling, for some reason, a little uncomfortable, "I ... I guess I do."

Half an hour later, Sarora spotted Master Racht and Zack walking up the hill to the training arena. Master Racht was wearing a green fighting tunic, covered by a green ceremonial robe, each with a gold pattern of some magical animal that Travis did not know.

Zack wore similar clothing. He wore a tan tunic and robe, but neither had embroidery on them. Both of their faces showed concentration for the task ahead.

Once they reached the field, Zack stopped in the middle, but Master Racht kept walking on to the opposite side. Once there, Master Racht turned to face Travis and Sarora, who were the only other members of the Acer council since there were no other living Acers. Even without the other members, they were still going to go through with the entire ceremony, word by word.

"Welcome," Master Racht began. "Today will be a day to remember as my eldest apprentice, Zachary, Honorable Apprentice, becomes an Acer.

"As is tradition, Zachary will begin by displaying the Apprentice forms one through four, and then performing his elemental fifth form, finding his movements only by the feeling that he finds deep inside himself. If everyone is ready, let us begin." He turned to Zack. "Please begin."

First, Zack bowed to Master Racht, and then to the crowd (Travis and Sarora). Then he began the elemental forms—these were the group of forms for apprentices who did not know their element yet.

When the first four forms were finished, Zack was already covered in sweat, and yet, he still looked full of energy and ready to go.

"Now, Zack," Master Racht began again, "it is time for your element to be revealed. Dig deep inside yourself and use the Element Fifth that speaks to your heart."

Zack turned and faced Travis and Sarora, and closed his eyes, deep in thought. Travis watched intently, excited to see what Zack would do.

Suddenly, Zack began; his fists tight and arms sweeping

to his side. His movements were focused and fluid. His first move beginning his form, but his second is what really started it.

Flash!

Zack punched the air, releasing a crackling bolt of lightning from his fist. Travis saw Zack's white teeth flash as he smiled, continuing on to the next move. Throughout the series of movements, random flashes of light streaked across the training field, some narrowly missing Travis, Sarora, and even Master Racht.

Finally, Zack finished his form with two high kicks, each shooting out lightning, and a punch that flashed and boomed like a roll of thunder. He held his position for few seconds, trying to catch his breath, before dropping his arms down and facing Travis and Sarora in his starting position. On his face was a large grin, even though he was still panting and out of breath.

Master Racht walked over to Zack and rested his hand on his apprentice's shoulder, "Well done, Zack. The electricity that now burns inside you will always be with you, helping you to save lives and complete missions. Now that one-half of your powers has been found, it is time to call upon your spirit animal.

"Your spirit animal can be called in only a few ways, but the most efficient way to call upon them is by reciting the words that I will be giving to you.

"Now, Zack, repeat after me, however when I name my element, you will name yours, and when I name my spirit animal, once again you will dig deep inside yourself to find who you truly are. Let us begin,"

"I call upon," Master Racht began.

"I call upon," Zack repeated Master Racht words.

"The element of earth,"

"The element of electricity,"

"To bring forth,"

"To bring forth,"

"The spirit of,"

"The spirit of,"

"The Foo Lion!"

"The Qilin!"

First, out of Master Racht's hand came a glowing green stream of flowing, visible wind. Likewise, out of Zack's hand came the same stream only in a yellowish-gold.

Both streams soon began to take shape. Master Racht's stream flowed together to create some bizarre-looking creature, the one Travis had seen many times on his robes. It had a large head that looked both similar to a dog's and a lion's. It had a strong, stocky build to its body, and a horse-like tail. The hairs on its tail and lion-like mane were more like pieces of a cloud than hairs at all. Its whole body, however, instead of being made of a solid substance, still remained the stream of glittery green.

Travis watched also as Zack's yellow-gold stream formed shape. In the shape, Travis saw the same strange, gazelle-like animal that he had seen on the book that Master Racht had given to him. The qilin had one horn instead of two like a gazelle, the tail of an ox, and the hooves of a horse, but the same basic body structure of a deer. However, just like Master Racht's foo lion, the animal was only made out of the stream that had come from Zack's hand.

Both animals' eyes were glowing; each seemed to look from one part of their surroundings to another. The foo lion seemed quite lax about the whole ordeal. However, Zack's qilin seemed quite fidgety around its new surroundings.

Travis was perplexed. He looked from the other spirit animals to Sarora and back to the others. The other animals were completely different from Sarora. Sarora had a solid body, flowing fur, many different colors to her body, and could speak. The other spirit animals were without a true body, more like ghosts than real animals, did not show any other color than that of their element, and showed no signs of being able to communicate with humans.

Travis badly wanted to blurt out his findings, but he remained silent. He would wait for the break in the ceremony before challenging Sarora.

Master Racht looked to Zack with a smile. "Zack, you have now just revealed what the Crystal of Justice holds deep inside of itself, a spark of electricity held within the spirit of the qilin. As is tradition, you will now be given until the sun sits just above the trees to study and plan how to use your new abilities to fight in battle against me, your master, for your true title of an Acer. Until then, you are neither apprentice nor Acer."

Master Racht turned to Sarora and Travis. "Now, let us leave him in silence." He turned back to Zack again. "We will arrive again when the time has come." And he led Travis and Sarora away from the training field back to the tent. They had roughly five hours before the rest of the ceremony. That would give Zack plenty of time to strategize.

As soon as they were at the tent, Master Racht turned

to them. "Stay here. I'm going to take a stroll. I have thoughts of the future to plot out in my head." He turned and walked away.

As soon as Master Racht was out of sight, Travis turned on Sarora. "Okay, start explaining!"

Sarora, who had absentmindedly been watching Master Racht leave, was taken aback in shock. "What do you mean, Travis?" she asked him, her eyes full of surprise.

"You know exactly what I mean!" Travis felt his anger continue to rise. "You lied to me, Sarora! You lied to me about being my spirit animal!"

Travis saw a flicker of recognition in Sarora's eyes as she flinched at his accusations. "Travis, I didn't mean to hurt you ..." she tried to explain.

"Didn't mean to hurt me?" Travis cut her off. "Not only have you have lied to me about not only being my spirit animal, but also about who you truly are!"

Sarora's eyes were beginning to water with emotion. "Oh yeah?" Sarora lashed back at him. "Do you think that I enjoyed lying to you? Do you think I take pleasure in keeping secrets? If you're so smart to figure out my white lie, then tell me, tell me, Travis, who am I?" she dared him with her words.

Travis looked away. He was full of hurt, questioning, doubtfulness, and other emotions that seemed to swell him up like an annoying bruise. He finally found the words to use and glared back up at her. "If you told me who you really were in the first place, then we wouldn't need to have this conversation."

This time, Sarora looked away. "If I had told you who

I really was in the first place, you wouldn't treat me like I should be treated."

Travis's mind kept flashing back to the moment when he had first asked for the true Sarora. "Who are you, Sarora?" he asked, his voice nearly a whisper.

Sarora let out a sigh. "Right now, I truly am the last living gryphon, but you are right. I am not your spirit animal, Travis. Never have I been, and never will I be."

AN URGENT MESSAGE

Travis sat in his room alone. The sun told him that he would only have to wait another couple hours until the finishing of the ceremony. Master Racht was still on his "little walk" that had taken longer than he had guessed it would. Travis really didn't mind him being gone for so long though, because it gave him time to think and sulk.

Travis was still furious with Sarora. After their encounter, he had stomped off to his room, hoping to forget about the whole thing. It was weird because part of him wanted to forget Sarora's lie and the other part of him wanted always to remember. That part of him wanted to be able to stay angry and hate Sarora, no matter how hard she had tried to apologize.

Travis lay on his back, tossing a small wad of rope into the air and catching it as it came back down. He just wanted to get away, from Sarora, from his troubles, from his hates, from *Firmara*, part of his mind said. He was surprised with himself for thinking such a thing, and yet, at the moment he actually missed the life he had back with his step-father.

Finally, deciding he had spent too much time wallowing in self-pity, Travis stepped outside the tent to find Master Racht sitting alone.

His master must have heard him coming, because he

turned and looked up at Travis. "Ah, finally decide to come out of your lair, have you?" he asked, smiling.

Travis forced a small smile. It wasn't Master Racht's fault that he felt bad inside, so why should he be angry with him?

"I see you're still ruffled up a bit," Master Racht commented as Travis sat down. "Yes, Sarora told me all about your little spat. There is no need for you to lie to each other, but there is also no need for the two of you to stay angry at each other. Well, at least, one of you shouldn't," he glanced at Travis and then looked away again.

"I, well, she just, she just makes me so, ugh …" Travis groaned as he couldn't find words to complain about Sarora. She was his best friend, how could he really be mad at her?

Master Racht chuckled. "See what I mean? You can't even stay mad at her for that long." He looked Travis in the eye. "You know that she would never keep anything from you unless it was important. Sarora's faced more hardships than even I've had in my entire life, and that is very hard to comprehend."

Travis looked up to his master. "Hardships?" he asked. "I know that she got ticked off when I pressed her about wanting to know who and where her family is, but is that really a hardship?"

Master Racht sighed and sat his hand on Travis's leg, "Sarora's family isn't part of a big picture in her life anymore. So, as you may understand, it's hard to deal with that kind of pain and still keep your chin up."

Travis looked away from Master Racht again, suddenly feeling even more regretful for all the times he had pushed Sarora to her emotional boundaries.

Master Racht put a smile on his face. "Come now, Sarora has already agreed to put the past in the past if you decide you are done with your hate rant. Why don't you go and say you are sorry for jumping on her like that and then the whole thing can be forgotten."

Travis nodded. "Yeah, I'll go and tell her right now." He began to stand back up.

Suddenly, Travis spotted a running figure from the corner of his eye. "Master!" he cried.

Master Racht looked to where Travis was pointing. A dark figure was running at them full speed. As it came closer, Travis could see what it really was—a wolf, possibly one of the wolves from Oberon's group. The wolf wasn't very muscular, it was very small, probably a younger pup. It had a tawny-colored pelt and its eyes were an anxious-looking amber.

Master Racht stood to his feet as the wolf arrived in front of them, panting, out of breath. He looked so tired that he could collapse. "I ... I have a message for Acer, Acer Racht," the wolf managed to speak through heavy, exhausted pants.

"I am he," Master Racht spoke, a look of concern and worry on his face. "What is the message?"

"Acer Racht," the wolf began to recite the message. "I, Timur, send a message of worry. Alpha Oberon has gone missing in a battle in the woods. I suspect (pant) that the enemy has captured him and plans to interrogate him for secrets of your location.

"I send this message, (pant) begging you that you will come and fight alongside myself and the other wolves to protect the portal to the human world, where they believe Sarora and Travis are still staying. Without your help, (pant)

233

they will launch an attack on the nearest city on either side of the portal, and innocent lives will be lost. I pray that you will come because we cannot hang on much longer.

"For the sake of the creatures magical or not, come. Sincerely, Al Timur Sonj, second in command."

Travis looked to see Master Racht's expression. It was hard to read, but Travis could tell that he was having to make a difficult decision and that he didn't like doing it one bit. Finally, after a pause that had seemed to last forever, he spoke. "Fine, I'll come. When were you given this message?" he asked the wolf.

The small wolf, still panting, looked up to Master Racht. "About five hours ago, in a valley in the middle of the woods. There is a shortcut to the portal from there."

A shortcut? Travis wondered. *Either Sarora never knew of this or it was another thing that she felt that she needed to keep from me.*

Master Racht cursed under his breath, something that surprised Travis because Master Racht never said things like that. "How do you propose I get there in time, then?" he asked the wolf, anger in his voice. "Did Timur ever think of how long it would take me to get there even through the shortcut?"

The wolf's eyes flickered with fear and the creature cowered at Master Racht's anger. "He said that your horse could run faster than any other and that it wouldn't be hard for it to get that far quickly."

"Seraphi may have the speed and stamina, but even she wouldn't last five hours with non-stop running. Did Timur think of a back-up plan?" he asked the wolf.

The wolf tilted its head to the side. "Sort of, he said that about an hour from here, in the same direction, is a Speed Spruce. He said if you could get there quickly enough, then you could practically teleport yourself to the battle."

Master Racht's eyes lit up. "That may actually work. The only problem left is that I have an apprentice that is at this very moment preparing for the second half of his ceremony."

"I don't have a solution for that," the wolf said, hanging its head.

Master Racht sighed again and looked up at the sky, as if he were searching for answers. Travis didn't know what he was going to do. Should he leave and save the others now? Or should he stay, properly finish Zack's ceremony and then fight?

Master Racht finally looked down from the sky and to Travis. "Hurry, go and get Zack. I'm going to leave right now, on my own. Once he is with you, each jump on your horses and ride to the Speed Spruce. From there, have Zack travel to the fight, where we'll count that as the last part of his ceremony."

"What about Sarora and I?" Travis asked his master.

"You two will wait by the Speed Spruce. If I need any help, I'll send someone for you. But if I can, I'd like to have you avoid any fighting. You're not far enough into your training for something as dangerous as this," Master Racht explained.

Travis wanted to fight alongside Master Racht and Zack badly, but he nodded, grudgingly ready to obey his master's orders.

"Now hurry!" Master Racht ordered Travis. "Go find the

others and explain everything to them on the way to the Speed Spruce." Master Racht let out a strange birdcall whistle. In a few seconds, Seraphi was there, ready to carry Master Racht to anywhere he needed.

Travis ran as fast as his legs would carry him. His heart pounded hard against his chest, sweat poured from every part of his body, and his breathing was shallow and labored. He wanted to stop and rest, but he had to keep running to get to Zack.

Finally, Travis reached the training field where he spotted Zack meditating in the middle of the sandy arena. "Zack!" he called to his friend, "Hurry! Get up! We have to go!" Zack didn't respond. *He must be taking this whole 'no talking while you prepare for battle' thing seriously.*

Travis panted as he continued at a jog to Zack. Once there, he patted Zack on the back. "Master Racht's orders! Get up! We have to go!" Travis though he saw Zack open one eye, look at him, and then close it again.

"Zack, come on! This is no joke! We have to go!"

Zack sighed and mumbled, his eyes still closed. "I must prepare for the fight."

"Yeah!" Travis yelled at him, "the one you'll be fighting alongside with Master Racht!"

This time, Zack opened both eyes and looked at Travis. "What do you mean?"

"I'll tell you everything as soon as we get Sarora and we are on the road!" Travis said.

Zack looked Travis directly in the eyes, as if to study him to be sure he was telling the truth. Finally, Zack stood up with a sigh. "If this is really Master Racht's order, then I'm coming. But if it isn't," his glare suddenly went from questioning to fury, "I'll know exactly who I'll blame for interrupting my ceremony."

Travis tried not to flinch at Zack's gaze as he nodded. Then he and Zack whistled for Shadra and Mesha, who came galloping to them at full speed. Bareback, Zack and Travis hopped on their steeds and told them to head to Sarora, wherever she was.

The horses carried them to the edge of the woods where Sarora sat alone, watching them come. "Sarora!" Travis called out loudly, "Quick! Run with us! There is no time to lose!"

Sarora gave Travis an extremely puzzled look, but then for some reason decided not to stop and argue with Travis and to run with the horses.

As they began their journey to the Speed Spruce, Travis explained everything that had happened and where they were going. Both Zack and Sarora were worried for Master Racht and forced the horses to go as fast as they could through the woods.

The two horses and Sarora were worn out when they finally reach the Speed Spruce. The large conifer stuck out like a sore thumb in the woods of deciduous trees. To Travis, it looked like any other spruce that you could find. However, the Speed Spruce was supposed to give anyone who ate one of its needles the power to move so fast that you were really only teleporting yourself.

Zack hopped off Mesha and looked to Travis and Sarora. "Now you two stay safe. I'd hate to lose either of you because you didn't listen to orders."

Sarora glared at Zack in a stern but caring way. "No, you

stay safe. You'll be the one trying to avoid getting killed."

Zack tried to put a smile on. "I'll try and make sure that my head isn't lopped off while my back is turned."

"Better yet, don't turn your back," Sarora suggested.

Zack nodded and gave her a quick hug before shaking Travis's hand (they weren't into the whole hugging each other thing because they were both boys). "Good luck," they told each other as Zack grabbed a needle off the spruce, ate it, and then disappeared, leaving a boy, a gryphon, and two horses together in the large expanse of woods.

THE BATTLE'S BEGINNING

Waiting for a sign from either Zack or Master Racht ate at Travis like a ravenous wolf. They had been sitting for about two hours, listening for any sound that might be the other two.

While they sat waiting, Travis had made up with Sarora. Even though he was still angered at her, he was able to hide the emotion from his face and his words. They needed to be close friends again if they ever needed each other in battle.

Travis paced back and forth while Sarora lay down on the ground, her head on her front legs. Her talons were tapping out a rhythm. Obviously, either Sarora was bored out of her mind or she was just as anxious as Travis.

"When do you think they'll be here?" Travis asked Sarora for about the seventh time.

"I said," Sarora began, annoyed but trying to keep a hold on her temper, "I don't know."

"Do you have any idea when they might be here?" Travis asked.

"Travis! They'll get here when they get here!" the gryphon yelled back at him, evidently sick of listening to his constant questioning.

The woods went silent again; even the birds had shut up when they had heard Sarora. But they were only silent for about three minutes before Travis spoke again. "Wait, I thought I heard something."

Sarora sighed again. "You thought you heard something ten minutes ago, a half-hour ago, and about three times before then! You're obviously hearing your own brain sputtering as it breaks down."

"No, seriously," Travis tried to convince her. "I could swear I heard something."

"Yes, you *could* swear you heard something but then you'd be swearing for no reason." Sarora looked away from him, her eyelids slowly beginning to droop. "Why don't we play my new favorite game? It's called, 'Let the Exhausted Gryphon Get Some Rest Before She Eats the Annoying Apprentice.'"

Travis finally gave up and sat down, trying to calm his nerves. But her couldn't relax because, this time, he really thought he heard something. Sarora must have as well because her head snapped up and she stood quickly.

"Heard that, didn't you?" Travis teased as he stood up as well.

"Shh ..." Sarora told Travis. "Open your ears, not your mouth." She continued to search the parts of the woods that she could see.

"Over there!" Travis exclaimed as he spotted a messenger wolf running at them.

The wolf was worn to the core. Its white fur was matted with both dried blood and dirt. It nearly collapsed as it came to a stop at Sarora's feet.

"Quick!" Sarora ordered Travis, "Get her some water from the small creek!" Travis obediently walked over to where a small stream of water ran next to the Speed Spruce, cupped some water in his hands, and brought it to the wolf to drink.

Eagerly, the wolf lapped up all of the water. Even though she was still panting heavily, she seemed to be able to regain her ability to speak.

"I, I have, have message for apprentices, Sarora and, and Travis," the wolf stammered as she continued to pant exhaustedly.

"If you are ready, then speak," Sarora replied gently, swiping her tail over the she-wolf's body.

The she-wolf gulped once before starting. "Master Racht is in terrible need of help. Zack is quickly wearing out and he needs someone to replace him for a few minutes in battle. He orders, (pant) orders that that the two of you come and help him in battle. But only if you promise to retreat if that is what it comes to."

Travis looked to Sarora; her expression was a blank worry. She looked to Travis. "We'd better go, now." Travis nodded.

"I'm, I'm supposed to lead you there," the white she-wolf spoke, her voice barely a whisper.

Sarora looked at the tired wolf with pity. "What you need to do is rest. Show me where to go and I'll take Travis there."

The wolf didn't respond for a few seconds, but she eventually nodded grudgingly. *Show her? How?* Travis wondered. He was excited to see what Sarora would do, but all she really did was press her beak against the crest of the wolf's head, and both closed their eyes, going into some trance.

About three seconds later, Sarora's eyes snapped open and she pulled her head back from the white wolf's. She then turned to Travis, who was eyeing the she-wolf suspiciously because she had not awoken from her "state" yet. "She's only sleeping," Sarora explained to him and Travis's heart continued to beat again in relief after its sudden halt.

Travis hopped on to Sarora's back, and Sarora ate one of the needles of the speed spruce, but not before telling Travis to hold on for dear life. Travis felt as if he was being sucked into a hole. Everything whooshed past them in a blinding light. Or was it them whooshing past the other things?

Without warning, Sarora came to a stop. They were at a small piece of woods that was not too far from where the battle was supposedly being held.

Travis gaped in amazement, "Wow, if we had had one of those needles on the way to Firmara, we would have been here the day we had left my house!"

Sarora shook herself, "Yes, but if we use them that much I'd nearly kill myself. They are useful, but if you take more than one in a range of two days, they'll poison you, and you'll bleed from the inside before you die in pain nearly a day later."

Travis's eyes widened in surprise. "Geez, sounds great! Sign me up for being the taste tester of every plant known in Firmara!" he said sarcastically.

Sarora ignored his comment and walked at a steady pace to where they could hear the battle. A wolf stopped them in their tracks just before they reached the scene of the battle.

His upper lip was curled in a small growl. "Are you Travis and Sarora?" he asked them. When they both nodded, the ferocious look on the brown wolf's face softened and he replied, "Then I'll lead you to the armory site."

While another wolf lead Sarora to where she would be fitted with her armor, the brown wolf lead Travis forward. "You've been trained?" the dust-colored wolf asked.

Travis replied, "Yes, I have been trained to fight."

"In armor?"

"Uh, no," Travis responded.

The large wolf turned his head to look at him, "Have you ever tried armor on?" Travis shook his head.

"Hmm ..." The wolf scrunched his eyes together, deep in thought. Finally, he looked up to Travis. "I think that I may have a suit for you. Just one question: Are you fast?"

Travis nodded. "Exceptionally."

"Good. Then I have the right suit for you. It's made of a lighter metal than most armor that is used, but it'll allow you to have more movement and to be weighed down less." The wolf turned and lead Travis to where he was fitted with the armor.

While another wolf helped Travis to put on the lightweight armor, the brown wolf spoke with him. "I've heard much about you, Travis. Yes, Timur was very impressed by how well you seemed to handle a situation even though you were very unaware of the dangers at hand."

"Um, thanks," Travis's reply sounded more like a question.

The brown wolf chuckled. "Oh, it was a compliment, believe me. I know my brother. Timur always hands out more than he is given."

"Timur is your brother?" Travis exclaimed, only to be cut short when the wolf helping him with his armor pulled the back together too tightly.

"Sorry," the second wolf mumbled and continued to help Travis with his armor.

"Yes, we are brothers. Half-brothers to be exact, but let's not go into details." The brown wolf chuckled again. "I am Bratislav. As for my position in command, I am just a general of a small patrol."

"Without the smallest of jobs, those larger could not survive. Therefore all jobs are honorable," Travis replied and then thanked the second wolf as it left.

Bratislav smiled at Travis. "You speak as though you have lived in this land since the dawn of time."

"Sometimes the people who you are with can change both your appearance and attitude."

"Ah, positive peer pressure. Nothing is better than the gift of friends." Bratislav spoke as Travis took his helmet off the hook. Like his breastplate, the helmet was silver. On the center of it was a five-pointed star. Travis stared into the mirror in front of him. Clad in metal, Travis was convinced that he looked nothing like himself.

"You remind me of someone I once knew." Bratislav stepped next to him so that Travis could see him in the mirror. "He was a great man. Not always the brightest star in the sky, and most of the time he was quite reckless, but still a great man all the same." Then Bratislav turned away from the mirror. "Time is wasting, we must get going."

When they met up, both Sarora and Travis were clad in silver armor. Instead of wearing his worn-out sneakers, Travis wore the pair of leather boots that Zack had lent to him a couple weeks ago. Travis also was given a battle sword. It wasn't of the highest quality, but it would do well enough for what needed to be done.

Sarora's armor was light but strong. She wore a version of a chest plate, a strange-looking helmet made just for her, and metal cuffs that she wore on each of her legs near her feet. On the helmet was a small, star-shaped jewel. Its clear, colored form was sparkling in the light. As well, each one of her cuffs bore a similar jewel in its center.

The silver on both of their armor shone brightly as they walked with Bratislav. He was explaining to them where they would be fighting and what to do in the fight. "You need to stay in your position the *entire* time. If you leave your post, then it'll weaken our wall of defense.

"Your jobs will be to hold off the enemies as well as defeat them. So you are allowed to kill in this fight. Any questions?"

Travis spoke. "Uh, yeah, um, I was wondering, who are we fighting exactly?"

"Many of the Midnight Lord's followers—wolverines, cormorant birds, and plenty of his human warriors," Bratislav explained.

"Cormorant birds?" Travis asked.

The brown wolf nodded. "Yes. They are fairly large birds. Not very sharp talons but piercing beaks. You'll know them when you see them because of their pitch-black feathers."

Travis nodded as they finished their walk to the battlefield. It was the same place where Travis had rode Shadra down the large hill.

Travis gaped at the sight. There were clusters of people

and animals here and there. Travis felt his stomach churn when he spotted a wolf corpse lying only three feet from where they stood. It was the same tawny-colored wolf that had delivered the message to Master Racht.

"Good luck to the two of you," Bratislav bowed his head and then retreated from the clearing.

Travis jumped onto Sarora's back and she quickly flew Travis over to where they were going to fight. Travis was almost deafened by the sounds of shouting and clangs of metal as the wolves and other creatures of the light side fought their foes.

Travis looked for any sign of Master Racht and Zack, but was unable to spot them through the endless sea of chaos, blood, and death.

Sarora landed on top of a cormorant bird, crushing it under her weight. Quickly, the dark figure of a man lunged at them, hardly giving Travis time to think. However, he reacted quickly enough to hold out his battle sword, which speared the attacking man, going through his cheap leather armor, his body, and out his back.

Travis shuddered as he pulled his sword out of the dying man's body. Was this really what it felt like to fight in battle? If so, then Travis hated every second of it.

Sarora and Travis continued to fight off their enemies by working together as a team. But no matter how many warriors they killed, more would always come and take their fallen comrade's place.

As he continued to parry off the blows of other swords, Travis continually had to move his legs to avoid getting them cut. Once, a cormorant flew alongside a knight clad in dark leather. Seeing the man, Travis swung his sword out in front of him prematurely.

With an evil grin, the man ducked and quickly used his sword to slice open Travis's arm. Luckily for Travis, the armor on his arms took most of the blow. All he had to show for his mistake was a small cut on his arm.

Seeing that Travis needed help, Sarora turned and easily dispatched both the cormorant and the man in a couple of swipes with her talons.

A few minutes later, Travis figured he had killed at least three people and dark animals, but the more he killed, the less he felt confident with his skills. Taking another's life was not what he was about.

Travis began to grow tired quickly. They had been fighting for at least half an hour by now and had still not seen any sign of their friends. Travis became used to the steady rhythm of the battle. He was so lost in it that he couldn't remember most of the battle, only the expressions on the faces of those he killed.

Sweat dripped down from Travis's brow and into his eyes, making them sting. He did a double-take when he spotted a patch of blond run toward them. Zack was coming to back them up—his sword was covered in blood and he had a small cut on his cheek, a larger wound on his leg, and he was covered in sweat and dirt.

"Zack!" Travis called to his friend. Zack looked to Travis with a nod, coming toward them.

"As big as Sarora is it took me forever to find you," Zack said to Travis as he stood next to Sarora, helping to fend off their enemies. "I need you two to help me find Master

Racht."

"What?" Travis asked. "But isn't he supposed to be with you?"

"If he was with me, I wouldn't be looking for him now, would I?" Zack forced a smile that quickly disappeared. "Sarora, can you give me a ride?"

"We are supposed to stay here," Sarora finally spoke as she used the metal cuffs to deflect another blow from a sword, "but we should find Master Racht. It's dangerous for him to be alone." Travis nodded and Zack hopped up on top of Sarora, behind Travis. Quickly, they were off and into the air.

As they scanned the scene in search of Master Racht, Travis cringed each time their armor scraped against one another's. They looked for about five minutes before they spotted Master Racht's golden armor. He was outside of the battle area, in a small clearing in the forest. He wasn't alone. There were two other figures standing in the tree-surrounded clearing.

Travis spotted Oberon's black fur next to Master Racht, but there was also another figure. "Oh no!" Travis gasped as Sarora descended to help Master Racht.

Oberon and their master were fighting Sievan.

A DANGEROUS FIGHT

Sarora let out a battle cry as Travis and Zack jumped off her back and she collided with Sievan. Both Travis and Zack rolled as they hit the ground. Travis felt pain all over his body—so much for a perfect landing from a 10-foot drop.

Travis and Zack struggled to their feet and ran over to Master Racht's side. He had a large slash cut through his golden armor where blood flowed. His left hand had a deep wound, making it impossible for him to use it. His arms were also cut in several places.

Oberon, however, was not so well off—the tip of his tail was missing, a large chunk was gone from his left ear, his paws were bloody and raw, he had several large wounds on his body and chest, and there was a large wound on the side of his head where blood flowed heavily.

"Zack! Travis!" Master Racht called, his voice filled with irritation. "What are you three doing here?"

"I'm sorry, master," Zack apologized. "I just felt that you would need help in some form or another."

Master Racht sighed. "If you must fight with me, then you must swear to do everything that I tell you to do, no matter what I say."

Travis exchanged a glance with Zack before they both nodded. Then all four of them looked to where Sarora was wrestling with Sievan. They were a blur of brown and black as they tussled about, each of their talons cutting into the other's hide.

Sarora let out a shriek of pain as Sievan flung her across the small clearing and into a tree. Blood oozed from her newly cut wounds and there was a small dent in her helmet. While Sarora was temporarily stunned, Oberon leapt to her aid. Sievan saw the wolf's move a second too late and the black leader was on top of the dargryph, his teeth sinking into Sievan's neck.

Sarora tried to stand but her legs had trouble holding her up. Quickly, Zack ran over to her and helped steady her. "Thanks," Travis saw the words form on Sarora's mouth as she finally regained her balance.

Oberon's attack didn't last long. Sievan quickly turned his head almost all the way around, grabbed hold of the alpha's neck, and flung him across the clearing into a tree not too far from Travis.

Without thinking, Travis ran to the loyal wolf's side. There was now another wound caused by Sievan's beak on Oberon's neck. His panting was fast and shallow as blood flowed fast from the deep gouge.

"Here," Travis offered, "let me help you."

"No," Oberon spoke, "there is no need. I am not going to make it much longer." There was a pause before the wolf spoke again. "Can you promise me something, Travis?"

Travis couldn't believe what he was hearing and yet, he nodded, agreeing.

"Promise me that you will tell Timur that he was and always will be the pup I never had. Tell him I loved him and

I wish that I was alive to see him become alpha of the pack."

Travis felt tears begin to well in his eyes. He didn't want the wolf to die, but he was going to anyway.

Oberon continued, his breaths coming even shallower. "And promise me that you will make a difference. Make a difference in the lives of the others. They all deserve to be free from the power of the darkness."

"But, Oberon—" A one-eyed glare from the dying wolf cut Travis off.

"Do you promise?" the wolf begged Travis.

Travis nodded again, tears streaming down his cheeks. "I promise, Oberon."

Oberon sighed. "And that's all I can ask of you, Travis. Be strong …" and the black wolf died with his head in Travis's arms.

Sievan let out an evil cackle, making Travis turn his head. "What a fool! One down hundredsss to go!" His eyes gleamed with joy and satisfaction at the sight of Oberon's body.

Anger was welling inside Travis's heart. In a fury, Travis stood and pointed his finger at Sievan, "You evil, foul, disgusting—"

"Keep them coming, child," Sievan sneered, "they'rrre all complimentsss to me." He cackled again, making Travis's anger boil over.

Without a second thought, Travis ran at Sievan, his sword held out tight in front of him, ready to rid the world of the dargryph.

Without much of an effort, Sievan stepped out of Travis's way and knocked the sword out of Travis's hand using only his wing.

Travis fell to the ground, dazed. He really had no clue why he had charged Sievan without a plan, and now, the dargryph could easily kill him with a swipe of his talons.

"How foolish of you, you insssolent child!" Sievan screeched at Travis. "Now sssay goodbye to the world you once knew!" Travis rolled over to see that Sievan was on his hind legs, preparing to come down and crush the life out of him.

Travis's past flashed before his eyes—his step-dad, his old home, the stories of the past, his mother's smile. Travis felt a pang of foreboding as he shut his eyes, waiting for death to come. But it did not.

Master Racht charged Sievan. Vines sprouted from his hands and grabbed hold of Sievan, immobilizing the dargryph. Travis quickly struggled to his feet, and got as far away from Sievan as he could. His heart was pounding hard inside his chest, giving his body a numb and shaky feeling.

Once Travis reached Zack and Sarora, he turned back to watch Master Racht fight Sievan. The large dargryph was struggling against Master Racht's power. But it looked as if the more Sievan struggled, the more weary Racht became.

Travis turned to his friends, "Come on, we have to help him!"

Zack's dark blue eyes were filled with fear. "What could we possibly do against Sievan?"

Sarora was still recovering from being thrown against the tree. "Why don't we attack Sievan while Master Racht has him all tied up?" she suggested.

Travis nodded, "Exactly, let's go!"

"Wait."

Travis turned to look at Zack. "What?"

"Let me use my magic first," Zach said. "Maybe my animal spirit could help."

Travis looked to Sarora, who nodded. "Let's allow Zack to go first, Travis," she told him. Travis nodded, finally agreeing.

Zack stepped forward, held his hand out in front of his body, and aimed at Sievan. "I call upon the element of Electricity to bring forth the spirit of the Qilin!" Zack shouted at the top of his lungs.

Quickly, the same strange animal that had appeared before came again. The Qilin stood in front of Zack and counted with its horse-like hoof.

"Now, attack!" Zack ordered the glittery, yellow animal. The Qilin sprinted forward at full speed. Sievan saw it coming, but he couldn't move out of the way.

Lightning sparks appeared on the Qilin's yellow-gold pelt. As it collided with Sievan, the sparks zapped the dargryph, and the spirit animal went right through Sievan, who was screeching in pain. As soon as it attacked, the Qilin disappeared into thin air, just as it had done after Zack had called upon it at the ceremony.

"Nice one!" Travis congratulated Zack, who was laughing with glee at the sight of beating up someone like Sievan. Travis also spotted Sarora's joy—her eyes were shining with hope that they may actually beat Sievan.

Travis looked back to his master, who was still struggling to hold Sievan in one spot. "I'll help Master Racht," Travis told the other two as he began to jog toward the older man.

Sarora stepped into his way, a stern look on her face.

"No. You stay here. Call upon your fire powers to help burn him, but not your spirit animal."

"Why not?" Travis asked, liking the thought of revealing his true spirit animal. "If I use my spirit animal, I could be of better help and—"

"And it might kill you," Zack cut in. When Travis looked at him with a confused expression, Zack explained, "If you use your spirit animal for the first time, it has to be on the day equal to your birthday." Travis was still confused. "Like for you, your next chance would be on the fourteenth day of your fourteenth year."

"Ohh …" Travis finally understood.

"I'll go and help Master Racht," Sarora began, "while the two of you attack him with fire and electricity. Who knows, we may actually win this time." And she turned and left them to help their master.

As Sarora helped to pin down Sievan, Zack looked to Travis. "You do know how to control your powers, right?"

Travis gnashed his teeth. "Uh, sort of." Zack glared at him. "No, not really at all," Travis replied again, quicker this time.

"Okay," Zack began, trying to explain quickly. "Reach deep inside yourself and find your fire. Once you've found it, pour it out of your hand, aiming at Sievan. And be sure not to hit Sarora."

"Uh, I only really was able to follow the last sentence," Travis admitted.

Zack shook his head and sighed in desperation. "You'll know when you do it. Feel your true emotions." Turning back to Sievan, he held out his hand, concentrated, and a strip of lighting shot out of his palm.

Sievan screeched in pain once more as he continued to try and struggle free of the vines and the gryphon that were holding him.

Travis, doubting that anything would happen at all, closed his eyes and tried to find the fire within him. His head was swarming with all sorts of thoughts: *What will happen next? Will we make it? Can I really call upon fire like I did once before? What will happen if we don't win?* Travis tried to push past those thoughts as he continued to search for his fire.

After several seconds, Travis opened his eyes. "Zack, I can't find it!" he called to his friend, who was having a difficult time aiming the bolts of lightning at Sievan.

"Then dig deeper!" Zack instructed him, still trying to concentrate.

"I ... I just can't!" Travis exclaimed, after trying again for another couple seconds.

"Dig ... even ... deeper!" Zack managed to grunt. A second later, Master Racht's vines withered and the older man fell backward, exhausted.

Now that Sievan was free of the strong vines, it was all too easy for him to shrug Sarora off him.

"You really thought that you could ssstop me?" Sievan taunted them and to Travis's fear, it looked as though their last couple of minutes of fighting really had had no affect on the dargryph.

Sarora was standing by Master Racht, trying to get him back up on his feet. Master Racht leaned against Sarora for support so that he was finally able to hold some of his weight while standing up. "We can, and we will," Master Racht grunted, pain beginning to cloud his eyes.

"Oh," Sievan spoke as he approached Master Racht and Sarora, "Isss that ssso? And how do you prrropossse that you are going to defeat me?" Sievan answered his own question, "Exactly. You won't be able to defeat me. Today isss the day of victorrry for Lord Trrrazon!" he screeched and then cackled at the sky, his red eyes glowing.

Zack ran at Sievan, his Acer sword held above his head. As he approached, Sievan jumped out of his way and knocked him over with a blow from his front legs.

Sarora attacked Sievan this time, but the dargryph was ready. He intercepted her charge by rearing up on his hind legs. When Sarora tried to rear as well, Sievan dropped back onto all fours and slammed Sarora in the stomach, knocking the air out of her.

Now it was Travis's turn. He ran at Sievan, his sword at his side. Sievan had just looked away from Sarora to find Travis running at him. Luckily, for Travis, Sievan wasn't ready to defend himself this time.

Without much of a thought, Travis spotted the scar on Sievan's left wing. It was the one that Sarora had given to him a couple nights before she had met Travis. With as much accuracy as he could conjure up, Travis swung his battle sword down Sievan's scar, reopening the healed flesh.

Blood sprayed over Travis as the wound began to flow uncontrollably. Sievan was now screeching in agony, but the pain didn't immobilize him. Before Travis could run, the dargryph turned on him and sent him sprawling across the clearing with one of his massive front feet.

Travis was dazed by the time he stopped rolling. He rose to his knees and felt his head. There were no apparent injuries, but his head was pounding with pain from the blow.

Travis slowly staggered to his feet as Zack approached him. "Travis! Are you okay?" he asked.

Travis nodded at first but his head throbbed even harder and he clenched his teeth at the pain. "I'll live," he managed to tell Zack.

Travis turned to see his friend looking at him with great concern. "Are you sure?"

Travis didn't nod this time but spoke again, "Yes, I'll be fine. Go and help Sarora fight Sievan, I'll help the two of you in a second."

Zack looked at his with doubt, but nodded and ran to help Sarora. While Travis struggled to recover from the blow, he watched Sarora and Zack try to tag team Sievan.

Sievan made the first move. He came at Sarora, aiming his beak at her eyes. Just before he reached his mark, though, Zack shot a bolt of lightning at the dargryph. His aim was off, but it turned Sievan's attention away from Sarora to Zack.

With a ferocious growl, (a noise that Travis had never heard from Sievan), Sievan leapt at Zack, preparing to crush him with his talon's unbelievable strength. Quickly, Sarora reached out with her beak and grabbed Sievan's snake-like tail. Sarora spun and tried to use Sievan's own speed and weight to swing him around.

Sarora's plan didn't turn out well, however, because Sievan's weight was much too great and his tail was slippery like a snake's. All she managed to do was halt Sievan's attack and annoy the dargryph.

With another growl, Sievan leapt at Sarora, who still held the tip of Sievan's tail in her mouth. Her eyes wide with fear, Sarora quickly jumped out of the way, biting the tip of Sievan's tail off with her beak. As he had many times before, Sievan let out a screech of pain as a trickle of blood came from his tail.

Although she saw his fury, Sarora held on to his tail, but this time, she bit higher up on it. Sievan's snake tail, once five feet long, now was just a small stump off the end of his rump, barely more than a foot and a half long.

Blood continued to pour from Sievan's wound, forming a puddle where he stood. The injury on his wing was bleeding even worse than his stump of a tail.

Sarora tried to dodge Sievan's next blow of fury, but the dargryph was quicker. His talons scraped over the front of Sarora's face. Thankfully, Sarora had closed her eyes, preventing the talon from splitting open her right eye.

Travis felt sick at the sight—Sievan's pool of blood, Sarora's newly cut wound over her eye, and as he looked at the back of his right hand, he spotted a large cut that he only now began to feel. It wasn't too deep, yet it startled Travis. He figured that Sievan must have cut it when he had sent Travis flying. The cut wasn't life-threatening, but it was bleeding pretty badly.

Travis placed his left hand over his right, trying to stop the flow of blood.

"Here, try this," a voice next to him said.

Travis nearly jumped, but his heart rate came back down when he saw that it was only Master Racht. He was holding out a plant leaf. It was a dark green and had a smooth surface. As Travis took it, Master Racht explained, "It's a healing herb here in Firmara. It'll help stop the bleeding for now." He was right. Not long after Travis put the leaf on his hand, the bleeding began to cease.

Travis looked up to Master Racht. "Thanks." He smiled.

Master Racht helped Travis to his feet. "No problem. Now let us go and help the other two."

While Travis had been distracted, Zack had suffered a small wound on his arm from Sievan, and Sarora was struggling to get back to her feet. Exhaustion showed in their faces.

Master Racht attacked first this time, a storm of green leaves erupting from an open-handed punch. The leaves hit their target, slicing small cuts into Sievan's wings.

Master Racht leapt out of the way as Sievan came at him with his talons. The dargryph landed a couple feet to the side of Master Racht, and about five feet in front of Travis.

With a quick flick of his wrist, Travis struck the blade against Sievan's crow-like beak. Even though he did not cause his mutated beak to bleed, it still left a mark that would scar Sievan for the rest of his life.

Although the attack had been somewhat successful, Travis had put himself in a bad position. Any direction that he could move in, he was still well within Sievan's striking range.

With an evil grin of delight, Sievan lunged for Travis. Travis had signed up for a death wish without even knowing it. He was too afraid to close his eyes so he left them wide open in shock.

Everything seemed to move in slow motion. Travis wasn't prepared for death, but he was sure that his was coming. As he watched Sievan leap at him, out of the corner of his eyes he saw Zack and Sarora's terrified expressions. "Travis! No!" he thought he heard Sarora's voice, though in slow motion everything was dreamlike and quiet.

However, just before the talons of death reached Travis, Master Racht leapt between the two of them. Travis's heart plummeted as he watched Sievan's talons rip through Master Racht's armor.

A DIFFICULT DECISION

After that, time seemed to speed up. Travis found himself able to leap out of the way as Master Racht's body flew past him. "No!" Travis screamed.

Master Racht hit the ground with a dull thud several feet from Travis. Filled with terror, Travis ran to his master as fast as his shaky legs would take him.

Master Racht lay on the ground, his breathing fast and hard. There were three deep gashes across his chest that ran through his armor and far into his body. The whites of his eyes shone brightly.

Travis felt his knees buckle as he came upon Master Racht. He was still alive, but things didn't look so well.

Sarora and Zack ran to them, both filled with horror.

"Master!" Travis called to Master Racht as Zack and Sarora arrived at their side, though they remained standing. "Master, come on. Let's get you up! Sarora can fly you to the nurse and she'll be able to save you."

Sievan's cold laugh echoed from Travis's side, though he was still several yards away from them. "Finally! Death hasss reached Racht! Oh, how happy Lord Trazon will be! The Last Acer! Dead!"

"No!" Travis screamed, trying to fight back the tears that welled at the back of his eyes, "He's not going to die!"

"Travis …" a weak voice spoke to him. Travis looked back to Master Racht, whose eyes were filled with sadness. "As much as I hate to admit it, Sievan is right. I won't make it another five minutes."

"No!" Travis shook his head in denial as tears streamed down his face. "You can't die!"

"But I am dying, Travis," Master Racht said, his voice was growing faint.

"But it's not fair!" Travis yelled, "You just can't die!"

"Travis, life isn't fair." Master Racht was still full of wisdom, even at his death. "And I must ask you to do something that no apprentice should ever have to do." Travis looked at Master Racht intensely, afraid of what was coming next.

"Travis, finish me off."

Travis's heart stopped and all seemed to go silent again. "But, I-I-" Travis stammered.

"Travis," a different voice spoke this time. It was Zack. "You have to. If Master Racht is killed by someone, the killer will inherit his powers."

"What!?!" Travis exclaimed.

Sarora nodded. "Travis, do as he says. Or Sievan will gain his power and his spirit animal."

"Travis, please," Master Racht began to beg. "It is my command and wish. Kill me and inherit my powers so to save Firmara from further destruction."

Travis still didn't want to believe a word. "I won't!"

"Travis!" Master Racht's weak voice was suddenly commanding, "Do as I say! You made a promise and now it is time for you to uphold it!"

Travis looked to the sword that he had dropped as he had reached Master Racht. Slowly, he reached out, grabbed hold of the handle and looked at his reflection on its blunt side. Suddenly, he remembered a lesson from long ago in the woods where he had traveled to Firmara,

"It's okay." Sarora had said. "We do not kill for joy or for sport, we kill to live."

... "But then what should we do about death?"

"Enjoy our life now, give thanks and pray that we live long lives, and accept it when it comes."

The voices of that day echoed in Travis's head, making him shake with fear at the thought of Master Racht dying.

Travis stood, his legs barely able to hold him and his head dizzy with words of the past, "No! I won't do it!"

"Travis—" Master Racht began.

"No!" Travis refused, "You can't ask this of me! You can't expect me to kill you after what we've been through!"

Master Racht's breathing was now becoming shallower and faster. "Travis," Zack spoke again, "do it, or I will!"

Travis looked at his friends and saw the seriousness in their faces. Sarora gave him a curt nod and Zack just stared at him with a glare that repeated every word that he had said.

Travis looked back to Master Racht and then to Zack again. He tossed his sword to Zack. "If you're so brave, you do it!"

Zack caught the sword by the handle and looked to Master Racht, who sighed and nodded, giving him permission to get the job done.

"Ha! You'rrre both too afraid to caussse death!" Sievan

cackled at them. "I'll have hisss powers and you will be able to do nothing about it!" he cackled again.

Zack looked away from Sievan once again, to his master, and then back to Travis. Finally, he broke the small lapse of silence. "For Firmara!" he cried as he brought down the sword on Master Racht, piercing through his armor and the other side of his body.

Master Racht's eyes widened with shock, and then quickly dulled as his spirit left him. Still holding the handle of the sword, Zack fell to his knees, his eyes tightly shut and streaming with tears. Many small sobs escaped the older boy.

Sarora hung her head as tears began to pour from her hawk-like eyes. "May Master Racht, Element of Earth, Spirit of the Foo Lion, and Last Acer, rest in peace forever."

"Rest in peace, Master Racht," Zack spoke, his words filled with pain. Travis repeated his words.

Sievan cackled again, waking them all from their sadness. "I have won! I will now announce my claiming on the portal!" Sievan flew away. From where he sailed above the war that had still been raging, they heard Sievan cry, "All hail the followers of darkness! Racht, Last Acer, is dead!"

There was a mighty cry of triumph from all of Lord Trazon's army as they celebrated their victory. Sievan called out again, "I now claim the portal in the name of The Dark Lord Trazon!"

"We have to get out of here," Zack was the first to speak.

Travis looked to him. Zack's eyes were red and puffy from crying, but his expression had returned to normal.

"But we can't leave Master Racht here!" Travis argued, tears still falling down his cheeks.

Sarora shook her head. "We have no choice. I can't support everyone's weight."

"Then you can carry him and Zack and I will run!"

Sarora shook her head, "That's not fast enough. We must fly on without him."

Travis looked at Master Racht's body. *Body?* he wondered to himself. How quickly a person became just a body after their spirit left them.

Zack was already on Sarora's back. "Come on, Travis. If it's safe later, I'll come back for him." Travis looked up to his friend and knew that they didn't have a choice.

He nodded and joined Zack on top of Sarora. Together, they flew away from the death and destruction of the battle and back to the safety of the tent.

MOVING ON

Travis sat alone in his room. It was his room now because they had decided that Zack would be the one to sleep in Master Racht's old room.

Travis studied his right hand where there was a dark scar. The cut Sievan had given him would most likely remain a scar for life. No matter how many times Travis and his friends used poultices to try to hide or remove the scar, it wouldn't leave. Therefore, Travis was stuck with an awful reminder of the day that had been fate-filled.

On his lap sat the book that had been given to him by his master. It had been almost two weeks since his master's death and it was Travis's birthday.

"Some birthday," Travis mumbled to himself. Being fourteen felt exactly like being thirteen, so what was the real difference? "One number," Travis managed to mumble again.

Pran padded into the room and rested his head gently on Travis's lap. Since Master Racht was gone, it only seemed right for the dog to be living with them. "Good afternoon, Pran," Travis spoke to the dog, trying to put a smile on his face. "And what mischief have you gotten into today?" The dog looked up at him with solemn eyes, as if to say, "Nothing, I'm totally innocent." But Travis had seen that look many times before.

"So, what did you eat?"

Pran sneezed, shook his head, and then wagged his curled tail.

"Uh huh, you say 'Nothing at all'? I find that hard to believe." Travis smiled at the dog, who panted with a dog's smile. Travis cringed as Pran's breath reached him. "It's a cross between a skunk and dirt hole, isn't it?" he questioned the dog as he tried to plug his nose from the awful stench.

Pran ducked his head and ran out of the room, probably afraid that Travis would yell at him as Zack usually did.

Zack had left to go into town to get a few supplies and Sarora was hunting for them out by the woods. As Travis should have figured, Zack was never able to recover the body of Master Racht. When he had risked going back to the area two days after the battle, their master's body had gone missing. Travis didn't want to think about what might have happened to it.

Travis had told his friends that he would share the book with them when they had both returned. He had never been able to bring himself to read the book. It only reminded him of Master Racht, and brought tears to his eyes.

To his surprise, when Zack returned, he and Sarora threw a party for Travis. They had even been thoughtful enough to each get him a present.

Zack gave Travis a new tunic. It was a leathery brown, and although it wasn't as fancy as the tunic that Zack had worn to his ceremony, Travis was happy. Not only would he now be able to go to the market with Zack, but he could wear something else besides the recently ripped white shirt (which was now more tan than white), and his destroyed blue jeans (which, just like the shirt, were no longer the original color).

Sarora gave him, out of her kind heart, an expensive-looking book that told all about the history of Firmara. She gave it to him saying, "It'll help with the Empty-headedness." Travis smiled and thanked both of them for the gifts.

Dinner was truly delicious. Sarora had successfully hunted for and killed two wild chickens (one for herself and the other for Travis and Zack to share).

Zack had also bought some pepper and salt to add to the flavoring of the chicken (it was a big deal because any spices were extremely expensive). Along with the chickens, they also ate Travis's favorite fruit–apples. In addition, for dessert, Zack surprised both Sarora and Travis with a small piece of taffy. They ate it slowly, trying to savor the flavor.

Now, with their stomachs full, they sat in the study room. Travis stood up while Zack and Sarora sat, intently listening for what Travis would read from the book.

"Okay," Travis began before he opened the book, "here goes nothing." And he swept his hand across the cover. As it had done before with Master Racht, in what had seemed to be forever ago, the three animals ran off the seal and the ribbon fell out of the seal's hold.

Nervously, Travis opened the book and began to read its contents.

"'To Travis, this book is here to reveal words that should have been spoken the day I had all three of you standing in front of me,'" Travis read Master Racht's handwriting.

"If you are reading this, then my time must have passed and I've left to be in a better place. Though you may be grieving, I want you to rejoice in my departing and be glad for the time that you had with me while I was still here.

"First, I would like to display my will and wishes—

"To Zack, I leave all my contents of the tent. Anything inside now belongs to you. Take good care of it. Also to Zack, I ask that you continue Travis's training. Even if your Acer ceremony never happened or for some reason, was never finished, you can still train him in the old ways even if you are not an Acer. My wish to you, Zack, is that you judge everyone equally and do not hold grudges. For the grudges that you hold strangle possible friendships.

"To Sarora, I leave the mentoring of Travis in the knowledge of any and all magical creatures. If Travis is to live here, you must not forget a single detail. This may seem like not much of a gift, but you will see its true meaning in the future. My wish to you, Sarora, is that you keep moving forward, no matter what struggles you face from the past, now in time, and in the future. Never let troubles be your doom.

"And lastly, to Travis, I leave one of my dear friend's swords. You will find it in the forest. Ask Seraphi to show it to you. The sword will give you the strength to keep moving on and the knowledge to fight those who wish you harm. And my wish to you, Travis, is that you know this one thing—"

Travis stopped reading and his heart stopped. His eyes widened in shock and he almost forgot to breathe. There was a dull thud as the book hit the ground. Travis had dropped it in shock.

"What?" Sarora asked, her voice filled with worry. "What is it?"

269

Travis couldn't answer at first. His head was spinning a hundred miles an hour. Finally, he spoke.

"Master Racht was my grandfather."

The adventure continues in the next book:

Spirit Hearts—
The Last Secrets

PRONUNCIATION GUIDE

Hello, and welcome to Firmara. No, don't worry, you have not left your own dimension. I was really welcoming you to learn how to pronounce the names of people, places and things. Some of these names are very hard to read using only sight as a guide. Here are the names that are easily mispronounced.

Abendega – ah-BEN-di-ga

Afon – AI-phon

Aitasen – ATE-uh-sin

Areem – ah-REEM

Arlen – (sounds as is spelled)

Blagasian – Blah-GAY-zee-on

Capricious – Ca-PRIH-tious

Derya – DAIR-ya

Donigan – DON-i-gan

Ferocia – fair-OH-sha

Firmara – fur-MAR-a

Foo Lion – (sounds as is spelled)

Gore – goar (Rhymes with or)

Lacerpenna Animi – lah-sir- PEN-na an-ih-mi

Lucidis – LU-sid-uhs

Mesha – MEE-sha

Mira – MEER-ah

Myrddin – MEER-din

Oberon – OH-ber-on

Pelagius – pel-ah-GEE-us

Qilin – CHI-lin

Racht – Ract

Sarora – sa-ROAR-a

Sendoa – zen-do-a

Seraphi – SAIR-i-fy

Shadra – SHA-dra

Sievan – See-VAN

Silva Woods – SILL-va Woods

Tantillus – TANT-ill-us

Timur – Tee-MOOR

Travis – (sounds as is spelled)

Trazon – Tray-ZON

Xue – Zoo

Zelophehad – Zeh-lo-PHEE-had

CHARACTER GUIDE

Here is a page of physical descriptions for the main characters of *The Last Acer*.

Travis – Thirteen-year-old boy with brown hair, and brown eyes. Holds the Crystal of Courage (Fire)

Sarora – Gryphon that is half-lioness and half-hawk with dark, golden-brown feathers and a lighter brown fur pelt.

Zack – Fourteen-year-old boy with blond hair and dark blue eyes. Holds the Crystal of Justice.

Arlen – Older man with white hair and bright blue eyes.

Master Racht – Old man with longer white hair and beard, and brown eyes. Holds the Crystal of Knowledge (Earth)

Sievan – A dargryph that has the body of a black leopard, the tail of a snake, and the talons, wings, and head of a crow. Beak has several jutting spikes that are set around the sides of the opening.

Oberon – Black wolf with amber eyes. Leader of the wolf pack.

Timur – Brown wolf with white underbelly, black-tipped ears and yellow eyes. Second in command of the Wolf Pack.

BIOGRAPHY

McKenzie Dempsey is a new author, who finds the inspirations for her writing through her experiences in life. She enjoys reading and writing in her spare time and always finds a chance to hang out with her friends. McKenzie lives in a small town in Michigan with her parents and her younger brother.

Breinigsville, PA USA
25 October 2010
247988BV00004B/2/P